Praise for Vivi Andrews's
Lone Pine Pride Series

"The author created a fascinating world and built up lots of suspense for the future books and the captivating characters..."
~ *Night Owl Reviews on* Jaguar's Kiss

"This is an amazing new series, with lots of exciting possibilities leaving you bouncing in your seat wanting to ask what and when and who, the mark of a first class author."
~ *Coffee Time Romance & More on* Jaguar's Kiss

"...this was an intriguing and exciting story. I enjoyed the visit to this interesting world with its various characters and will definitely look for future installments."
~ *Long and Short Reviews on* Taming the Lion

"Vivi Andrews has written a complex, fun and easily readable tale in *Taming the Lion* which follows on from *Jaguar's Kiss* and precedes *Hawk's Revenge*. This adult romance fantasy series will prove addictive."
~ *Fresh Fiction*

Look for these titles by
Vivi Andrews

Now Available:

Reawakening Eden
Ghosts of Boyfriends Past
Superlovin'

Serengeti Shifters
Serengeti Heat
Serengeti Storm
Serengeti Lightning
Serengeti Sunrise

Lone Pine Pride
Jaguar's Kiss
Taming the Lion
Hawk's Revenge

Karmic Consultants
The Ghost Shrink, the
Accidental Gigolo & the
Poltergeist Accountant
The Ghost Exterminator
The Sexorcist
The Naked Detective
A Cop and a Feel
Finder's Keeper
Naughty Karma

Print Anthologies
Tickle My Fantasy
Shifting Dreams
Serengeti Sins
Midnight Justice

Hawk's Revenge

Vivi Andrews

Samhain Publishing, Ltd.
11821 Mason Montgomery Road, 4B
Cincinnati, OH 45249
www.samhainpublishing.com

Hawk's Revenge
Copyright © 2015 by Vivi Andrews
Print ISBN: 978-1-61922-807-8
Digital ISBN: 978-1-61922-322-6

Editing by Christa Soule
Cover by Kanaxa

First Samhain Publishing, Ltd. electronic publication: February 2015
First Samhain Publishing, Ltd. print publication: February 2015

Dedication

Dedicated on behalf of Lea Eldridge to Melina Horn, "the best BFF a person could have". Happy Birthday, Melina.

Chapter One

They say you can't keep a good man down, but the truth is with enough horse tranquilizers, you can drop just about anyone.

Adrian drifted up through the layered fog of his consciousness, the sensation oddly familiar, mirroring the memory of his wings catching air current above air current to lift him higher into the sky. The *distant* memory.

Panic wanted to arise, but the fog wouldn't allow it. The pharmaceutical cocktail they'd been feeding him was thorough, dulling everything. His senses. His thoughts. His ability to shift. But not his will to fight. That still burned, an angry ember in his gut, fueling this latest push toward consciousness.

He became aware of his body in a hazy, detached way. Muscles heavy and aching. Head throbbing. How long since he'd moved his arms and legs? He didn't want to think about how badly his muscles must have atrophied by now.

His throat was so raw and dry it felt like it had been lined with sandpaper and his eyes stung and burned from a dozen needle pricks. An endless source of fascination for the bastards, his eyes. Gauze and surgical tape bound the top half of his face—either in a half-assed effort to bandage the latest wounds to his corneas or an attempt to blind him, hooding him like the raptor he became, as if that would make him more docile.

He'd often overheard them talking—when they didn't realize they were in range of his hawk-fine hearing—complaining about how troublesome he was, debating how to deal with the difficult subject. Fucking with their experiments was one of his few sources of pleasure and he took a fierce satisfaction in being as disruptive as possible, refusing to be cowed.

The rough fabric padding the restraints at his wrists itched, chafing the skin. Instinctively, he tried to call to the hawk, but the dense, syrupy fog blocked his other half from rising.

It was a mistake, he knew. The block. The doctors had argued for hours about whose fault it was. One of the drugs they'd given him was designed to force a shift so they could observe the process—but it had been designed for felines, and avian shifters were a different breed entirely.

His body had rejected the shift, violently, and at the time he'd been viciously satisfied. Served the bastards right if they broke their own fucking toy because they were too busy shooting him full of shit with side effects they didn't fully understand.

But now—however many months later—the vindictive satisfaction had faded and he felt the loss of his feathers like a missing limb, a piece of his soul that had been hacked away with pharmacological amputation.

The door slid open with a pneumatic whisper. Soft footsteps. A whiff of delicate, feminine perfume.

"Hello, Hawk. Waking up again, love?"

He jerked, twitching against his restraints.

There it was. The voice. That same fucking voice that always whispered in his dreams. Soft and ladylike, with that genteel southern lilt.

The voice of his betrayer.

It sounded different now. Edged with cruelty. Or maybe that was just the sound of his illusions being stripped away.

He wanted to snarl at her not to call him *love,* but his tongue was sluggish and uncooperative.

Anger sharpened his thoughts, rushing him up through the last few layers of drug-induced morass until he could open his eyes. The gauze was thin and the light in the room harsh and bright enough to let him see the outline of a woman leaning over his bed. His memory eagerly filled in the details he couldn't see—the curve of her cheek, the chocolate brown curls and bright, save-me-protect-me-trust-me clarity in her rich brown eyes.

She wasn't meeting his gaze now. He hadn't had a good look at her in months—or what he assumed was months. Not since his capture. She was always just outside the edges of his vision, weaving in and out of the drug-induced fever dreams with her silky southern accent and soft touches that could turn excruciating in a heartbeat. And the laughter, always the laughter.

But he didn't need to see her to know she'd still be just as heart-stopping as ever. The backstabbing bitch.

"How are you feeling, darling?" A caress drifted across his forehead and he jerked, avoiding her touch as much as the restraints would allow. She heaved a sigh, the melodramatic sound striking him as out of character—but what did he really know about her? He'd thought he'd known her, thought she could be his mate, the one he'd do anything for and she for him, and then she'd jabbed a needle full of sedative into his shoulder and stood by while her bosses at the Organization collected his body for testing.

Good work, Dr. Russell.

He'd been paralyzed, all but unconscious, his system shutting down one sense at a time, but those words had been clear as a bell. Matter-of-fact. Just another day at the office. *Good work, Dr. Russell.* Adrian couldn't cling to the hope that she'd been coerced, forced to betray him, not with those words playing on repeat in his brain.

And not with the way she spoke to him during her visits over the last few months. She was an Organization power player, he now knew, higher up than he could have imagined. All those months when she'd been helping shifters escape from Organization cells, funneling them to Adrian on the outside so he could whisk them away to safety, all those *years* had been a lie, designed to lure him in.

11

He could almost admire her perseverance, if he didn't despise her with every fiber of his being.

Her outline drifted out of his line of sight, returning a moment later. "You must be thirsty."

A straw pressed against his lips. Probably another serum. Another poison corrupting his body so they could observe the effects, but his throat was jagged with thirst and he knew from experience they would only force a tube down his throat if he resisted.

Adrian sucked greedily, the relief of the liquid worth the risk. When he was confident he could get the words out, he spat out the straw and grated out the one question that mattered: "The date?"

He needed to know how long he'd been out of it this time, helpless and senseless as they used his body as their personal science experiment. How many months he'd be adding to the prison sentence he was constructing for the angel-faced doctor for the day he got out of this hell hole. Because he *would* get out. And she *would* pay for every second.

He'd tried to do the math, tried to add it up. It was hard to string the lucid moments together and he couldn't be sure, but he thought they'd had him for two months. Maybe three. Hell, for all he knew it had been three years—his only source of information was what he managed to overhear from the doctors. No one ever told him shit. He wasn't a person, after all, just another animal.

"September twenty-ninth," she answered, and he flinched.

Jesus. Six months. Six months of his life gone.

If she could be believed. He didn't know why he bothered to ask her. He knew from bitter experience Dr. Russell wasn't exactly reliable with the truthfulness. He'd learned that lesson all too well. Six months in captivity could really drive home a point. If it was six.

"You're being transferred," that genteel southern lilt continued. "I'm afraid you aren't going to enjoy your new habitat. The C Blocks are...something of a hostile environment. But I can help you, if you'll let me." A fingernail traced the side of his neck and he swallowed back his revulsion. "We have reason to believe you were part of a conspiracy to remove shifters from our facilities. Obviously you couldn't have done this alone. You'll save yourself a lot of pain if you tell me who your contact on the inside was."

The drugs were fucking with his brain. What the fuck kind of game was she playing? *She* was his accomplice on the inside. She didn't need to make a show of asking him—

Unless she was still working to free them. Still maintaining her cover so she could get more shifters out. He wanted to believe it. Wanted with an ache in his gut to believe she'd only betrayed him so she could continue to do their work. Someone could be listening to them now. Perhaps someone was forcing her to interrogate him. His Rachel could still be innocent. Still be *his*. She wasn't this creature.

The idea was too seductive to be trusted.

But on the off chance that she was the woman he wanted her to be, he played along. "I don't know what you're talking about."

"I think you do." The words were silky, awash with sensuality. "I can make it good for you if you cooperate, love." Her hand slithered down his pecs, over his stomach and toward his waistband. "All you have to do is talk to me and I can make sure you feel so good. You won't get another offer like that."

"I'll take the torture, if it's all the same to you." He'd been trained to withstand it. He'd die before compromising the safety of the shifters he'd relocated in the last three years.

"Shame." She released another dramatic sigh. He saw her shadow move, heard her adjusting the machines at his bedside. "I suppose the C Blocks it is. You will be a challenge," she purred. "And I do like a challenge."

The words started to blur and bleed into another as the familiar fog of the drugs surrounded him.

"Sleep well, my hawk. When you wake up...well. You'll probably wish you hadn't."

And when I get free, you'll *wish I hadn't...*

It was the thought he clung to as the world washed away.

Chapter Two

Rachel flashed her ID badge at the gate, fighting to keep her smile natural and easy as her heart climbed up her throat and she waited to see if the guard would look too closely at the fudged clearance area marker. She wasn't allowed to be here, but this guard didn't know that.

She was relying on complacency—and, yes, the typical masculine reaction to her appearance—to keep him from asking questions she couldn't answer. Like what the hell a reproductive specialist was doing at a transfer station visiting a patient who was no longer under A Block jurisdiction.

The guard smiled, a little too broadly, as he scanned her ID, focusing more on giving Rachel an appreciative look than inspecting her badge—*Thank heavens*—and waved her through.

Only when she was through the gate and well clear of the guard post did she let herself breathe. First obstacle cleared.

Eleven million and two to go.

In all the extractions she'd ever done, this was perhaps the worst plan she'd ever concocted. She never would have attempted it if she hadn't been desperate. And if this wasn't going to be the last.

They were onto her.

She'd bought herself some grace when she'd betrayed her hawk, but that was gone now.

Her co-conspirators were already in the wind, some walking out with classified data in their pockets and computer viruses in their wakes. Those who could get out, anyway. The others were burrowing in and hoping for the best.

Rachel reached over, nervously checking the backpack in the passenger seat, though it wasn't as if the thing could have vanished into thin air in the five minutes since the last time she'd touched it. A plain green nylon bag. With three hard drives and a sheaf of papers inside. Everything she'd been able to steal with the help of a computer tech who was now halfway to Costa Rica.

Each of the hard drives was encrypted, with two possible password keys. One which would unlock stores of innocuous medical data to match the decoy papers and a second to display the real intel. Financial records for the Organization. Schematics for their facilities. Files on all shifters known to the Organization.

Those three hard drives were the key to bringing the Organization down, if she could get them into the right shifter hands. And she knew only one man who she would trust to deliver them. The Hawk.

Unfortunately, he wasn't likely to trust her at the moment.

She almost hadn't been able to do it. Jab that needle into his back. Take away his freedom. It had been so much harder than she thought it would be.

Even six months later, she could still remember the exact expression on his face when he'd fallen. The confusion. The shock. The flash of rage. The surge of disgust. She hadn't been able to escape the memory of her betrayal. It revisited her every night in her dreams.

Her biggest mistake. It didn't matter that she'd been aggressive in the last six months, freeing as many shifters in that time as they had in the previous three years combined. She still wished every day that she could go back and do it differently. Tell him the truth. Fight with him. Run away with him. Anything else.

One hundred seventy-three days, thirteen hours and twelve minutes. That was how long her hawk had been in captivity.

She hadn't been able to let his capture be for nothing. His sacrifice—even if it wasn't voluntary—had to mean something. And it had meant the lives of all those shifters.

But the recent extractions hadn't been without risks. She hadn't been as careful. Some of the shifters were moved on the fly, with thrown together identities and relocations. The famous Hawk wasn't on the other end anymore, making sure that part went off without a hitch. Rachel got them out, but over the last couple months, some of them had started coming back, being recaptured—which, considering they were listed as dead in the Organization databases, had raised some serious red flags.

The Board of Directors knew now they had a problem. They were actively looking for a mole and Rachel had been in too many of the right places at the wrong times.

They weren't certain. If they had been sure, she would've been in a cell somewhere in the C Blocks. Or dead in a ditch on the side of the road, the victim of a convenient accident.

But they were suspicious. Far too suspicious. They'd been pushing her, testing her loyalties, and she was afraid she wasn't fooling them anymore.

Time was up.

The second she helped the Hawk escape, the last shred of her cover would be blown and she would have to disappear too. No more helping the others—but security was tightening another strangling notch and their chances of success with any other extractions were rapidly dwindling anyway.

Besides, he was scheduled to be sent to the C Blocks—the torture division—and if they broke him, if they managed to get at the information he carried, then all of her work for the last three and a half years was forfeit.

No. Better if he escaped. If they both did.

Not exactly what she'd had in mind when she'd envisioned herself running away with the man of her dreams.

Rachel parked her Civic in the lot beside the transfer station. She grabbed the backpack and climbed out, locking the doors by habit, though there wasn't really any point. If everything went according to plan, she wouldn't be back for the car.

The Organization guarded the roads leading into this valley, no escape that way, but the wilderness at its back was all but ignored—an oversight Rachel had always thought indicated an arrogant lack of understanding about shifter strengths. With the Hawk at her side, Rachel could vanish into those woods.

At least that was the idea.

She flipped the backpack onto her shoulder, hoping the move looked casual and her grip on the shoulder strap less desperate than it was as she strode toward the front door of the transfer station as if she had every right to be there.

The C Blocks always seemed to be overcrowded—never enough torture chambers for all the intended victims—so these transfer stations had been set up to keep the shifters drugged and waiting for their turn in the chair. Rachel had only been to one once before—when a particularly volatile cougar female had been believed to be pregnant and the Board wanted Rachel's expert opinion on her gestational state before they decided whether she belonged to the A Blocks or the C Blocks.

The cougar had been pregnant. And she'd gone to the C Blocks anyway. Rachel hadn't been called back to a transfer station since.

The guard at the front door took a much closer look at her badge, frowning when she told him which captive she needed. "Popular guy."

She jolted, jumpy with adrenaline. "Sorry?"

"Ms. Clarke is with him now."

Rachel fought to keep the sheer blinding terror from showing on her face. "Oh? Maddie's here?"

The people who worked for the Organization could generally be divided into three categories, in Rachel's experience. Those who were paid to be there—typically the guards who got off on the power and barely veiled sadism of their jobs. Those who were coerced to be there through threats or blackmail—often scientists and doctors with unique specialized knowledge, like Rachel herself. And the third, most terrifying subset of Organization employees—the True Believers. Like Madison Clarke.

"Rachel!" As if called up by the thought of her, Madison came striding around the corner at the end of the hall, her long legs eating up the yards between them. From a distance, looking at Madison was like looking in a mirror. They were a similar height and build, but Madison was more muscular, her brown hair curlier, and on closer inspection her features were a little too pointed and sharp to fall within the boundaries of the classical beauty that an accident of genetics had given Rachel. A scattering of tattoos on her left wrist, the back of her neck and her collarbone leant Madison's appearance an edginess that contrasted Rachel's own feminine, southern style. Rachel had always found her eyes too hard and her intensity a little terrifying.

"I didn't know you were going to be here today," Madison called as she approached.

Because I'm not technically authorized to be. It wouldn't take much for Madison to figure that out. The fudged clearance marker would fool a lazy gate guard who wanted to get Rachel's phone number, but it wouldn't hold up against Madison's scrutiny for a second. She was too smart and too much of a stickler for protocol.

The guard handed back her badge and buzzed her through, obviously satisfied now that Madison had proven to know her. Rachel quickly pocketed the incriminating badge and moved to meet Madison halfway.

Her mouth was dry, but her prepared cover story came easily. "I heard the avian was being transferred. We never did manage to get sperm samples. Be a shame to waste the only avian we've ever had in captivity."

"You need the Hawk?" Madison came to a stop in the middle of the hallway, casually blocking Rachel's way. "Isn't your access to him restricted?" she asked, too sweetly.

Maddie knew damn well that Rachel hadn't been allowed within fifty feet of him since she'd assisted in his capture. *Not your concern, Dr. Russell. Tend to your own work and leave the Hawk to us.*

Rachel swallowed around the knot in her throat. "Special circumstances. The breeding program is high priority."

"I suppose. Though you're going to have a time getting samples out of him now. I just dosed him. He's doped up to kingdom come at the moment."

She'd expected as much. Drugging the shifters was standard operating procedure at the Organization. Unless lucidity was required for a test, they were kept so out of it they couldn't fight their restraints or try to maul their captors. Much. She'd known he would be surfing a chemical cocktail—which was why she'd brought a pair of syringes to shock him out of it—but she could hardly admit as much to Madison.

"Depending what he's on, I might be able to get my samples without waking him," she said instead.

Maddie chuckled. "*I might be able to get my samples,*" she mimicked, imitating Rachel's accent with eerie perfection.

Madison had always had a disturbing chameleon-like tendency to try on other voices—one she frequently engaged to manipulate shifters desperate to hear from loved ones they'd been separated from. Blindfolded and bound, shifters would hear the voices of their loved ones—pleading, crying or sometimes even playing the role of torturer. The skill had made Madison a cornerstone of the C Blocks interrogation teams. If she'd been with the Hawk, had his inquisition begun already?

"You must love your work," Madison snickered in her own voice.

Rachel bristled, but kept her expression placid. "It pays the bills."

Madison snorted. "Look at you, all righteous and disapproving. You feel sorry for them, but we're doing good work here, protecting the human race from these creatures. If the world at large knew about the shifter threat, they would thank us for our work. They're animals, Rachel. I know they can seem very human at times and it's easy to get attached to them, but thinking of them as real people is a mistake. It doesn't pay to be soft with them. It's like having a pet tiger—you have to maintain control at all times or you wind up like Siegfried. Or was it Roy?"

She didn't seem to want an answer, so Rachel ignored the question. "The avian?"

"Hm? Oh, right. Down this hall, first left gets you to the cells. You want number five." She smiled, catty and snide. "Good luck, Doc."

"Thank you." When Madison stepped to the side, Rachel strode past her, hyper conscious of every movement. She was good at this game after years of practice. Don't walk too fast. Don't look guilty or try too hard to look innocent. Breathe normally.

Even when it felt like a semi was parked on her chest and her lungs refused to expand all the way.

She didn't breathe any easier when she was around the corner and out of sight. With Madison here, her entire plan was a thousand times riskier. The guards could be counted on to do the bare minimum, but Madison was a different beast. And a much more frightening one.

Rachel paused in front of number five.

Thanks to the computer tech now on her way to Costa Rica, the code she punched into the access panel both opened the door to the cell and sent an "upgrade" into the security system that would play hell with their video and audio surveillance systems for the next half hour. They would have privacy. Provided Madison didn't come to investigate.

Rachel stepped into the room and the door slid shut behind her. Only then did she let herself look at the figure on the bed—and a soft, horrified cry escaped her lips.

"*Noah.*"

It wasn't his real name. It had been too dangerous for her to know his real name when they first met as two links in the underground railroad to free shifters from Organization captivity. She'd picked the name for him that first night she'd seen him in person, loving the way his firm, unsmiling lips had twitched up at the corner when she teased him about rescuing enough shifters to fill an ark.

They'd already been corresponding for nearly three years by that point, working together to free the shifters being held and experimented on by the Organization—Rachel on the inside, Noah whisking them to freedom once she got them out. Nearly seventy shape-shifters disappeared into the night and wiped from Organization records. She'd often wondered, during that time, what her counterpart looked like. She'd built up an image in her head of a knight in shining armor, glowing with goodness like some Arthurian legend.

When she had finally met him in person, he hadn't looked at all like she'd expected. He was supposed to look so *good.* Honest and wholesome and pure. Like all the good deeds he'd done, all the lives he'd saved, would have shaped his face into soft, easily trustable lines. Her Galahad. But no, from the very first glance it was obvious he was dangerous. Hard. Chilling. His extraordinary yellow eyes harsh and unyielding.

In retrospect, it had been naïve of her to expect him to be anything else.

His face was all angles and edges. Every mannerism quick and sharp and purposeful, a predator in the guise of humanity. He was tall, with a lean narrow build and the slight hunch to his shoulders that some tall men developed to adapt to the shorter world around them. His hair was dark and cut short, in an almost military style, as if he'd never quite gotten away from his Special Forces background.

Her partner. Her counterpart on the outside. The man she'd secretly hoped would be so much more.

For all his fierceness, he had only ever been gentle with her—and with the dozens of shifters they had worked together to rescue. Firm. Commanding. But never cruel.

Cruelty was more the Organization's forte.

It showed in the wasted figure lying on the bed, drugged out of his mind. He'd never been heavy, but now he was so thin his skin seemed stretched over his bones.

She'd promised herself, when she pushed that syringe into his back at the hotel, that she would do everything in her power to make sure he wasn't hurt in Organization custody, but her access to him had been all but nonexistent. Whatever they'd done to him had wrung him dry and left him a shell of himself.

Her hawk. She hadn't known what kind of shifter he was— hadn't known about his fame as *the* Hawk in shifter circles, until the Board of Directors had called her in and insisted she help capture him. Avian shifters were rare to the point of near myth, but it was easy to visualize him as a bird of prey. It fit him. Her Noah. Her hawk.

His eyes were bandaged, but his file indicated it was more to blind him than to protect his eyes. She set the syringe aside and quickly set about removing the gauze. Without the bandages his face seemed even more hollowed out, the shadows darker and more menacing. She let her fingers linger along the line of his stubbled jaw. "What have they done to you?"

Blinking back the moisture in her eyes, she reached purposefully for the IV snaking out of his arm, sliding the backpack off her shoulder and pulling out a syringe. Shifters and humans were physiologically different in thousands of ways, but the pharmaceutical mix in this syringe was as close to an adrenaline shot to the heart as she could get. In the chemical trials it had never failed to wake up a shifter. And it woke them up fighting.

Hopefully he didn't try to kill her.

She hesitated, fidgeting with the needle.

One syringe had broken his trust. Could this one bring it back?

She couldn't be sure how quickly she could bring him out of his drugged stupor or how soon he would be able to move, let alone run. So many variables.

So many unanswerable questions. And one louder than all the others.

What if he didn't cooperate at all?

She'd done so much to destroy his trust he might—quite understandably—refuse to do anything she said. He may try to slice her open with his talons as soon as he was lucid enough to shift. And if he did, could she blame him?

Rachel pushed down the plunger.

Chapter Three

"Noah."

His eyes flew open, blood surging through his system like fighter planes being launched off an aircraft carrier—though his thoughts still swam with the syrupy fog of the drugs.

The light was brutal, harsh and painfully bright, but when he squinted that vicious light wrapped lovingly around a chocolate brown curl. A curl that fell forward to rest against the sweet curve of a familiar cheek, caressing a face that made his chest ache.

His heart shuddered in his chest. *Rachel.*

Adrian wasn't a beast—his animal side had always been as distantly calculating as the man—but even the civilized hawk had to bite back a growl. If only he could have called his talons, slashed them through his bindings, raked them across that creamy cheek. The fantasy was so vivid he could almost smell the blood.

"Noah, we haven't much time. I need you to focus for me."

He was breathing hard, strangely energized even as the world continued to bend and warp like a Dali painting. He locked his eyes on her face, fighting for coherency. Why was he being allowed to see her face now? And why was she calling him Noah again? It had been "Hawk" for months. What was this new game? She'd told him the next time he woke up he'd be in the information extraction department—what strange torture was this?

"Can you hear me, darlin'? We don't have much time."

Something about the endearment helped him focus on her eyes. He fucking hated her eyes. The dewy compassion in their dark chocolate depths. The regret. The strain that pulled at their corners. The silent pleading for him to forgive her.

Never in this lifetime, sweetheart.

"Fuck off," he said—or would have, if his throat hadn't been stripped raw with rusty nails—the drugs always dried him out. The words were a sick croak.

Rachel ignored him, weaving in and out of his field of vision in a rush of movement that made his world blur and spin. He heard a rattle of medical instruments as she pulled a tray up next to the bed. The snap of a surgical glove. The smell of talcum powder. A scalpel gleamed in her hand.

Ah, and now we get to the torture.

She was talking, but the words seemed to warp into one another. The world did the wave again and he closed his eyes in self-defense, though the sensation of movement didn't abate. This made the worst hangover he'd ever had feel like a walk in the park, his body a thousand raw nerves.

He felt her touch then, feather light, undoing the strap pinning his shoulders to the bed, cutting away his shirt to expose his chest to the chill, overly air-conditioned air. Her fingertips were cool and sure against the fevered warmth of his skin and his body reacted, even through all the drugs.

Fantasy. That's what this was. Even after her betrayal, she still infiltrated his dreams with her soft voice and softer hands. She might be a soulless bitch, but she was still the most beautiful thing he'd ever seen in his life. And she kissed like her mouth had been made for him alone. He hadn't forgotten that.

"I'm sorry. This is going to hurt."

Yep. Definitely a dream. Everything would be sweet and sultry and erotic until the moment she apologized and stabbed him in the back. His subconscious knew this routine. It was a well-worn path.

Adrian didn't bother opening his eyes, waiting for the inevitable prick.

But the pain wasn't the jab of a needle followed by a rush of oblivion.

Something sharp sliced into his upper chest, just beneath his clavicle and he hissed, jerking against his bonds, his eyes flying open only to be assaulted by the angry light and swirling world again.

"I'm sorry," she whispered, her face once again floating above him. "We don't have time to do this the gentle way. I would have done it while you were unconscious, but I didn't think you'd trust that I'd taken it out unless you saw it yourself."

Fingers probed into his chest, nails scraping beneath his collar bone and he would have shouted, would have screamed, but his throat was still too raw to form the sounds. Beneath the haze of pain he felt a jerk, a rip, and then her bloody hand rose between them, her expression grimly pleased. "There. Done."

She stripped the bloody gloves, wrapping them around something that looked like a hearing aid with dangling cords dripping bits of his gore. Had she just pulled that out of his chest?

"I'll patch you up better when we're clear, but for now this will help."

Clear?

Something warm and slimy smeared over the wound, stinging briefly before leaving a soothing numbness in its wake. He fought to hold on to the pain. Numb was bad. Numb was a precursor to oblivion.

He felt her fingertips, so cool against the itchy heat of his skin, tugging on the bindings at his wrists. Loosening them? No, that couldn't be right. They never moved him unless he was drugged to hell and back. She wouldn't be untying him.

The restraint on his left wrist came free with a jerk.

She was.

What the hell?

He heard that name again. Noah. She was speaking, he realized. Had been for some time. He tried to tune in to the words floating around his head like butterflies, but for a moment all he could make out was the pitch of her voice, low and urgent, the southern accent more pronounced than ever. He began collecting the butterfly words, putting them together like puzzle pieces.

"...only five guards...small outpost...lazy...believe what the computers tell them...your tracker here...cameras off-line...won't even look...by the time the 'upgrade' program finishes screwing with all the primary surveillance systems we should be long gone. I hope. But with Madison here..."

His right wrist released and dropped limply to the mattress. Through that same distant, shifting, butterfly-puzzle awareness, he felt her move to the foot of the bed and start on his ankles. "Can you walk? You have to walk. Or shift. If you can fly—dang it!" She hissed and he caught a flash of red before she shoved her finger into her mouth, sucking on the wound in a way that reminded him more of a little girl than a genius doctor. Her hands were back on his bindings almost instantly, though he saw lines of pain on her face—her face seemed to be the only fixed point in the Dali painting of his world. He felt a drop of moisture soak into the sock on his ankle, the fabric sticking to his sensitized skin. Was she bleeding?

"Can you sit up at all? How are you feeling? Dizzy? Nauseated?"

He felt like his mind had been put in a blender and someone had hit puree, but he managed to lever his upper body a couple inches off the bed, the effort of it pathetically intense. Then he saw her hands.

The fingernail on her right forefinger was bent back at a sixty degree angle, detached from the nail bed and bleeding a steady red stream onto the crisp white sheets, but she kept working steadily at his bindings using all her other fingers.

She freed the ankle strap with a soft sound of triumph. "Can you get the last one?" She started away from the bed, but he just looked at his hands—confused to find them free—and she made a low, impatient noise and returned to yank at the last cuff.

"This is taking too much time," she murmured. "Madison probably already suspects me. For all I know, the Board could have dispatched a team as soon as my badge was scanned at the gate." He had the feeling she was talking for her own benefit as much as his. Nervous chatter. Some people were like that during an op.

Was this an op?

Where had that thought come from? This wasn't an op. It was a fantasy. Just a fucking weird one where his chest hurt like hell from where she'd cut something out of it and she'd accidentally ripped one of her fingernails off trying to free him. Not his usual brand of fantasy, but the subconscious worked in mysterious ways.

"We need you off the grounds before the surveillance upgrade decoy finishes running. If they suspect anything and hit the alarm, even my badge won't get us out of the exterior doors—they only open from the outside during lockdown and then only if your clearance is higher than mine. But if we can— There!" She straightened, his last bindings falling away. "Can you stand?"

She reached for his arms, and he flinched back, crossing his arms over his chest. A flash of hurt was quickly masked on her face. "I'm helping you," she said, low and calm. "We're escaping. You and me. I know you have no reason to trust me right now, but why would I lie about this?"

Why? A thousand whys instantly jumped into his head—not butterfly puzzle pieces but a hive of angry bees.

To fuck with him. To trick him into revealing something. To trick him into shifting so they could observe it. Hell, he wouldn't put it past the Organization to actually let him go so they could follow him and use him to capture other shifters.

Rachel must have seen his doubt. Her expression hardened. "I'm not lying, Noah. Hawk. Whatever you want me to call you. I'm sorry about what happened before—more sorry than you can know—but it was for the greater good. I hoped you would understand that." She shook her head. "We don't have time for begging forgiveness right now. They've begun to suspect me. You're my last extraction. Please just let me help you."

She reached for him again and this time he let her touch him, let her hands close around his upper arms and guide him to the edge of the bed where he tried to put weight on legs as wobbly as a newborn fawn. His stomach pitched violently and he cursed under his breath, digging deep, dredging up all his will and every last reserve of shifter strength and it was barely enough to get him vertical.

She muttered something and dove into the backpack at her feet. She straightened with a syringe in her hand and Adrian jerked back so fast he collapsed back onto the bed.

"It's energy!" She raised both hands like he'd told her to stick 'em up. "Artificial strength. You'll feel like Superman for the next couple hours and then you'll crash harder than ever, but we have to get out of here. Understand?"

"No drugs," he growled in his raked-over-glass voice, swallowing hard to keep his stomach from sending its contents up to visit with his tonsils.

"You can't run. You can barely stand and we don't have time to wait for you to recover. It's this or a lifetime in Organization custody and that life sentence might be pretty darn short since they were planning to transfer you to the torture division."

"No drugs." He thought he managed to say the words aloud, but it was hard to tell—even her face wasn't steady anymore, dancing like a fucking Cheshire cat's.

She sighed. "You can hate me later." She moved fast—it couldn't have been shifter fast, he knew she was only human, but it seemed shifter-fast to his muddled senses. The syringe was needle-deep in his thigh before he could blink and then warmth was slithering through his body on a strange, invigorating tide.

"I already hate you," he tried to say. But it was working.

Strength. Fuck. She hadn't been kidding. This stuff was *incredible*. It did almost nothing to clear the cobwebs from his mind, but damn if his body didn't feel like it was puffing up like Captain freaking America. His stomach settled and the quaking left his legs. He wouldn't have been surprised to see his muscles visibly swelling, but when he looked down he was still the same wrecked, shriveled bag of bones.

"Put these on." He recognized the light-weight sweats that she tossed at him from the corner cabinet. They were standard "exercise" wear for the captives during endurance experiments.

He was tempted to throw them back at her, but he really was starting to feel like Superman. If he could overpower her, perhaps he really could escape. And if it really was September, he was going to need something warmer than a bloody half-shredded T-shirt when he did.

Adrian quickly changed, not giving a thought for modesty. Dr. Russell blushed and averted her eyes and he snorted as he pulled on the sweats. "Nothing you haven't seen already, sweetheart."

"Hurry up," she said, making a point of checking her watch rather than looking at him. "We have sixteen minutes left to get clear of the building."

"Let's go then." He crowded up behind her. He'd never been in the habit of using his height to intimidate, but he found he loved the way she flinched when he towered over her.

She darted toward the door, swiping her access card and tapping a number sequence into the panel until it beeped and clicked open. She silently held up a finger and he stayed back, stayed quiet. He may not trust her any farther than his atrophied muscles could throw her, but he'd ride this out and see how far it would take him. Whether she was really rescuing him or just playing at it to mind-fuck him, it didn't do him any good to balk now. So he played along.

She poked her head out into the hallway, then opened the door all the way, nodding to him to follow her as she darted into the hall. He stayed on her six, the instincts of a lifetime in special ops making his fingers itch for a weapon even as he hurried silently in her wake.

The facility wasn't large, he quickly realized. Two short hallways, two quick turns, and they were at a door marked *EXIT* in bold red letters.

The intercom crackled. "Dr. Russell, please report to security. Dr. Russell to security."

Rachel stiffened, sucking in a sharp breath at the sound of the impersonal female monotone floating through the hallway and all of Adrian's doubts coalesced into an angry knot of certainty.

Another trick. That's all this was. Another fucking game. He didn't know why he'd believed, even for a second, that Rachel might be helping him. That he might actually be able to get free of this place. He longed again for his missing talons, for blood dripping from them.

He wouldn't go back to the cell. He'd make them hunt him through the short white corridors of the outpost like a rat in a maze first.

Focusing his eyes was still a challenge, but he managed to home in on her face, saw the decision form, the determination settle there. She pivoted, swiped her card over the panel next to the exterior door and let out a soft sigh of relief when the door beeped twice and popped open.

She grabbed him by the shoulder and shoved him through the opening into the shadow of the building. Disorientation shuddered through him. Sunlight. He didn't know why he'd been so sure it was night, but the sunlight filtered through the trees and cool breeze rode the air. A fall breeze. Jesus, he really had lost months in there. The trees were pines, the slope rising behind the building steep enough to qualify as a mountain. He had to be three hundred miles from the city where he'd been taken, but for all he knew it was closer to two thousand. *Dorothy, we aren't in Vegas anymore.*

A backpack hit him square in the chest, the backpack he hadn't noticed Rachel carrying. "Remember, schematics, roster, financials."

"What?" He clutched the backpack automatically.

Frustration suffused her face. "Haven't you been listening?"

The words, he remembered. The butterfly words. Had they been important? Then he realized she was speaking again, these words quick and angry, a hive of bees.

"Three hard drives. Schematics and locations of Organization facilities, a roster of all known shifters, and financial records of all Organization dealings. You have to get them to shifters who can use them to bring the Organization down."

Tracking devices, probably. So the Organization could locate the largest and most organized shifter opposition.

"Repeat it back to me. Schematics, roster, financials."

He didn't for a second believe that was what was in the bag, but he parroted obediently. "Schematics, roster, financials."

"One more time."

"Schematics, roster, financials. I've got it."

"Good." She threw a glance behind her, back into the building where the intercom crackled again with another request for her to report to security. "We're in Wyoming. Northwest corner of the state. Near Cody."

Something in him shuddered at the thought. Shit. That had to be nine hundred miles. Nine hundred miles they'd transported him without his knowledge. Like so much luggage.

She pointed to a small black dome in the eave above the door, standard surveillance camera. The building was smaller even than he'd thought. Just a few hundred square feet when he'd always envisioned the Organization facilities as bigger than the Pentagon.

"The cameras should be offline for another six minutes. They only go a hundred feet past the tree line and the motion sensors were deactivated because they kept tripping for local fauna. Get into the forest and you should be clear." She put a hand over the backpack. "Run, Hawk. Run like hell."

"So you can hunt me?" He didn't realize he'd growled the words aloud until he saw the hurt flicker briefly across her face, but she didn't reply to the jab. All business, his Rachel.

"We're getting out, Noah. This facility is backed up to a National Park and they won't want to draw the attention of the rangers, so you should have the advantage. I'll buy you as much time as I can and be right behind you. By now they've figured out I'm not entirely on the straight and narrow. Hopefully they'll be too distracted by me to come after you right away. When I can get clear of them, I'll post to the old message boards."

"You expect me to believe you would sacrifice yourself for me? After everything you did to me?"

Irritation flashed in her warm chocolate eyes. "It was never about *you*," she snapped. "None of it. Now go." She slipped off her watch and grabbed his wrist, putting it on him. "Four minutes." She placed a hand over the backpack he still held to his chest, almost as if it was a child she was praying over. "Make it count, Noah."

She went up on her toes so quickly he didn't have time to react before her lips were pressed, soft and sweet, to his. He jerked away, tempted to spit out the taste of her, but she was already whirling, bolting back inside, the door clanging heavily shut as she left him there, quite literally holding the bag.

Adrian cursed.

He knew it was all a trick, all a lie. The Organization bitch would never have released him into the wild. He was probably carrying enough tracking devices to be seen from space—if that even made sense. His brain felt like it was three-quarters mush. Luckily his instincts were still online, and they were urging him to run like hell. Even if he was being used as bait, he could be bait that got the hell away from here. He ran.

Chapter Four

There were certain defining moments in a person's life, moments that gave you the opportunity to test your true nature and see if you were really the person you thought you were. In a crisis, would you save the day or be a lump of useless, shocky flesh? You never really knew until you were tested.

Rachel had often wondered if she would truly be able to sacrifice herself for others. Or if, when push came to shove, when it was the moment of truth, if she would give in to self-preservation and fight for her own survival instead.

When she'd first discovered that her "patients" at the Organization weren't there voluntarily, she'd told herself the shifter captives wouldn't be helped in any way by her disappearance—but she'd still called herself the worst sort of coward because she had let herself be cowed by the Organization's thinly veiled threats.

She knew now that her bosses hadn't been bluffing. She'd had colleagues vanish when they started asking the wrong sorts of questions. The local authorities had never investigated—the Organization selected their personnel carefully. No family attachments, unless they could be exploited as leverage. The preacher and his wife who had adopted and raised Rachel had both passed by the time she was recruited into the less-than-legal side of the Organization.

They were careful. No one would raise a ruckus if a scientist notoriously terrified of flying decided without warning to jet off to Mozambique to pursue a research grant. There was always a barely plausible story to explain the disappearance, and anyone else within the Organization who was thinking rebellious thoughts heard the warning in the faulty explanations. *You could be next.*

In the Organization there were two options—toe the line and advance, or rebel and vanish. So Rachel had toed the line, and told herself it was for the best, that through her treatment she was at least better for the shifters than some other less humane doctor might be. She told herself there was nothing she could do.

Until God had seen fit to give her an opportunity to prove her true mettle again.

It had been a clerical error. A glitch. *A sign.*

The shifter on her table had been very much alive, but somehow the file had been marked deceased. There were no additional transfer orders, no one who was expecting to receive this shifter for the next round of tests because as far as the system was concerned, the slim, dark-haired wolf was dead.

It had been convenient that the video surveillance systems had been knocked out in a lightning strike the day before, impulse to dress the woman in a spare pair of her scrubs, and pure luck that the guard at the gate hadn't looked under the blanket in the backseat of Rachel's car. That first time had been completely unplanned and her heart had been thundering out of her chest the entire time, but she'd done it. She'd saved a life. She'd proven that she wasn't only a coward. She could be more.

So she'd begun planning and recruiting. Finding those who seemed dissatisfied within the Organization and cautiously approaching them. Computer techs, other doctors, even the occasional—rare—guard. They'd developed a system that wasn't without risk, but it had succeeded. Five times. Ten. Rachel had been heady with the victory, but she'd still worried about what was happening to the shifters after she set them loose into the world. Some of them were so weak, so damaged. What was to say they wouldn't be captured again?

It was one of the escapees—a young lynx with eyes too old for his face—who had given her the contact information for a shifter who could help them from the outside. Forged identities. Safe houses. Picking up where her operation left off.

Noah. Her hawk.

They'd worked together for years before they'd met, freeing over sixty shifters before that night in the woods when he'd stepped out of the shadows and straight into her heart.

Betraying him had been another of those defining moments. She could still feel the syringe in her hand. The wrongness of it. He'd had his back to her, gun in hand, ready to defend her with his life, if that was what it took, and she'd done it. Taken him down. Handed him over.

She told herself it was for the greater good. A thousand times she'd told herself that, but it still felt like a lie, even if she knew it to be the unvarnished truth.

The Organization had already known about him when they approached her to acquire him. They'd known that she was seeing him, but not that Rachel was involved in the shifter underground or even the extent of the Hawk's involvement, as they called him. If they'd kept digging, it would have compromised the entire operation and endangered the lives of all the shifters they'd whisked to freedom, not to mention those they had yet to free.

All those lives had meant sacrificing one, so she'd done it. And hated herself every day since.

But today she got to make amends.

Madison's voice crackled over the intercom again, demanding Rachel report to security for the third time, an edge of impatience creeping into her sedate intercom voice.

Sorry, Maddie. A little busy at the moment.

Rachel swiped her card over the access panel for the pharmacy storage, expelling a little gasp of relief when the door beeped and glided open. At least her card was still working; they hadn't gone on full lockdown yet.

She made quick work of grabbing the vials she needed, shoving them into her pockets and filling syringes on the run as she trotted down the hall to the cells. The first cell door beeped and whooshed open, revealing a muscular Caucasian man with dark-hair just going to gray, unconscious and strapped to the bed. Rachel shot the Wake-Up Juice into his IV, jammed a chair in the doorway to keep the door propped open, and ran to the next cell. Hopefully he could get himself free of his own restraints because she didn't have time to untie him.

Three cells later—one empty, one with a wiry African-American female and one with a slight Asian male who looked even more emaciated than Noah had—Rachel heard a distinctly feline roar from the first cell and changed direction, diving into the empty cell and pressing herself against the wall. She wasn't wearing a lab coat—nothing to identify her as an Organization doc other than the fact that she didn't smell like a shifter, but somehow she didn't think the enraged cat was going to ask questions or care that she was the one who had freed him.

With a scrabble of claws against linoleum, the cat took off down the hall, a streak of tawny fur past the open doorway. As soon as the coast was clear, Rachel darted out of her hiding place and ran as fast as she could in the opposite direction— back toward the door where she'd left Noah.

How many minutes had it been? It must have been more than four, so why weren't the alarms—?

As if on cue, the intercom squawked and a deafening siren began to wail, the agonizing screeches reverberating off the walls. A headache immediately blossomed between her temples—and she didn't even have a shifter's sensitive hearing.

She reached the door, swiping her card over the access panel, but the light stayed stubbornly red. She swiped again, frantically, but it was no use. Lockdown.

Rachel spun, pressing her shoulder blades back against the door. What now?

Her thoughts began to drift. Floating. Flying. *Noah is clear.* He had to be. If he'd gotten away, it would all be worth it.

The African-American girl staggered out of her cell and collapsed, fingertips twitching.

At the end of the hall, a large predatory cat snarled. The cougar. *Puma Concolor.* No, that wasn't right, that was the species name for the feline. This was a shifter. A much more dangerous beast.

I'm going to die. The thought hovered without a tether in her mind.

The cat lunged forward, his steps strangely awkward and clumsy.

Gas, she realized in that same tetherless, moorless way. Of course the guards would gas them. You don't try to take a cougar in hand-to-hand combat. Or a hawk. Her knees buckled and she staggered, falling to all fours. The linoleum was chilled beneath her palms, gritty with tiny particles of dirt the janitors had missed.

The cat continued to rush toward her—probably less affected by the gas thanks to the Wake-Up Juice she'd injected him with.

Her dizzy thoughts spun, as if stirred by a lazy finger. She really should have expected this. There was a sort of justice in it. A symmetry.

She should probably be upset about this, she thought vaguely as her arms gave out and her cheek took up residence between her palms on the dirty floor. If the cougar didn't kill her, the Organization would. She'd betrayed them and her employers did not take that sort of thing lightly.

At least Noah had gotten away. He'd taken the hard drives. The shifters had a shot now. They would know what they were up against. With the roster they could protect themselves, with the schematics they could fight back, and with the financials they could attack the head of the beast, go right to the source.

She really should be sad that she wasn't going to be alive to see it, but as her thoughts finally fogged to match the lethargy swamping the rest of her body, she found herself...relieved.

She was done. Done with the Organization. Done with the intrigue. Done doing the wrong thing in the name of the right thing. Done pretending obedience and living in an isolation bubble where she couldn't allow herself to confide in anyone or care about anyone because they would only become a liability. Only one thought disrupted the perfect relief, one fear as she realized these might be the last conscious moments of her life.

Had she been forgiven?

Sure, she'd explained, she apologized, but how much of what she'd said while she was untying him had he been able to process? She thought of them as still friends, still allies, she'd seen them as partners in one last grand rescue...

She still loved him.

More the fool her.

The cat was impossibly close now, teeth and claws at the ready. Moment of truth...

The cat leapt over her and threw himself against the barred door, claws scrabbling, but he had no more luck than she had. Trapped.

The alarm cut out with an aborted squawk, leaving her ears ringing with the silence. The cougar rumbled queasily and thudded to the ground, his hindquarters landing on her legs, the substantial weight pinning them down—not that she would have been able to move anyway. Her body was beyond her control. She clung to consciousness by her fingernails—and in spite of her desperate grasp it was flaking off and peeling away.

Footsteps rushed down the hall. Faces in gas masks loomed above her. Madison. She couldn't see the features, but she knew one of them was Madison.

"Not smart, Dr. Russell," the woman scolded, a malicious smile in her voice.

No. Perhaps she hadn't been smart today. But she'd done right. She'd made amends. Noah was free.

Rachel's lips curved in a smile as her vision went dark and the mortal world fell away.

Whatever happened next, Noah was free.

Chapter Five

Adrian dreamt of a soft touch on his brow and the sharp jab of a needle into his hand. He tried to jerk away but something pulled at his wrist, holding him down. More restraints. Another IV. Back at the Organization labs. *Fuck.*

"Easy now." The voice was unfamiliar. Masculine. "It's just fluids."

"Rachel," he groaned, without managing to drag his weighted eyelids up. Was she here? Was that her holding a cloth to his brow? Her hand on the needle?

"What was that?" the man asked.

Adrian tried to speak again, but his lips wouldn't move and his mind went into a flat spin, sending pieces of his awareness flying off like leaves on a merry-go-round. Another unknown voice spoke into his silence, this one female.

"It's Rachel, I think. He calls out for her all the time, though I haven't figured out if he's asking for her or cursing her."

The male voice chuckled. "It's a woman. Probably both."

"Nice, Doc."

"Don't take it personally, Moira. You know I don't think of you as a woman."

"Just digging yourself deeper, Doc."

"Hormone levels are still dangerously high. His body isn't shaking off the effects of the drugs the way I'd like."

Adrian tried to hold on to the words, the names, the information—if he could just hear a little more he might learn where he was—but the flat spin was accelerating now, more pieces of him flying off into oblivion as the merry-go-round twirled faster and faster, and he lost his grip on the world.

Time slid sideways. He woke again, sometime later. Or perhaps he dreamed. In the dream, he'd made it safely to Lone Pine. He had the vague sense of other people entering the room, one of them so massive he could only be the pride's Alpha. Adrian tried to tell them about the backpack—he'd buried it somewhere, hadn't he? Just in case it was riddled with tracking devices—but he couldn't be sure how many of the words he was actually managing to get out in coherent order.

Then the carousel kicked into warp speed and he flew off into senselessness.

When the world fell back into place around him, the room was quiet, punctuated by the rhythmic whirring and beeping of medical monitors and the soft, regular breaths and steady heartbeat of someone a few feet to his left.

He opened eyes that felt gritty and saw an unfamiliar blonde woman sprawled out on the chair beside his bed, reading off a tablet.

His head was only throbbing—which was a relief after the tornado-like spin-cycle it had been going through every time he rose up to semi-consciousness for the last god-only-knew how many hours or days.

His limbs felt wrong—achy and shivery and chilled, like the cold was radiating from the bones outward rather than the skin in. His chest ached when he tried to breathe and his throat was so dry his own saliva burned like acid when he tried to swallow.

The blackness was easier. So much more comfortable. He wanted to sink back into it and let oblivion wash away the aches of his body, but something held him back.

"*Rachel.*"

The woman's chin jerked up, gaze lasering in on his and her lips quirked up on one side in a wry, smart-ass grin. "Don't you recognize me? I'm crushed. After all the lovely talks we've had."

She stood, flicking the tablet onto the chair where she had been sitting and crossing to his bedside to examine him with a briskness that spoke of long experience even if her bedside manner was more go-fuck-yourself than Florence Nightingale.

"I'm Grace, you're Adrian Sokolov," she said, with that same aura of an often repeated routine. "I'm a lion—" She half-shifted her hand and wagged a paw at him, flexing her claws, "—and a field medic, as well as a lieutenant at Lone Pine Pride. That's where you are. We found your sorry ass unconscious in the woods three days ago. Xander thought you were dead, but Xander's a dumbass, so don't take that personally. Someone pumped you full of all manner of nasty shit and you've been in la-la-land off and on for the last few days as it played hell with your limbic system, though you've been boring as hell for the last twenty-eight hours—very inconsiderate of you, if I do say so myself—because you've been in what Doc Brandt calls a *healing trance* or some such shit. Feeling better now?"

"Much." His voice cracked and she lifted a cup with a straw to his lips. He drank, his throat still raw as hell, but surprisingly, his answer wasn't a lie. His body was drained, but his brain was working in nice linear lines now rather than whirling in spirals and circles.

"Good. You look less like hammered shit too. Though I wouldn't try running any marathons just yet. And don't freak if you can't shift. You're still recovering from the shit they pumped into you." The woman—Grace, apparently—moved away from his bedside then, sitting on the arm of the chair she'd recently vacated.

She was tall and strong, as many lionesses were, with blonde hair just long enough to curve next to her chin and an average, angular face made extraordinary by her pale blue-gray eyes rimmed by blue so dark it was almost navy. He didn't know many prides with female lieutenants, but she exuded strength and authority in a way that made the claim easily credible. One foot swung idly as she studied him with those incredible eyes.

Could this really be Lone Pine?

The Lone Pine Pride in Montana wasn't far from the Wyoming border. He vaguely remembered trying to get here, dragging his body north.

The pride was the biggest and strongest in the country. If anyone could take on the Organization, it was Lone Pine. They were also one of the only prides in the world that didn't treat non-lions as vermin to be exterminated with extreme prejudice. Non-lion shifters told stories about them the same way people talked about Shangri-La. As this distant perfect place where no one was ever persecuted or rebuffed, where shifters who didn't have the protection of packs and prides could finally find safety.

A lioness could be held captive at the Organization and forced to impersonate a medic for Adrian's benefit, but he'd trusted this woman enough to give her his full name and his instincts told him this was the real deal.

"We recovered the hard drives."

Every muscle in his body tensed with Grace's words—which, considering the state of his muscles, hurt like hell. He had only the vaguest memory of ditching Rachel's watch and burying the backpack beneath a big rock. "Did you check for tracking devices?"

"Nah, we thought it would be fun to lead the Organization right to our door." She rolled her eyes. "Of course we did. They were clean. Though even if there had been a tracking device you might have managed to drown it. The backpack was wet as a groupie at rock concert. Apparently you swam through an ocean or two on your way here. I didn't know birds were into swimming."

"We aren't." He frowned, trying to remember the details of his escape, how he could have gotten wet, but everything after the Superman juice wore off was a black hole. If the backpack was wet... "Were the hard drives salvageable?"

Grace pulled a face. "We have our best people on it, but the Alpha and his heir both want to pick your brain as soon as you're back in the land of the coherent, which you certainly seem to be. You've managed to focus on me for almost five minutes now and you haven't called me Rachel more than once."

Rachel. If that was even her name. He had the move elusive snippet of a memory of overhearing a guard call her something else. But when he tried to grasp it, it slithered away as if it had never been. And maybe it hadn't.

But the memory of her thrusting the backpack into his arms was so real he could almost feel the nylon. *Schematics, roster, financials.* If she hadn't lied about that… No tracking device—that they'd found. She could really have been trying to bring down the Organization. Unless she was playing an even longer game than he thought. *Schematics, roster, financials.* If that was what was really on those hard drives…if the information was authentic…then she was innocent—at least of that—and he had left her there to…what? Be killed for her part in his escape?

"You have to access the information on the hard drives."

"We're trying."

"Try harder," he demanded. "Those hard drives may contain schematics of the Organization locations, rosters of every shifter in the Organization files and financial records of where they are getting their funding."

Grace went preternaturally still. "Are you serious?" She must have read the confirmation on his face because she didn't wait for a verbal response. "Don't move. I'm getting Roman."

Don't move. As if he could.

Seconds after Grace blasted out of the room, the doctor walked in. He was tall with military short salt-and-pepper hair and surprisingly thick hands. The woman who trailed after him was petite and tawny-colored, her hair, eyes and skin all in muted shades of brown, with a round sweet face that would always be called cute though she looked a decade past the point of appreciating that word as a compliment.

No one would ever call Rachel cute. Stunning. Gorgeous. Heart-stopping.

"Adrian, how are you feeling?"

The doctor moved to the bed and immediately began checking the same vitals Grace had just checked, also running through a gamut of questions asking him how every inch of his body was feeling, as well as how many fingers he saw and who was president. Adrian responded automatically, listening with half an ear, the rest of his attention locked on the nurse. She was so quiet, so peaceful, he couldn't imagine her as a lion. There was nothing commanding or regal about her. She was mild and almost servile, gentle and distinctly submissive. He'd heard that Lone Pine allowed non-lion shifters into their ranks, but seeing it for himself was still jarring.

As the doctor interrogated him, the woman bustled to the far side of the room and cracked the window. The sounds of a busy pride instantly rushed in to meet his ears. Layers of unfamiliar voices calling to one another. Children laughing, the rhythmic squeak of swings on a playground.

The Organization wouldn't know enough to fake a soundtrack for his hawk hearing.

Jesus.

He was really here. Lone Pine.

It was a strange feeling, both welcoming and confining, being here with so many others of his kind—even if they weren't exactly his kind. He'd visited a wolf pack or two and knew a little about the lion prides, but his parents had raised him in a secluded cabin, far from the company of other hawks, let alone other shifter breeds. Whether by nature or nurture, he had grown into a solitary man. The army had forced him into a community, but it had been that same combination of welcome and uncomfortable, and ever since his discharge he'd been on his own. Until Rachel had contacted him and he'd become part of her team. But even then, he hadn't gotten invested with anyone besides her. He'd moved shifters efficiently, without getting attached. Vegas had been a perfect base of operations—

the kind of place where lots of people vanished and popped up again unexpectedly, where no one looked too closely at anyone else.

Rushing footsteps announced the arrival of Grace with the big Alpha. Adrian vaguely remembered the man looming over his bedside, but little else.

The massive blond man radiated command as only a born leader could, but the doctor turned to the larger man with a stern expression. "Fifteen minutes, no more. No tiring the patient."

With that, he and the nurse slipped out, the door clicking shut behind them.

Grace fixed Adrian with a don't-let-me-down stare. "This is Roman. Tell him exactly what you told me."

Wasting no words, Adrian explained to the Alpha what Rachel had told him. When he was done, the big man couldn't have looked more stunned if he'd been hit in the face with a two-by-four.

"Holy shit," he muttered under his breath, eyes narrowing. "How did you get all that?"

Adrian didn't flinch at the Alpha's obvious suspicion. He would have been an idiot not to mistrust such a gift. "I stole them when I escaped."

"And they were just lying out where a stoned-out shifter would trip over them on the way out?"

The backpack hitting his chest. Brown eyes staring intently into his. "There was a doctor," he said, inexplicably reluctant to let them know about her. She was *his*. "A woman."

"She helped you?"

Had she? His memories were so warped, but it seemed that she had, that day. But on another day, six months earlier, she'd betrayed him in the worst way. He couldn't seem to accept her help this week at face value. There was too much history there. But the facts didn't lie. "I think so. It's hard to be sure. My memories are all jumbled up."

"But you remember what's on the hard drives."

"She kept repeating it." He remembered that much. The butterfly words. And if she really had helped him escape, what possible reason could she have for lying? Unless... "You checked my body for tracking devices?"

"Before we brought you back here."

He lifted a hand, rubbing absently at the bandage on his chest where Rachel had dug something out. "And the hard drives? You had the backpack checked as well?"

"It was clean."

Clean. No tracking devices. No ulterior motives. No tricks. She may have genuinely been trying to make right what she had done when she betrayed him.

He couldn't seem to stop thinking about the lines of strain on her face, the hunted shadows in her eyes. She was in trouble—or a damn fine actress pretending to be. She had rescued him, but she was also the reason he was in Organization captivity to begin with. He refused to care about the extra stress on her face, the fear in her eyes. He had gone against his better judgment once for this woman and look where it had gotten him.

"I wondered if she was setting me up. Tricking me into escaping so I would lead them to Lone Pine. But I wanted so badly to get out of there, I didn't even care if I was endangering all of you by coming here." It was a miracle he'd found the place at all.

Roman surprised him by not railing at him for the risk. "We've heightened our security. So far there has been no indication that you were followed."

"There won't be." Even if the Organization was coming for them. "They're good at what they do." He swallowed, his throat convulsing with the effort. "If they aren't using me to try to get into Lone Pine, the information on the hard drives could be legitimate." Or the information itself could be the trap. "But if they know I took it, they'll begin moving people." Moving Rachel.

Imprisoning her. Torturing her. "If we want to have any chance of rescuing them—"

"We would need to go fast," Roman finished.

"I want to go with you." Adrian shoved himself up higher in the hospital bed, knowing he looked like a liability right now, but trying to force strength into his body. He needed to find her. Before it was too late. He wasn't sure whether he wanted to save her or imprison her himself, but either way, she was *his*. "Even if we can't get any of the data off the hard drives, I might be able to lead you back to where I was held."

The odds that Rachel was still there were slim, but it was all he had.

Roman nodded. "I'll pass that along to the Alpha."

Adrian frowned. This wasn't the Alpha? Who was? The Incredible Hulk? "I just have one condition."

Roman, Not-the-Alpha, cocked an eyebrow in question.

"The doctor. Rachel Russell. I don't want her hurt." Not by anyone else anyway.

"She works for them?"

"I'm not sure she has a choice." It was instinctive, defending her. But he found himself wondering if the words were true. He'd been so focused on the betrayal, so foggy with drugs, he'd never really thought about the bigger picture. There was always a bigger picture. Adrian's energy abandoned him and he sagged back down on the bed. "She wanted to leave with me. I thought she was lying. That she couldn't be trusted. So I left her behind."

"And now you want us to endanger our people rescuing her." The Not-Alpha was visibly unimpressed by that idea.

"No," Adrian argued. "I just don't want her killed when we're rescuing *our* people. Make her a prisoner here. I won't object."

"We don't usually hold prisoners."

Adrian met Roman's eyes, making his gaze unmovable. "That's my condition." Rachel was not negotiable.

Chapter Six

"So this Rachel. Do you love her?"

Grace spoke as Adrian lunged for a higher grip on the climbing wall. His concentration splintered, the tiny hold slipped off the pads of his fingers, and he cursed, instinctively trying—and failing—to shift as the ground rushed up to meet him with punishing force. A puff of dust rose around him in a cloud as he hit. Luckily he'd only been about ten feet off the ground, but it still hurt like a bitch. He groaned as Grace leapt down, landing gracefully in a crouch at his side.

"Nice," he grunted.

"Did you break any of your delicate little birdy bones?"

"Fuck you."

"You asked me to train you. Part of my training is ensuring you're mentally sound. If you're mooning over this Rachel bitch and fall off a cliff, I don't want the Alpha taking it out of my ass. So are you in love or what?"

Adrian grunted and shoved himself up onto his forearms. Nothing felt broken. Thank God. The incursion team set to strike the first Organization installation—the one where he'd been held—was scheduled to leave tomorrow and there was no chance they'd delay if he broke his ass on the obstacle course today. He'd be left behind and he *refused* to be left behind—which was why he'd asked Grace to get him back up to fighting trim.

And as much as he hated to admit it, the lioness had a point. He couldn't be distracted by his feelings for Rachel—whatever the hell they were—while they were on a mission.

"No. I'm not in love with her." Even if he had once thought she might be The One. Even if he'd felt like a freight train of emotion had flattened him the first time he saw her. Even if he'd once believed in True Love and Love at First Sight and all the romantic platitudes. Even if he had seen his unborn children in her arms more than once in his mind's eye—none of that mattered. That had all been before the needle. No love could survive six months of being used as a lab rat. Not when she was the cause.

"So what's the deal with her?" Grace pushed. "Why are you so obsessed?"

He lurched to his feet, his muscles shaking with the effort, and Grace straightened beside him, placing a gentle hand on his shoulder. "Take it easy. That's enough for now."

Even healing shifter-fast he was pushing the limits of what his body could handle. The pride doctor had cleared him for the mission, grumbling the entire time, and Grace was helping him get his body back into military form—but he was still light-years away from his usual physical condition and the weakness was constantly infuriating. He hated being this man. This invalid.

It didn't help that he was only a man. He still hadn't been able to take his hawk form. His blood tests were clean now, the last of the drugs finally loosening their hold on him, but still nothing. Not a single fucking feather—though several of the cats had reported his eyes would partial-shift when he was worked up. Dr. Brandt thought that was a positive sign, a sign that he wasn't completely cut off from his animal side, but Adrian wouldn't feel like himself again until he felt the wind ruffling his feathers.

Grace guided him over to a bench on the side of the practice course—and at least he made it there before his legs gave out. They sat side-by-side, watching as other pride members made use of the course. Young soldiers training, veterans keeping their reflexes sharp.

Lone Pine was bigger than he'd dreamed. He'd heard of prides having up to fifty members, but the Lone Pine numbers were well over a hundred and growing every day. They allowed non-lions into their ranks and welcomed shifters in need of refuge at a much higher rate than any other shifter group he'd ever heard of—and there were more and more shifters in need of refuge these days.

The Organization was starting to get a reputation among shifters in the south—even if they hadn't known what to call the mysterious scientists who were abducting their kind. More and more lions and non-lions alike had come to Lone Pine for protection as the rumors got worse—even breeds who were typically more isolated, like cougars. And hawks.

Though there were no other bird shifters at Lone Pine.

He'd heard that his kind were on the verge of extinction and the lack of a single other avian shifter seemed to support that. Adrian Sokolov. Last of his kind. And he couldn't even fucking shift anymore.

Grace bumped his shoulder. "You didn't answer my question."

"Question?"

"Why the obsession with the evil doctor?"

"She isn't evil." He didn't know what she was, but he knew she wasn't evil.

"She isn't good," Grace countered.

"I'm not obsessed."

"Just because you're careful not to mention her name now doesn't mean I can't see the obsession pouring off you in waves."

Adrian didn't have an answer for that, so he let his attention be caught by a sleek feline form darting through the obstacle course at stunning speed. The Siberian tiger was as large as any of the lions and should have been slowed by all that bulk and muscle, but the big cat seemed to defy the laws of physics with each leap and twist, unnaturally agile. "Jesus," he whispered.

"Yeah. He's a royal prick, but Dominec can sure move."

"That's *Dominec*?"

He'd met the surly asshole a handful of times, but never seen him in feline form. Or moving like *that*.

The tiger finished the course easily and turned his head to scoff at the rookies scrambling desperately in his wake, the move revealing the shiny, ridged scars that marked one entire side of his face in both feline and human form. His head swiveled slowly until he was staring fixedly at where Grace and Adrian sat watching on the bench.

Adrian didn't know much about feline behaviors, but he had a feeling the sustained eye contact was intended as aggression, especially when Grace stiffened beside him. They were working with Dominec as part of the incursion team that would stage the attack on the Organization. He was an asshole, but a smart one—and of everyone on the team, he seemed the most inclined to watch Adrian with barely veiled mistrust.

Apparently through with the staring contest, the tiger leapt off the back of the course and disappeared into the woods with a flick of his tail.

"Don't mind him," Grace muttered, slouching back onto the bench beside him. "He's just being a dick. Per usual."

"He doesn't trust me." And he wasn't the only one. Sometimes he would catch even Roman—who Adrian had learned was the Alpha's chosen successor—staring at him with hints of suspicion.

"He doesn't trust anyone."

That much at least was true. Dominec wasn't exactly known for making friends among his pride mates. His scars had marked more than just his face. Adrian didn't blame him, but he was cautious around the tiger—he seemed too damaged to be relied on.

"He'll come around," Grace went on, though her tone was dubious.

Adrian knew as well as anyone that this first mission was a test. A test of the materials Rachel had given him and a test of his own trustworthiness. A test Dominec seemed convinced he would fail. He helped them plan and the leopard leading the team acknowledged that he was an asset strategically, but everything he said was weighed.

Adrian was allowed freedom within the pride, but there were always eyes on him. Frequently those eyes were Grace's. Though she seemed to be a friend and never acted like a jailer, he couldn't help wondering if she had been assigned to guard him. Keep him from learning anything too sensitive about the pride until they knew for certain where his loyalties lay.

Grace cringed as one of the rookies took a hard fall, but it was Dominec she spoke of when she said, "He doesn't understand why you want to protect an Organization doctor. None of us do."

Everyone he'd met in the pride seemed to have their own reason for hating the Organization. Adrian just as much as anyone else. Of course he hated Rachel. She'd betrayed him. She'd tormented him during his captivity, seeming to take pleasure in his pain, calling him a mindless animal—each insult more biting because of what he had once thought she could be to him.

But there was still that idiotic hope that she had only cursed him because she was forced to, that she was still his Rachel beneath it all. The memories of his time in Organization custody were foggy and disjointed, while his memories of the time before remained vivid and fresh, screwing with his heart and mind.

He remembered with absolute clarity the first night he'd laid eyes on her. And all the nights after.

He'd known that every meeting was a gamble, known that she could be a plant, a spy, and that even if she was exactly what she advertised herself to be, she was still one of them. But every time they met, he felt it. The tug at his soul. His mate.

He'd believed she was The One, but he'd been wrong. And none of that could matter now. He wouldn't let it.

Adrian had only one—justifiable—reason for protecting Rachel. He said as much to Grace. "She's an ally. She's helped dozens of shifters escape and we need what she knows. Killing her would be shooting ourselves in the foot."

Provided she wasn't already dead. She'd said to check the message boards where they'd once scheduled their meets online, but they taunted him with their silence.

Tomorrow the team would leave. Two days after that they would arrive at the Organization facility where he had been held. He might know what had happened to her in as little as seventy-two hours.

"Be careful picking your friends, Hawkeye," Grace said softly, still watching the runners on the course. "Some are dangerous to have."

She stood, leaving him then. But he knew he wasn't alone. He wasn't one of them yet. He'd never be left unobserved. But perhaps he could be. If he could take Rachel prisoner. Prove to them all that she was not his obsession. She was his tool, his weapon to be used against the Organization. Nothing more.

Not anymore.

There was a dent in the door and scratches in the steel that could only have been left by claws. Adrian stared at the marks, the same thought that had been rolling around slowly in his brain since the second they'd seen the facility rising again to the forefront.

Rachel was gone.

The facility had been completely abandoned. This was the place. His memory of that time was far from sharp, but he knew this door. Knew he had let it close with Rachel still trapped inside.

There was no blood. He would have thought that was a good sign, if not for the overpowering stench of bleach that had all the feline-shifters in the room gagging and covering their sensitive noses.

It was all gone. Not a scrap of paper left behind. Even the electronic pads sealing all the doors and windows had been stripped. All that was left was a husk of a building. But a husk that perfectly matched the schematics on the hard drive. That was a victory, he supposed. The data looked to be legit.

Adrian stared at the dent in the door.

One hundred and three. There were one hundred and three more Organization facilities scattered around the world. One hundred and three other prisons and laboratories and way stations where Rachel could be. One hundred fucking three.

Dominec whirled, putting his fist through a wall. "We were too slow," the asshole tiger snarled, and for once Adrian agreed with him.

They'd waited too long. Waiting for his feeble body to be up to the trip.

"We'll try the other locations," Kye, their usually reticent snow-leopard leader, said. "They can't evacuate them all."

But they all heard the lie in the words. The Organization *could* evacuate every facility they knew of. One hundred and three empty buildings.

"We aren't giving up," Roman vowed. "This is just the beginning."

The Alpha's heir hadn't been supposed to be on the incursion team, but on the second day Roman and a slim, dark-haired cougar-shifter named Patch had joined them. The two had been in constant physical contact with one another ever since. The other lions on the mission whispered about the Alpha's heir and the cougar, but Adrian kept his head down and his focus on the mission at hand.

The failed mission.

Now the Alpha's heir reached over and cupped Patch's nape. "We aren't giving up," Roman murmured, the words so low that no shifter without avian hearing would have caught them. "We'll find her."

Her. The reminder was sharp. Everyone on the incursion team was looking for someone. Patch's mother was in captivity and her father now believed to be dead, thanks to the information on the hard drives. It wasn't just Rachel they had failed to find. In fact, she would be so far down their priority list her name probably fell off the bottom of the page.

But for Adrian, finding her had just become priority one.

The door was dented.

It was a small thing, but he couldn't stop staring at it. Only a shifter would have the strength to do that to a steel door. She'd released someone. Someone who could have attacked her and dented the door in the process of spilling her blood. Or they could have been trying to bang their way out together while he was running up the hillside as fast as that fucking super juice would carry him.

He still wasn't sure how he felt about her. The emotion that burned in his chest was too complicated to examine. He'd put it in a box, figure it out later.

He simply knew that he had to find her. It was his mission. And the Hawk always completed his missions.

Chapter Seven

"Are you being good, Dr. Russell?"

Rachel froze, her fingers hovering over her keyboard, suddenly incapable of typing another word into the report she'd been compiling. "Good?"

She didn't look behind her. She didn't need to. Madison Clarke's particular brand of poisonous sweetness wasn't the sort of thing a person forgot. Her footsteps were nearly silent as she came farther into the lab, but Rachel heard them clearly—it felt like even her heart had stopped beating so there wasn't much to mask the sound.

"I hear you've been a model citizen these last few weeks."

Not that I've had much choice in the matter. Her mama had always told her if you can't say something nice, don't say anything at all. She'd been very silent the last few weeks—a policy that had probably kept her alive.

"I suppose you haven't heard the latest news, holed up down here in your lab."

Locked up was more like it, but again Rachel said nothing, staring blindly at the screen in front of her.

"Would you believe three of our facilities have been attacked in the last month? Someone seems to be trying to liberate our shifter friends. You wouldn't know anything about that, would you, Dr. Russell?" Madison propped her hip on the desk beside Rachel's arm, spinning some kind of small remote control between her hands.

Rachel was certain she did not want to know what that remote controlled. "Me? How could I?"

She hadn't had any contact with the outside world in weeks. They could hardly accuse her of conspiring against the Organization.

"A certain shifter was spotted at the site of the last attack—right before they disabled the security measures as if they knew exactly where each and every camera and sensor were located. How would your boyfriend know that, Dr. Russell? Hm?"

Her boyfriend. Noah. No, the *Hawk*.

Suddenly her heart was beating again. Too fast. Too loud. Drumming out a tattoo against the inside of her ribcage. He was alive. He'd made it. For weeks she hadn't known, could only hope that Madison's irritation was a sign of his survival, but if they were launching attacks, he'd not only survived, he'd made it to the other shifters. Her plan, her stupid crazy half-assed plan had worked.

For everyone except her.

"The Board would like to know what you know, Dr. Russell. Typically that would mean the C Blocks, but you're special, aren't you?" Madison purred.

Rachel barely heard her.

Was he still angry with her? Did he ever wonder what had happened to her? Did he ever think about her? She couldn't seem to stop thinking about him. Trapped inside her lab, day after day, forced to work for the devil just to keep on breathing.

She'd discovered she liked breathing. Another defining moment.

Often it was him she thought about as she worked to further the Organization's cause against her will. She hoped he would respect that she was doing what she needed to survive, but couldn't help fearing he would prefer she had eaten a bullet instead.

"You and I are going to get to know one another better," Madison went on, apparently having tired of waiting for a response from her. "Plenty of time for that when we get to your new lab." Rachel looked up at that and Madison smiled. "We're moving you. You have twenty-four hours to pack your research."

Rachel bit her tongue and held her breath until Madison's near-silent footsteps faded and the door whispered shut behind her. Only then did her brain latch on to her last words like a drowning woman gasping for air.

They were moving her. Did that mean Noah was coming here? Did they know something about the shifters' plans? Or was it just a precautionary measure? They were careful, doubtless evacuating all the locations the infamous Hawk might know about.

She was more than a little surprised they hadn't moved her to the C Blocks to try to get the information out of her. She was too valuable to be tortured, apparently. Just like she was too valuable to be killed. Her unique understanding of shifter reproductive science was the only thing keeping her alive.

Rachel scanned the lab, mentally prioritizing each item, deciding what to pack first. As tempting as it was to tell the Organization to screw themselves and smash every instrument in her prison, she knew the only ones who would suffer from her tantrum would be the shifters who would be put through the same tests all over again to reclaim any data she destroyed.

She hadn't been allowed to have any contact with her patients, which wasn't much of a surprise. Ever since she'd woken up in this lab after Noah's escape to find Madison eyeing her with her chilly gaze, her low voice calmly explaining how disappointed she was in Rachel, she'd known things weren't going to be like before. She wasn't the Organization golden child anymore. She was a traitor. A prisoner.

She stood, the anklet weighing heavy against her left ankle. It had been locked around her ankle when she woke up that morning with Madison standing over her.

Think of it as house arrest, Dr. Russell. This lab is your house.

And if I leave?

Thirty seconds later, boom. You're an amputee. Don't try to leave, Dr. Russell.

Her life stretched out in front of her—days and nights locked in this lab, or another one just like it in another facility. Unless Noah came for her. That was what she dreamed about each night on the cot tucked against the far wall. Noah bursting into the lab, armed to the teeth, bristling with strength and purpose as she'd seen him that night in the hotel. Not as she'd last seen him, emaciated and staggering, each step a struggle as she rushed him through the sterile Organization halls.

She dreamt someone would rescue her, just as she'd rescued over a hundred shifters, but she, better than anyone, knew the odds, and they weren't in her favor.

She didn't bother going to her cot to collect her personal items—there weren't any. She wondered, sometimes, when the nights were long and the whirr of the lab equipment kept her awake, what had happened to her things at her condo. The photos and keepsakes she'd brought from her parents' house when her mother passed could be gathering dust in her empty apartment. All of her bills were set to autopay and she'd practically lived at her work before she was forced to literally live at her work, so it could be months or even years before anyone realized she wasn't in her condo anymore. Or had the Organization swept in and collected all her things so it would look like she had moved? Had they taken her things, moved them to some storage unit somewhere filled with the possessions of the hundreds of shifters they'd kidnapped over the years?

The Organization had chosen well when they hired her. No one would miss her.

Sure, she'd had occasional email contact with friends from college and med school, but everyone had grown up and grown apart, gotten busy with their own lives, their own families and practices. Her schedule had never made it easy to cultivate friendships outside the Organization and with her family gone, who would even notice she wasn't around anymore?

No one, apparently.

It was a sobering thought. Thirty-two years on the planet and if she simply vanished off it, no one would know or care. That wasn't what her life had been supposed to be. This wasn't who she was.

She shook away the depressing thought. There was no sense dwelling on it now when she should be packing. She had a lifetime to dwell on it when they got her to her new prison, wherever that was. Though wherever it was, she was sure it wouldn't be on any of the hard drives she'd smuggled out with Noah. They were taking her beyond his reach.

Rachel rubbed her fist against her sternum, pressing against the ache there. She hadn't forgotten the look of betrayal in his eyes when she'd jabbed him with the needle. The idea that he would fight his way into an Organization facility just for her...ludicrous.

But still she hoped for it, with the part of her soul that still believed in miracles.

The lights flickered and a fraction of a second later, the building shuddered.

Rachel stumbled, bracing herself against the wall as the room went dark. Power failure alarms began beeping insistently on the machines around her and emergency fluorescent lighting kicked in, casting the room in an odd, muted orange glow. In the distance, several floors above her head, a siren began a cascading whoop.

"*Noah.*"

It had to be him.

And she couldn't go to him. She couldn't help. She couldn't do a damn thing, trapped in her lab while all of the machines seized from lack of electricity.

"Oh no. No no no. Not the incubators."

She raced over to the large, box-like machine, but it was still humming softly, the lights on the status panel a comforting green, indicating the battery backup had kicked in. Rachel offered up a quick prayer of thanks. She hadn't been able to see patients, but her work continued nonetheless. Test-tube shifters were the Organization's current goal. Once they could breed them, they were convinced they could be trained—as even the youngest shifters they had captured seemed resistant to Organization training. Her two mandates were to produce a viable shifter fetus—something the Organization had yet to achieve—and to develop a gene therapy to activate shifter abilities in humans. All of her research pointed to the second mandate being impossible, so she focused her energy on the first, working slowly, methodically, showing only enough progress to keep them from killing her, and guarding the biological resources she was given. Any ova that failed to fertilize was another shifter female being subjected to having her eggs harvested—so Rachel treated the test-tube products in the artificial wombs like gold.

It had been instinct to run and check on them. But if Noah had really come for her, none of that mattered.

She listened intently, trying to pick out the sounds of battle, but she was too deep in the bowels of the building. From things other doctors had let slip when they were brought in to consult with her, she knew she was at least three floors below ground. Any fighting on the surface was well beyond the range of even shifter hearing.

Were the shifters winning? Was Noah all right? She paced in the tight confines of her lab, imagining the Hawk striding through the halls, her white knight with piercing yellow eyes. The Organization security forces would flee before him—

Pop! Pop pop pop!

Gunfire. That was gunfire. Goose bumps spread across her arms. She retreated to the back of the lab, the phrase *fish in a barrel* echoing ominously in her mind as the sound came again and again. Rachel crouched down, wrapping her arms around her knees and closed her eyes to focus her hearing.

A door splintering. Another burst of gunfire. Closer this time. Right next door. Shouts—pain, shock, anger—then silence. Deadly, chilling silence.

The sequence repeated across the hall. Door, gunshots, shouting, silence.

Someone was systematically working their way through the lower level labs, shooting everyone he found.

That couldn't be Noah, could it? He was fierce, but this was something else. Something cold and—

The door to her lab cracked under the force of a blow from the outside. A second strike and it sheared off the hinges, ricocheting off a centrifuge and smacking to the ground.

The man who filled the doorway was like something out of a horror movie. Blood covered him in a fine mist, but Rachel had a feeling none of it was his. One side of his face was ridged with heavy, ugly scars and his eyes were utterly devoid of emotion. The Hawk was a warrior. This man was a killer.

Her heart stopped beating, as if it knew what was coming and didn't want to waste the effort of a last few beats. "Please," she whispered.

The muzzle of the gun lifted, aiming unerringly for her face. "Sorry, sweetheart. I don't do requests."

Chapter Eight

Where the fuck was she?

Adrian cursed under his breath as he stalked through the halls of the Organization base. He'd been so sure she would be here. It was the biggest target they'd struck so far and from the schematics, it seemed to be the most scientifically oriented. When she hadn't been at either of the first two prison-like holding areas they'd taken out, Adrian had become convinced she was being forced to work at one of the labs. Today, when they'd surrounded the building, he'd felt that itch, that little scratch between his shoulder blades that screamed to him that she was here.

He'd been so fucking sure. So where the fuck was she?

He strode past Grace, who was baring all-too-pointy teeth at any of the scientists who threatened to step out of line as she herded them into an office. In another office, Mateo, their computer specialist, was mining the system for information while the team leader Kye guarded his back, keeping track of the rest of the team via his earpiece.

"Hawk," Kye called out as he passed. "Dominec isn't reporting. He was supposed to be checking the maintenance area on the lowest level for stragglers. Go check on him."

There was a particular weight behind the words that Adrian didn't have to question. Dominec was unstable on the best of days and the last few missions had only widened the visible cracks in his sanity. Adrian didn't know how the tiger had gotten his scars. He didn't particularly want to know—but he knew Dominec personally blamed everyone and anyone related to the Organization for what had happened to him.

If he wasn't also a one-man SWAT team, they never would have brought him with them on the missions, but he was too much of an advantage to leave behind.

Adrian jogged down the stairs to check on their resident psycho. From the stairwell, he could hear the distant *pop-pop-pop* of gunfire and he swore under his breath. "Shots fired," he snapped into the coms, doubling his pace.

The hall below was no maintenance area. Clearly another research area that hadn't been on the schematics, it was painted in orange fluorescent light and blood. Dominec stood halfway down the hall over the remains of a door, covered in a fine red mist that indicated he'd taken the time to get up close and personal with at least a few of the bodies lying lifeless on the floor. He hadn't noticed Adrian yet, too fixed on whatever target he'd spotted inside the room he'd just breeched.

"*Please.*"

A sudden surge of adrenaline made Adrian's muscles twitch. He knew that voice.

He couldn't have flown down the hall any faster if he'd gotten his wings back.

"Sorry, sweetheart. I don't do requests," Dominec sneered—

And Adrian slammed into him broadside, striking the wrist of his gun arm with enough force to shatter the bone of a human. It wouldn't break Dominec's, but it did force his hand to open so Adrian could strip him of the weapon, before they hit the ground. He twisted quickly, pressing the advantage surprise had given him, and planted his knee on Dominec's carotid artery, the gun shoved hard against his temple.

"This one is mine," he snarled, with all the animalism of a rabid wolf, the calm, distant hawk totally subsumed by the need to stake this claim. "Understand?"

Dominec gurgled unintelligibly—he probably couldn't say much with Adrian kneeling on his larynx—but his claws snapped out.

If he chose to use those claws, this could go to hell in a hurry. Adrian couldn't win against the enraged tiger. He knew that. It was only because Dominec had been distracted by his own bloodlust that he'd managed to take him down at all. If the tiger went on the offensive, Adrian would have to pull the trigger—and while he might not like the crazy bastard, he didn't want to do that. Especially since he wasn't sure what that would do to his relationships in the pride. He couldn't afford to piss off the Alpha. Roman had recently taken over the top position in the pride and while he thought Roman liked him, that probably wasn't enough to let it slide if Adrian killed a shifter to protect an Organization doctor. Even the Organization doctor who had gotten them the schematics.

"*Mine*," he growled again.

Dominec's eyes were fully feline and Adrian reached for the battle calm, curving his finger more securely around the trigger. The tiger didn't look like he would mind dying, and Adrian was willing to do him the favor of taking him out, if that's what it took.

The door to the stairwell at the end of the hall banged open.

Their struggle had taken them through the doorway into the lab. They couldn't see whoever had arrived, but they both heard Grace's disgusted, "Dominec, what the fuck?" as she took in the carnage in the hall.

The tiger's claws retracted, his eyes going human.

"Get off me," he grunted, when Adrian shifted enough of his weight off the knee bearing into his throat that he could speak.

"No one touches her but me," Adrian reiterated, but he got to his feet, even helping Dominec to his—though he didn't go so far as to return the gun.

Grace's footsteps slowly approached down the hall, checking in the other rooms as Adrian would have done if he hadn't heard Rachel pleading for her life.

A soft rustle of fabric came from the far side of the room, but he didn't look at her, his focus still locked on the feral tiger. "Kye said you weren't reporting."

Dominec shrugged—he'd never shown much appreciation for authority. "I was busy."

Busy killing half the scientists on the Organization payroll.

A little whimper from the far side of the room finally called Adrian's gaze in that direction. And again it happened. The sight of her hit him like a punch.

Big chocolate eyes, rich brown curls, and that aura of innocence and hope. The building seemed to shudder around him—she could move his fucking world—then a piece of rubble fell from the ceiling and he realized it was actually shaking.

Rachel cowered against the wall and unwanted emotion surged up, a conflicting mess of feeling that was distinctly unwelcome in the middle of an op—including a bizarre unnatural rage that she hadn't run into his arms. His true mate would have. He should be relieved she hadn't distracted him during his altercation with Dominec, but all he felt was irritation that he'd saved her life and now she was looking at him like she wasn't sure whether he was her savior or her doom.

The hell of it was, he wasn't entirely sure himself.

He'd pictured her bruised and battered, tortured himself with images of her torture.

There wasn't a mark on her.

He'd thought she would be chained and restrained, helpless and vulnerable. A quick glance confirmed there wasn't even a lock on the door.

Every hair was in place. She was clean and healthy and whole. And the longer he looked at her—looking so fucking *good*—the more his rage built.

He'd come to save a prisoner and here she was, not a prisoner at all. One of them all along. He should have fucking known.

Vivi Andrews

He spoke without taking his eyes off her. "Dominec, go check in with Kye. I'll bring her."

He expected the tiger to snarl at him on principle—Dominec wasn't exactly known for taking orders—but his scarred face tipped into a lopsided smirk. "She is pretty damn hot. I'm not sure I should leave you alone with her. Who knows what could happen?"

"You were about to kill her," Adrian reminded him with little more than a growl.

"It would have been a clean kill. There's honor in a clean kill."

Not for the corpse. "Go."

Dominec propped a hip against a lab table. "I think I'll stay."

Adrian knew better than to tangle with the tiger, but the urge to dig his talons into the unscarred side of the bastard's face was fierce enough his knuckles ached—but nothing happened. His shifting was still fucked to hell and back.

Light, quick footsteps continued down the hall and Grace appeared in the doorway, tranq gun in one hand, Glock in the other. She stopped abruptly when she saw Dominec lazing there as if they were about to have tea. Adrian used her momentary focus on the tiger to move, quick and subtle, putting himself between Rachel and both Dominec and Grace.

The lieutenant frowned. "I would ask if you boys were playing nice, but I've seen the evidence to the contrary—" Grace broke off, her gaze landing on Rachel. Her expression went instantly and completely blank. "Is that her?"

Adrian gave a minute nod, his body tensing instinctively, weight rolling to the balls of his feet. He trusted Grace, but if she had orders he didn't know about...he wasn't taking any chances.

"Her who?" Dominec asked, looking entirely too intrigued for Adrian's comfort. "This that Organization bitch you've got a thing for, Hawk? That explains why you went apeshit on me. I

70

know she's hot as fuck, but trust me, the only good Organization doc is a dead Organization doc."

"Shut up, Dominec." Grace threw him a glare. "You're in enough trouble."

"Me?" Dominec asked with exaggerated innocence.

"Yes, you. What is your fucking damage? You just decided to go all slasher-movie and thought no one would notice?"

He shrugged. "They resisted."

"Sure they did." The building shuddered again and Grace cursed. "Come on. No more fucking around. We can sort out the details later." She jerked her chin toward Dominec. "Dumbass over there used too much explosive. The building is going to come down."

"Then I used exactly the right amount of explosive."

"Shut *up*, Dominec. And go fucking report to Kye already."

The tiger bowed mockingly, but obeyed her command, slipping out into the hall.

Grace tipped her head to better see the woman half-hidden by his body. Rachel had been silent, but chose that moment to whisper, "Are they all dead?"

With Dominec gone, Adrian let himself turn sideways to look at her. Her shoulder blades were pressed against the far wall of the lab and she was shivering, arms wrapped around herself, her pupils as big as dinner plates.

"Fuck, she's in shock," Grace groaned, coming the same conclusion he had. "You need a hand getting her out?"

"I've got this."

He caught her nod out of the corner of his eye, never taking his focus off Rachel. With quick, near-silent footsteps, Grace retreated down the hall after their resident psycho. Leaving Adrian alone with the woman he'd once thought would be his salvation—and an inexplicable, directionless rage.

Rachel had tried to be invisible as the Hawk and the scarred one fought over her like two feral dogs over a juicy steak. She'd held her breath when the tall woman with the short blonde hair and Rambo's arsenal strapped to her body had appeared in the doorway. She'd managed to hold it together until the woman mentioned the *slasher flick* in the hallway. And then she'd started to shake.

The Hawk was supposed to be her savior, but when that yellow gaze swung back to lock onto her, she knew her fantasies about a heroic rescues were just that—fantasies. She'd pictured this moment a thousand times in the last few weeks and it had always been some stupid movie-perfect scene. No blood on the face of the maniac backing him up. No disturbing scent of death wafting in from the hallway. No fear. In her fantasy, this moment was triumph, not horror. Her brain couldn't seem to reconcile the two. Even the air she was breathing felt wrong. Thick and strangely cold as the world got fuzzy around the edges.

Shock, the blonde one had said. Yes. That sounded accurate. She tried to remember the treatment, but her brain wasn't connecting the dots. Shivers rippled over her body, radiating out from her spine.

"Rachel." The Hawk flicked his fingers at her, an impatient summons. "Come here."

Her gaze traveled from the beckoning hand across his body to lock onto the other one, held loosely at his side and still gripping the gun like an extension of his arm.

"I'm not going to shoot you," he snapped, clicking on the safety and tucking the gun into his belt with a practiced motion. In the same move, the Hawk withdrew another, strangely shaped gun from its holster at his waist. "This goes faster if I don't have to tranq you and carry you out. *Come here.*"

There was anger in the words. Anger in his eyes. She couldn't make sense of it. This wasn't Noah, who had kissed her like she was his salvation. This wasn't even the man who'd been all business as he'd been her partner on countless shifter escapes. This man demanded he come to her merely to assert his authority.

"They're all dead, aren't they?"

He cursed softly and reached for her, the movement so fast she flinched away with a squeak of alarm before she realized he was simply taking her wrist to feel her pulse, a detached calm cooling the fire in his gaze. "Not all of them," he said.

Not all of them were dead. That was supposed to be comforting?

Who had survived? Madison Clarke? She seemed like a survivor. She'd been here earlier, but she had a feeling Madison would have an escape route mapped out for just this kind of occurrence and she would never allow herself to be taken alive. It would be the average working stiffs like Rachel who were left to fend for themselves when it was time for the Organization to answer for its sins.

The faces of all the people she'd seen and worked with in the last few weeks passed through her mind in rapid succession. How many were dead? Sure, none of them had helped her even though several had to know she was there against her will, but many of them were in the exact same position she had been. Prisoners in their own way. No one who worked for the Organization was wholly innocent, but no one deserved to be blood spatter smeared on the face of the scarred shifter.

"They weren't all bad," she heard herself protesting, the words distant and muted.

"I know." Noah still held her wrist, his grip gentle as he began pulling her toward the door.

"No." She resisted, it was important that she stay here—*the bomb*—but her efforts didn't have any more strength and focus than her fuzzy, swimming thoughts.

"Come on, Rachel. We have to go. We never stay long enough for them to send in reinforcements."

She couldn't imagine the Organization sending reinforcements. They seemed more the types to burn the place to the ground until nothing was left but a napalm scar. Either way, she couldn't leave. *The anklet...*

"I can't."

He turned on her so swiftly she stumbled, his rage briefly penetrating her shocky haze. Only his hard grip on her arm kept her upright as he snarled down at her. "Why the fuck not? Are you so loyal to them now?"

Loyal? She would have laughed if she hadn't been so busy gaping at him incredulously. He actually thought she was loyal to the Organization. After she'd gotten him out. Gotten a hundred and fifty shifters out. Admittedly, she was to blame for the months he spent in Organization custody, but he had to know she hadn't had a choice in that. Was it so much to ask that he trust her for five minutes?

Anger cut through the fog, clearing away her daze and sharpening her next words to a razor's edge. "I'm not loyal to them, you ass. I have a bomb strapped to my ankle."

Chapter Nine

The light on the anklet still blinked green, thank God. Along with the emergency lighting, whatever sent the signal to her anklet to keep her from blowing up must be supported by the back-up generators. Which meant she hadn't been blown to kingdom come when the power was cut, but it also meant she couldn't get out now, even if the walls were about to come down around her ears.

At the word bomb, the Hawk spun back to her so quickly she swayed away and would have fallen if he hadn't caught her by the wrist. He steadied her for only a second before kneeling and shoving her loose pant leg up to reveal the anklet it had partially covered.

"If I leave this room, it explodes."

His hand wrapped gently around her calf—making her shiver in distinctly inappropriate ways before he cursed low, without looking up from the device. "You can't leave," he repeated.

"I tried to tell you—"

But he hadn't been listening. Just as he wasn't listening now.

"Kye," he barked into the empty room, and it took her a moment to realize he was talking into some kind of communications device. "Who do we have who can diffuse a bomb in a hurry?"

Rachel held her breath, waiting through the long silence that followed before he looked up. "He's sending someone," Noah explained. He glanced back down at the device and jerked his hand away from her leg as if startled to find he had still been holding her, his thumb gently brushing her skin.

The building shuddered again, releasing another spray of rubble from the ceiling and the Hawk lurched to his feet. He cursed and began to pace in the tight confines of her lab. Two steps to the incubator. Two steps to her cot. Two steps to the centrifuge. Back to the incubator.

"You should go," she murmured. "No sense both of us being trapped down here if the building comes down."

He didn't deign to respond beyond a single fuming look.

Two more tight circuits of the room and then the Hawk came to attention, calling out, "We're back here," long before she heard the thud of running footsteps.

A slim young man with a pretty, boy-band-worthy face skidded to a stop in the doorway, looking a little green. "Motherfucker," he swore, "the hallway is full of—"

"Get it together, Mateo," the Hawk snapped, cutting him off before he could say what the hallway was full of, but from the smell of it, Rachel had a pretty good guess. Noah pointed to her ankle. "We need you to disable that so she can leave without setting it off."

A calm focus instantly fell over young Mateo and he rushed to kneel at Rachel's feet for a closer look. He made a soft humming noise and pulled a set of tiny tools out of his back pocket. As he poked at the anklet, Rachel's heart rate tripled. Noah stood back, arms folded tightly across his chest as he watched the proceedings like the proverbial hawk.

"You're awfully young for an explosives expert," she said softly, trying not to distract the boy, but needing the reassurance that he knew what the hell he was doing.

"I don't know shit about explosives," Mateo said matter-of-factly, doing nothing good for her blood pressure. "But I know electronics and almost all triggers are composed of computer elements these days. Diffuse the trigger, you diffuse the bomb. Usually."

Usually. How comforting. "And you know how to diffuse the trigger?"

He hummed again, peeling away the outer casing of the anklet to reveal the wires and chips within. Mateo cursed under his breath.

"Mateo?" she squeaked.

"What is it?" the Hawk snapped.

"It's not good news, but it's not terrible either," Mateo said, looking toward the Hawk rather than her. "They used the good shit. To short this mother out, we'll need to seriously fuck with the temperature of the main chip. Dry ice, an acetylene torch—something extreme. See what you can find."

"There's liquid nitrogen in a canister in the second freezer over there." Rachel pointed and both men shot her incredulous looks—doubtless wondering why anyone would keep liquid nitrogen on hand—but the Hawk quickly collected the canister and knelt beside Mateo. "Try not to give me freezer burn," she requested, feeling a little light-headed at the idea that she could have frozen off the damn anklet detonator at any time, but also terrified that it wouldn't work and they'd all be blown to pieces.

Rachel closed her eyes, lacing her fingers together in old habit and praying fervently. The last few years had been hard on her relationship with God, but she was still a preacher's daughter. She gathered up every last ounce of her faith and poured it into the prayer.

She didn't look when she felt the chill of intense cold close to her skin, holding her breath and redoubling her prayers. There was a crack, like ice breaking, and the pressure that had been a constant around her ankle for the last several weeks abruptly loosened.

"Mateo, you're a genius." Noah clapped him on the shoulder as she opened her eyes, both men straightening.

The building groaned ominously around them. Before Rachel could thank the young man, he was swearing and bolting for the door.

Noah caught her hand and met her eyes, and for a brief, flaring moment she thought she saw something in them. Something fierce. Something tender. Something that held the promise that perhaps she hadn't killed everything between them with that sedative injected into his back.

He swore under his breath and wrapped one hand around her nape, the warm weight unbearably familiar. Then he was bending to take her mouth with a kiss that was dominant and demanding and seized absolute possession, reasserting his claim on her soul, as if there had ever been a doubt.

Another of those defining moments, that kiss. When she realized she was the kind of woman who would always melt for this man, even when the world was falling down around them.

It didn't last long.

The soft pneumatic snick was the only warning she had before a sharp pain pricked her arm.

She jerked back, confused to see the tranquilizer dart sticking through her sleeve. She wanted to ask why. And why now, when he could have just tranqed her the second he walked in the door. But those thoughts were quickly drowned by the drugs flooding into her blood stream until only one thought remained.

I guess I deserved that...

Adrian caught Rachel against his chest as her legs buckled, tucking away the tranquilizer gun and lifting her over his shoulder. She flopped there bonelessly as he charged from the room. His feet skidded a bit on the blood-slick linoleum of the hall floor, but he found his footing and raced past the lifeless faces of her colleagues.

He hadn't planned on tranqing her. In his anger, he'd wanted her to see the bodies, as a warning, a reminder that he was the only thing standing between her and a violent end—but then she'd looked at him, her big, brown eyes so open and trusting, so fucking *hopeful* and he hadn't been able to do it.

Tranqing her was the easiest solution. He wouldn't have to explain to anyone why he'd done it. They would all assume she'd resisted. No one needed to know it was his own unwanted softness toward her that had prompted him.

And no one needed to ever know about the kiss. It hadn't happened. It was already forgotten.

She wasn't light and though he was almost back to top shape, he was breathing hard by the time he reached the top of the stairs and wheezing like an old man when he burst out of the building into the parking lot beyond where Kye was organizing the loading of the bound prisoners onto a van.

Whether or not to take hostages from the Organization strikes had been hotly contested at the pride. Many wanted everyone who would threaten them exterminated to make a point. Others didn't want anyone who had ever been involved with the Organization anywhere near pride lands. But in the end, Roman had prevailed on his pride to accept the wisdom of containing their enemies, at least until they knew more about them.

The first few incursions had been against Organization facilities that specialized in holding shifters, the transit points— so there had been far more refugees released than hostages captured—but this was a different sort of installation. This facility was almost all Organization scientists—so the prisoners far outnumbered the rescued shifters.

Adrian hitched his own prisoner higher up on his shoulder and crossed to Kye to get his assignment for transportation back to the pride. They would split up, dozens of cars taking multiple routes and changing vehicles multiple times to ensure no one would lead the Organization back to the pride.

For the first time, Adrian found himself resenting the necessity, eager to get Rachel back on pride lands where she would be safe. Though he still wasn't sure whether he wanted her protected or at his mercy. Both perhaps. His feelings for her were far from clear—though his body still undeniably wanted her. The press of her thighs against his forearm as he held her in place over his shoulder was enough to stir his blood.

Inside the van, one of the prisoners huddled against the window, peering at him through the glass, eyeing Rachel's unconscious form slung over his shoulder. She was a frail-looking brunette, with her hair falling forward over her face, nearly obscuring her wide, terrified blue eyes. She looked too much like Rachel, and he avoided looking at her, not wanting to soften toward either woman.

Kye started to tell him to put Rachel with the rest of the prisoners, but must have realized who she was by the look on Adrian's face and quickly changed his tune.

A couple of the shifter soldiers nudged one another and pointed as he carried her to their designated car, whispering among themselves. The general attitude toward Rachel in the pride had changed drastically in the last few weeks. After the first successful raid, someone had leaked that the schematics had come from her and shifters rescued by her group began to fall out of the woodwork at the pride, singing her praises. His own reputation had improved as well when rumors had begun to fly about the infamous Hawk, doing a lot to smooth his way and gain the trust of the other lieutenants and soldiers. But where he was admired, she was *worshipped*.

Adrian tucked Rachel inside the car as behind him the building groaned and shuddered. It still hadn't collapsed, in spite of all their haste, and he overheard some discussion of whether they should intentionally blow it up now that everyone with a pulse had been evacuated.

If the choice was left to him, he would have flattened the fucking place, but he didn't stir himself to enter the argument. He wasn't a full member of the pride. He knew when to pick his battles. And it sounded like the argument was tipping in his direction anyway.

Five minutes later, Grace gave the order and the shifters all paused to watch as the building blew with a satisfying *boom*. Then they all dove into the cars—and some shifted and dove into the wilderness—scattering like cockroaches when the kitchen light came on and leaving nothing for the Organization to find but rubble.

Now if only he could be as decisive about what to do with the lovely doctor.

Chapter Ten

The air smelled of winter—or what she'd always imagined northern winters must smell like while she was growing up in the South. Pine and cold—if cold had a smell. Rachel focused on that—did cold have a smell?—distracting herself from the throbbing in her skull.

This must be what a hangover felt like. She'd always been careful not to overindulge in the past—initially because she didn't want to disappoint her parents and in recent years because losing control while the Organization was watching her was a dangerous business. But this definitely felt like hangovers she'd read about. Throbbing head. Achy muscles. A heavy reluctance to open her eyes.

And a chain around her ankle.

Rachel frowned, shifting again, and again heard the clink of metal and felt the weight of it dragging at her leg. That opened her eyes in a hurry.

She sat up, flinging off the light blanket that had covered her and groping for her ankle. This time instead of the detonator that had been her constant companion for the last weeks, her fingers met cold metal. The two-inch band of silver was smooth and shiny. New, by the look of it. Loose enough not to chafe, but snug enough that she'd have to break several bones in her foot to get it out. The chain was long and slack, trailing off the bed and across the floor.

She wore the same clothing she'd had on when they captured her at the lab—slacks and a turquoise long-sleeve button-down blouse that was now hopelessly wrinkled. Her shoes and socks were nowhere in sight and a bandage stretched over the ball of her left foot. Rachel frowned, wiggling her bare feet and felt a cut stretch and pull on the bottom of her foot, though there was little pain. Had they put a tracker in her? Taken one out?

It wouldn't surprise her if the Organization had tagged her from day one. Perhaps it was for the best that she hadn't been able to escape with Noah. She may have led the Organization right to them.

He was nowhere in sight, her hawk. He'd left her, alone in a cabin of some kind. The only light was courtesy of a weakly flickering camp lantern dangling from a hook near the door and the moonlight sneaking through holes in the threadbare curtains, but it was enough to see the rustic timbers crisscrossing on the ceiling and the rough-hewn furnishings that looked like they could have been pulled out of a Jack London novel.

The long snake of a chain was secured to a black pot-bellied stove in one corner, giving her full play of the single ten-by-twelve room and access to a smaller-than-standard door—which she desperately hoped led to a bathroom, considering the pressure on her bladder.

She scrambled out of the bed, pulling the chain behind her, and rushed to make use of the facilities—which were, thank heavens, of the modern variety and not a latrine to match the rest of the backwoods décor. Her body's needs seen to, she washed up and splashed water on her face to banish the last of the drug-induced lethargy. There was no mirror, but she didn't need one to know she probably looked like something the dog had been keeping under the porch. Her mama would be horrified by her lack of gentility, but Rachel didn't have time for vanity.

She quickly took stock of her surroundings—the bathroom was unextraordinary. Narrow shower, toilet and tiny pedestal sink all crammed into a space smaller than most closets. There was toilet paper and a cake of brittle soap beside the faucet, but otherwise no toiletries to speak of. Certainly nothing that could be used as a weapon or a tool to help her escape. Not that she was planning an escape—but it certainly spoke to Noah's frame of mind that he hadn't even left so much as a toothbrush for her to use against him.

The main room was just as bare. There was a small kitchenette—but the cupboards were empty. Not even a box of Cheerios to reward her for her efforts. The cooler held only bottled water and, realizing how dry her throat was, she snagged one and popped the seal, drinking half of it as she studied the rest of the room. A slab of a table with two heavy-looking chairs, a bed that was more glorified futon than proper mattress, a sturdy footlocker with a massive padlock at the foot of the bed, and, of course, the pot-bellied stove, squatting beside a pile of firewood.

She nudged one of the chairs out from the table and perched on it, once again scanning her limited range. She couldn't quite reach the windows or the largest door, the one she suspected must lead outside. She could be two feet from another building or two hundred miles and she wouldn't know it.

Was this a shifter commune? Or some remote cabin where they kept their prisoners who could not be trusted on their land?

Night had fallen, but her sense of time was all muddled. She must have lost at least nine hours, but for all she knew she'd been drugged for days. The Organization had been known to move shifters around the world while they were unconscious. She couldn't put it past the shifters to have done the same to her. Heck, she hadn't even been a hundred percent sure where she was *before* Noah captured her at the lab, so figuring out how far she'd been taken was pretty much a lost cause.

Noah...why wasn't he here? It seemed wrong that they would just leave her alone, unsupervised. Though the chain around her ankle was enough to keep her from going anywhere. She wasn't a super-spy. Not like him.

Where the hell was he? Didn't he *want* to see her? He hadn't kissed her like a man who was going to leave her to slowly starve to death in the woods.

The shifters wouldn't kill her. There was no point in it. She wouldn't believe Noah could be so vengeful. And he was still Noah beneath the angry layers of the Hawk. She was convinced of it.

This could be a test to see if she would try to escape. But he couldn't know her so little that he thought she would run.

Though really, how well did they know one another? They'd worked together for years, courted for a few weeks, and then she'd had him imprisoned and experimented on before helping him escape and becoming a prisoner herself. Theirs wasn't exactly the kind of relationship that had been conducive to sharing soul secrets. Not that she ought to be thinking in terms of relationships. She bet he wasn't.

But what *was* he thinking? If she could just see him, just look in his eyes while she asked him what they had planned for her—

The door opened as if in response to her half-thought prayer, and there he was. A tall, thin silhouette with a slightly stooped posture. If he'd cultivated the slouch to be less threatening, it failed abysmally. He still radiated that fierce intensity, yellow eyes seeming to glow in the dark shadows of his face.

"Noah." The name slipped out on a whisper, absent her intent. She stood, hovering uncertainly behind the table.

He stepped over the threshold, hooked the door with his foot to flick it shut and dropped a heavy bag to the floor with a thud before turning those gleaming yellow eyes on her again. "Don't call me that."

Right. Of course he wouldn't want to be reminded that she'd helped him build his ark of shifters, escaping two by two. She was the enemy. How dare she forget? "What do you want me to call you? Master? Sir?"

"Adrian," he snapped, cutting her off.

She caught her breath, shocked. "Is that your name? Your real name?"

He smiled, and it wasn't friendly. "No point hiding it from you now. I'm going to personally make sure you're never in a position to tell any of your Organization buddies about me."

She clenched her teeth, biting back her irritation. *Do not argue with your jailer.* "I don't have Organization buddies," she said, ignoring her own counsel, one hand fisting where it rested on the table.

"No? Then it won't bother you to know we leveled that building and everyone who was still inside it?"

"Of course it will bother me. Death is always a loss—"

"Not all death." His face, always sharp and angular, seemed even more jagged with the ferocity of his expression as he stalked closer, looming over her in a way that made her grateful for the table between them. She was tempted to sink back into the chair, but forced some starch into her spine.

Her emotions were a mess—so grateful to be here with him, away from the Organization, and so frustrated with the injustice of the way she'd been shackled and treated like just another Organization villain. Injustice won. "Have you forgotten everything I did for the shifters for the last four years?"

"I haven't forgotten *anything.*" He propped his fists on the wood, looming closer. She fought the urge to fall back.

"You have to know I didn't have a choice. When I sedated you at the hotel—"

"I don't want to talk about that," he snapped, shoulders stiffening.

"The schematics worked, didn't they? I got you out. I got you information that could take down the Organization. *I did that.*"

"So you're the victim here, are you, Doc?"

"I may not be a victim, but I'm not the only villain in the room, *Adrian.*"

He jerked at the sound of his name and straightened, pivoting away from the table and storming to the kitchenette— though it was probably an unsatisfying distance to storm off, since the room was small enough he made the stove in two steps.

She swallowed thickly, able to get a full breath now that he'd stopped eating up all the oxygen in the room with his proximity. She studied the lines of tension in his back. He'd grown strong again since his escape and there were muscles there again, where once he had been skin and ridges of bone. Remembering the way his body had been all but concave when she found him in the labs, her irritation retreated, leaving only a wash of guilt. She sank uneasily back into the chair, gripping the edges of the seat.

"Where are we?" she asked tentatively.

He didn't turn, but she saw his fingers tracing the lines of the sink, as if remembering the shape of it would sooth him somehow. "Does it matter?"

"As long as we're far away from the Organization, no. It doesn't." She wanted to rise, to go to him, but something about his rigid posture stopped her. She didn't know how to deal with this version of him. "Thank you for getting me out of there."

He did turn then, frowning. He studied her for so long she grew self-conscious, smoothing her hair and tucking the stray strands behind her ears. He'd once told her how much he loved her hair, twirling it around his long fingertips and using it to tug her close, his lips just teasing hers on the edge of a kiss.

It had been a risk, being with him, but desire had made her reckless, the danger adding a delicious tension...or maybe that was just him. The world was always sharper and brighter in his arms.

"I can't make you out, Dr. Russell," he said finally, folding his arms.

"Ask me anything. I won't lie."

And for the first time in what felt like a lifetime, the words were wholly true.

She didn't have to lie. She didn't have to smile for her bosses while her stomach churned at what they were doing. She didn't have to feel her heart beating out of her chest as she smuggled out a shifter, praying desperately that all the pieces were in place and all the codes she'd been given were still active.

No one was going to catch her now. Noah—Adrian— wouldn't kill her if she failed to cooperate. The shifters had an honor the Organization had never possessed. It was why they were at such a disadvantage in the silent war.

For the first time in an age—hell, maybe *ever*—Rachel was free to tell the truth. To be herself. It had been so long, she wasn't entirely sure she remembered who that was anymore, but she was finally free to find out.

Free.

The chain around her ankle was tangible irony, but it couldn't diminish the feeling that rose up in her chest and filled her eyes with tears.

Adrian's raptor gaze immediately locked on the moisture and his frown darkened. "Crying won't gain you anything."

"It's not a ploy," she said, her tone sharpened by his lack of trust. "I'm just relieved."

"Relieved," he repeated dubiously.

"I don't have to lie anymore."

"All right." He crossed back to the table, pulled out one of the heavy chairs and spun it on one leg like it weighed nothing more than a feather. Resettling it with the back braced against the table, he straddled it and braced his forearms across the back. His yellow eyes gleamed. "Tell me all this truth of yours then."

"All of it?"

"Backing out already?"

She wet her lips, mind racing. This was a test. She'd always been good at tests. Her emotions would go quiet, her mind calm and sharp, and she'd see the answers rising out of her memory, clear as day. But this wasn't like other tests. She had a feeling he wouldn't let her retake this one if she failed to give him the right answers.

There were thousands of truths she'd been swallowing over the last four years, but only one that seemed to matter. One regret that swallowed everything else. "I would never have betrayed you if there was any other choice that would have saved your life."

His eyes went distant. Yellow always seemed such a bright warm color; she'd never known it could be so icy cold. "Is that so? And the way you were with me, they made you do that?"

"No, Adrian. Everything between us was real. They came to me, when we'd been seeing one another for a few weeks, called me before the Board of Directors." She remembered the terror of that meeting. The way her heart had beat so fast and hard she'd been grateful there were no shifters in the room to hear the blatant tell. Mr. Washington, the Chairman of the Board, had watched her with his eerily pale gray eyes, unblinking as he slid photos across the table. Photos of her with Noah. "They'd been following us. They knew who you were, but they didn't know what we were doing. The shifters we'd helped escaped were still safe from Organization hunters. They didn't suspect me yet. They said if I helped them acquire you, it would prove my loyalty."

"So you proved it."

"What else was I supposed to do?" She started to reach for him, but pulled her hands back when his expression darkened, knotting her fingers at the edge of the table. "They knew who you were already. They would have kept hunting until they acquired you, one way or another, and if I tipped you off they would have known instantly that I wasn't to be trusted. Everything I'd done in the last three years would have been called into question and they might have uncovered the entire operation. At least this way, I was still in a power position in the Organization. I was able to get more shifters out and start working out an exit strategy for both of us."

That was what she'd told herself, over and over again, as she'd gone to meet him that night, knowing what she would have to do.

She'd told herself he knew the dangers as well as she. Some part of her had been expecting discovery for weeks, waiting for the other shoe to drop. And then it had—like a ton of bricks on her chest, making it hard to breathe normally.

She was good under pressure—quick on her feet. If she hadn't been able to think with adrenaline rampaging through her system, she would never have survived as long as she had—but that day as Mr. Washington had interrogated her, her brain had short circuited and she'd known only fear. Luckily, the illusion of cooperation had been her only play for so long it was second nature. They'd thought she was just a gullible female, a pretty face with an advanced degree being taken in by a shifter con artist. *How long have you been seeing this man, Dr. Russell? Have you told him anything about the Organization? When will you be seeing him again? Think of this as an opportunity for advancement, Dr. Russell. A chance to prove your loyalty. Of course, we want to believe you're loyal. You're the best we have at what you do. That's why you're still with us, my dear.*

That subtle emphasis on *with us*. That thinly veiled threat...

Adrian shook his head, eyes dark and unforgiving. "You should have come to me. Told me what they were asking of you. I could have—"

"What? Waved your magic wand and made it all better? They were monitoring me. I couldn't risk sending a message to you. Too many lives were at stake." She shook her head, brushing furiously at the frustrated tears that threatened her eyes. "And even then, even knowing it was the best move to turn you over to them, I still almost didn't do it. That night, I tried to warn you, tried to get you to fly away, but you wouldn't listen."

"So it's my fault you stabbed me full of sedatives and let them have me?"

"I didn't say that." She scrubbed at her face, not even wanting to think of how wretched and puffy she must look right now. So much for vanity. "I swore to myself that I would do everything in my power to protect you while you were in Organization custody and I kick myself every day for not being able to watch over you better."

He went rigid, eyes blazing. "That's what you call it? Watching over me?"

"I know I failed you."

"*Failed* me?" he parroted incredulously, lurching up and away from the table.

She could hardly blame him. "Maybe I made the wrong call, maybe we should have run—but we wouldn't have those schematics now if I had. We wouldn't have their rosters or their financials. We wouldn't be able to mount a successful offensive against them—like you were always talking about. And there are over seventy shifters free today who would still be in Organization custody if I'd run then. Children, Adrian. So forgive me if I took a gamble that hurt you in the name of the greater good. I shouldn't have made the choice for you, but would you honestly have wanted me to make a different one?"

His eyes narrowed as he stood over her, his firm jaw locked. She felt his gaze like a touch—on her shaking hands, her breasts as they rose with each gasped breath, the tears that still clung to her lashes.

"You're very good." It didn't sound like a compliment.

Rachel huffed out a sigh and looked away from him, that sense of frustrated persecution rising again. If she even had the right to feel persecuted after everything she'd done to him. She'd tried to balance the scales with everything she'd done *for* him, but it may never be enough.

Did he hate her now? She wanted to ask but was afraid to hear the answer. Afraid she already knew.

"What do you want me to say?"

"Sorry wouldn't be a bad place to start."

"*Sorry.*" She released a humorless laugh. "I am sorry. I am so sorry. I must have said that to you a dozen times. How many times do you need? A hundred? A thousand? Would you like it in writing? Or maybe I should get a tattoo."

"You haven't said it. Not to me. Not once."

She'd said it. She knew she had. He may not have heard it, but she'd spoken the words over and over when she was helping him escape. And in his ear before she stuck him with the needle, begging him to forgive her. But she would gladly say it again.

Rachel looked up, meeting the chilled yellow stare head on. "I'm more sorry than I can express for everything that I have done that has caused you pain in any way." She wet her lips, knowing she should leave it at that—but Rachel had never been good at leaving well enough alone. "Can you say the same?"

Chapter Eleven

Adrian stared down at her across the table, trying to pin down why he couldn't just do as the Alpha had instructed and present the bargain the Lone Pine Pride had come up with for the woman who was both Organization doctor and savior to so many shifters. He'd come in here to do that and only that, but one look at Rachel and all his good intentions had burned away.

She wasn't lying helpless on the bed like he'd expected, but sitting at the table, looking beautiful and rumpled and still somehow so elegantly composed and so damn *beautiful*, as if she didn't need him at all. And once again she hadn't flung herself into his arms, damn it.

He'd wanted to push her, to punish her, to rage at her and to beg her forgiveness all in a single breath. He wanted to reach across that table, drag her into his arms and kiss her until they both forgot why they were angry and all this awful, awkward distance between them melted into heat.

When she'd spoken his name, he'd gotten half-hard. When she'd cried, he'd felt a simultaneous spike of vicious satisfaction and the achy need to pull her into his arms and croon that everything was going to be okay. She pulled to the fore in him the most protective and most vengeful sides of his nature, this woman he'd once dreamed would be his mate.

More fool he.

Could he say that he was sorry for everything he'd done to hurt her? He was sorry—the regret that he'd left her behind had been riding him hard ever since he'd woken up at Lone Pine—but he choked on the words. If he gave her even an inch, it would feel like cracking open his chest and giving her a free shot at his heart.

He ignored the question.

Laying his palms flat on the table, he fought to make his face as impassive as possible. "We have a deal for you."

Her beautiful brown eyes flared wide with surprise, soft lips parting. "A deal?"

"Regardless of my personal feelings for you—" which was lucky because he didn't have the first fucking idea what those feelings were, "—and taking into account the fact that you did work for the Organization, the shifters I've been working with still feel that you've been a friend to our people. You did help many of us escape—" including several who had made their way north to join the Lone Pine Pride and seemed intent on deifying Rachel as some sort of Mother Teresa goddess who had rescued them from a fate worse than death, "—and, like you said, without you, we wouldn't have the hard drives which have been so useful in our efforts against your employers."

"Former employers."

"As you say." He couldn't be more civil than that. Not when her only explanation for tormenting him in captivity was her *failure*.

Those pretty eyes narrowed, and the urge to yank her across the table and plunder her mouth returned with a vengeance.

"The deal?"

He straddled the chair again—less likely to lunge for her that way. "You'll tell us everything you know about the Organization and their plans." And everything she said would be checked and cross-checked a dozen times because Adrian wasn't going to be tricked in the name of the greater good again. "In exchange, you won't be killed."

She glared at him, unimpressed. "I was going to tell you everything anyway. I want to *help*."

"And you will. But you'll *forgive* my suspicion," he said, emphasizing the word she seemed to like so much, "if we don't give you free run of the place."

"I take it the chain stays." She shifted her feet and the metal rustled.

He hadn't thought of it actually. The chain had just been all he could come up with on short notice to make sure she stayed put if she woke up while he had to run down to the main pride compound to get supplies and check in with Grace. "It does."

"For how long?"

He didn't answer, just lifted a brow. Her face flushed, eyes flashing—she really was entrancing when she was angry.

"How long? Two weeks? A year or two? Fifty? Are you going to keep me chained up in the woods until we're both eighty-five and too senile to remember why you brought me here in the first place? Because if I don't have any chance of earning my freedom, I don't see why I should help you."

"I thought you wanted to help."

"I do and I will, but I'm not the enemy and I don't deserve to be treated—"

"Don't tell me how you deserve to be treated, Dr. Russell." *Everything between us was real,* she'd said. Even those moments when she'd tormented him, laughed at his pain. "Every second I was in Organization hands I dreamed of this moment, of having you at my mercy. I will treat you however I damn well please. You're *my* prisoner, not the pride's." That had been his condition. No one got to say a word about how he treated her. She was *his.*

One would think that would worry her, but her attention had caught on another word.

"A pride? Is that where we are? With lions?"

"Lions and tigers and bears," Adrian said dryly.

Her expression turned skeptical—as if he was the one whose word couldn't be trusted. "I thought the shifter species rarely mixed."

"This place is the exception that proves that rule." He waved his hands expansively. "Welcome to Lone Pine."

"Does the Organization know about this place?"

"That's one of the questions the Alpha is hoping you will answer, Dr. Russell." Adrian had been hesitant about being so forthcoming with her about the pride, but the Alpha's mate had lobbied hard to be open about who and what they were—within reason—in an effort to gain Rachel's full cooperation.

Rachel shook her head, her long loose hair sliding against her cheeks. "I was never involved in field operations. I know very little about that side of things."

"Then what good are you?" He said the words just to taunt her and her glare said she knew it. She didn't bother answering.

"When do I get to meet this Alpha of yours?"

"Not of mine. He doesn't rule me, so don't go thinking you can charm him into making me let you go."

"I wouldn't dream of it."

He frowned. He'd never seen her like this. Snarky and sarcastic. Angry and letting him see it. Before his capture, she'd always been the sweet, biddable Southern lady, yielding readily to his greater knowledge in tactics and strategy. In the cells she'd been viciously pleasant. He'd never heard this spunk from her before, this fight, though he supposed he should have suspected it was there. She couldn't have survived inside of the Organization for four years without a will of iron beneath all that gentility and silk.

"So this Alpha?" she prompted when he was too long studying her. "Is he on his way now? Should I whip up some lemonade like a proper hostess?"

Adrian shook his head. "It's after midnight. We'll go in the morning."

"Go? You mean leave this palace? Aren't you afraid I'll see something and betray you?"

Jesus, once she went sarcastic, she went all the way. "You'll be blindfolded," he said, just to piss her off.

He would have preferred she stay here, where none of the other pride members could see her, but there wasn't enough room in the tiny shack for all the pride's lieutenants who would need to listen in on her debriefing. So he'd take her up to the main house on the goddamn hill, in full view of the pride and everyone. No matter how queasy that idea made him.

There had already been several attempts made by small packs of angry shifters against the Organization prisoners before they were tucked away in a building with armed guards. The security forces weren't terribly keen on hurting their own people in an attempt to protect those who had hurt them in the past, so it was only a matter of time before someone broke through and got the vengeance they were all hungry for. Dominec had been reprimanded for the slaughter this morning and taken off the incursion team that would be going on the next raid—but that hadn't stopped him talking to anyone who would listen about how good it had felt when the warm blood of his enemies had painted his skin.

Anti-Organization sentiment in the pride was higher than ever—no surprise there, many of their newest members were so recently rescued they still woke screaming at night—and Adrian couldn't predict how the other shifters would react to Rachel. Sinner or saint? Monster or savior? He had a feeling it would be some of both and he wasn't going to allow anyone else to lay a finger on her. She was *his*.

"I'll need shoes, if it isn't too much trouble. And a change of clothes and some shampoo wouldn't hurt."

"Making demands already, Dr. Russell? Was I allowed those things when I was your guest?"

"Just a suggestion. I'm less likely to be bothered by my stench than your people are. I wouldn't want to offend the shifters' sensitive olfactory systems." A rustle of chains beneath the table. "Why is my foot bandaged?"

"Tracker," he grunted.

"Meaning you tagged me or you removed the Organization's tracker?"

"The latter. Though tagging you isn't a bad idea, now that you mention it. I'll get Mateo on it."

They almost hadn't caught the tracker in her foot. It had seemed like overkill when that same foot would have been blown off if the anklet detonated, but all the Organization prisoners had been scanned—and every single one of them had pinged the system with their left feet. Dr. Brandt was getting good at extracting them—practice made perfect. Rachel's incision was tiny and already healing well.

"How long was I out?"

He shrugged, tempted to lie, tempted to tell her six months—the same amount of time she'd stolen from him—but in the end he told the truth. "Not quite a full day."

"And this place? It's yours?"

He stiffened, irrationally defensive of the shabby hut.

He'd moved out here to the far edge of the pride lands, well away from the main complex, as soon as he was able to leave the infirmary. The shack was old, but sturdy, equipped with all the necessities, though little in the way of luxuries. Exactly how he liked it. But somehow bringing her here—Doctor Barbie who was probably used to the finer things—the place felt bare rather than utilitarian.

"As much as anything here is," he muttered, ready for the blade of her sarcastic tongue, but she surprised him. Her gaze slid sideways to the beat-up futon mattress resting on a plywood frame.

"You don't mean to stay here with me, do you?"

"Concerned about your virtue? It isn't like you have any charms I haven't sampled. Or any that would appeal to me now." The words felt like a lie, but he willed them to be true.

"Concerned about the size of that mattress, more like."

His blood instantly heated. She hadn't said it suggestively, but it was too easy to picture the two of them together on that undersized futon. God, it had been so long.

But that wasn't why she was here. She wasn't his lover anymore.

He had planned to stay here, but he hadn't given sleeping arrangements a thought for a second. The idea of sleeping in her presence seemed so wrong to him that it hadn't even occurred to him to worry about the bed. He would be awake, his instincts screamed, guarding her—though whether he was guarding her to keep her safe or guarding against her treachery, he couldn't say.

His raptor gaze quickly scanned the room, finding the solution. He'd prop the heavy chair he sat in now against the door and sleep there. She wouldn't be able to reach him to strangle him with the chain, and anyone trying to get to her would have to go through him. Perfect. It wouldn't be comfortable, but it wouldn't be the first time he'd slept sitting up, nor the worst place he'd ever slept by a long shot.

"The bed is all yours, princess."

"I'm not tired."

He rolled his eyes. "Then sing *Ninety-Nine Fucking Bottles of Beer on the Wall* to entertain yourself until morning. You won't bother me."

"I'd like to take a shower."

Another memory hit him like a sledgehammer of lust to the groin. He swallowed thickly and feigned disinterest, waving to the tiny bathroom—which had only required minor plumbing tweaks to make livable when he'd moved in. "Be my guest."

"And how am I supposed to get these pants off with the chain around my ankle?"

With my help. "Very carefully, I imagine."

She glowered at him. "Are you enjoying being an ass to me?"

He paused, giving that one the thought it deserved. "Yes. I believe I am."

Misery loved company and as uncomfortable as the erection he was concealing behind the table was, she had a lot of misery to make up for.

She muttered something uncomplimentary about his lineage and stood. He heard himself laughing, the sound rusty and strange. "And here I thought you were the virtuous preacher's daughter who never let a word stronger than *shucky-darns* pass your lips."

She paused in her stomp to the bathroom, half-turning to face him over her shoulder, he shifted to keep her from seeing what she'd done to him.

"My daddy taught me every swear I know. He always reckoned the Good Lord wasn't afraid of a little language."

Her accent had grown thicker as she spoke about her father, the southern lilt coating the words in sugar and sex. It had to be the first time he'd ever been turned on talking about God. "Then why do you blush every time you curse?"

"Oh hush up." She turned and sashayed into the bathroom, as much as she could sashay while dragging the chain, her exit only slightly marred by the fact that she couldn't get the door to shut properly with the chain wedged in the way. She struggled with it, cursing some more, but couldn't manage to get the door to close that last inch.

"Relax," he called out. "I'm not going to peek." His memory was sharp enough without needing a refresher course.

She went still, all noises from the bathroom ceasing, then shouted back, "Fine, then."

He would have heard her if she'd whispered. Just like he heard the whisper of cloth, the rustle of the chain as she struggled to shimmy her slacks down over it. Soft thumps as she hopped and lurched against the wall.

He knew the second she was naked. Even before the faucet creaked, the old pipes groaned and water splashed into the narrow shower stall. He could picture every inch of her, hear the sound of the first droplets hitting her skin.

He cursed his sensitive hearing, closing his eyes against the temptation to peek through the crack in the door, but that only made the sounds more vivid and fired his imagination even hotter.

She was still the most gorgeous creature he'd ever laid eyes on in real life. And she was six feet away. Wet. Dripping. Her skin silky and slick. Water droplets beading on the high curves of her perfect breasts. He could hear her. The sound of her stroking her hands across her stomach. Sliding soap over her long, sleek legs. Up along the softness of her inner thighs and higher, into her warm, slippery folds.

Adrian groaned and lurched up from the table, half-tripping over the chair and scrubbing both hands hard over his face. He had to get out of here. He couldn't stay here, fixated on every nuance of sound coming from the bathroom. He adjusted his jeans around his painful erection, hissing out a curse of his own.

He remembered every detail.

She'd been the most seductive combination of shy and wanton when she caught fire in his arms. He'd worshipped every inch of her, wanting to remember every second of their first time together. And every time after. His Rachel had been so much more than scratching an itch. She'd been everything. He'd seen his future in the light of dazed pleasure and adoration in her eyes.

A light he would never see again. He could never let himself be such a fool a second time.

He stalked from the cabin, instinctually reaching for his hawk, but again, nothing was there. And he could still hear the damn water. Frustration compounded on frustration and he snarled out a string of curses, tearing into the night.

Chapter Twelve

Rachel heard a sound like a door slamming while she was in the shower and flinched, instinctively covering herself. "Adrian?"

Nothing.

She shut off the water, listening hard, but couldn't make out a single squeak from the other room. Had he left her?

Rachel dried off as best she could with the scrap of a towel she'd found and wriggled back into her clothing—a distinctly undignified contortion thanks to the chain dragging at her ankle. Decent again, she yanked open the door and found the main room empty once again.

Dang it. She shouldn't have stomped off and taken a shower. She should have taken advantage of the fact that he was there and willing to answer questions, taken the opportunity to ask him everything she could think of. But when he'd been sitting there across from her, arms folded, looking like the king of the universe, she'd just wanted to prove to him that she wasn't cowed. That he wasn't the boss of her—even if he was. And now her bout of immaturity had landed her right back where she started. Alone and ignorant.

Though she knew a bit more than before.

She knew she would meet the pride Alpha tomorrow. She knew she was at Lone Pine Pride—and Adrian was watching over her.

Adrian.

She knew his name now. It suited him. Adrian. Her hawk.

She sat on the futon, tucking her legs up tailor fashion, and finger-combed the worst of the tangles out of her hair. He'd left no clues as to where he'd gone or whether he would be coming back tonight. He'd told her the bed was hers, but not where he would sleep. Perhaps he had a warm bed waiting for him.

A bed being warmed by a lissome lioness.

The thought made something unpleasant clench in her chest and she kicked herself for caring. Of course he would have someone here. He wouldn't stay celibate forever. He was a handsome man. Okay, not handsome, perhaps, but compelling. Magnetic. Undeniably attractive. The raw shifter animalism was more contained in him, but no less seductive for that control.

It was probably that blonde she'd seen at the lab. Tall and strong, obviously a warrior—she'd be attractive to a man like Adrian. A fellow soldier who would fight shoulder-to-shoulder with him in the battle to free the shifters. Perhaps she was even a hawk like him. His mate.

Rachel had read a lot about hawks in the wild in the last several months. Little was known about avian shifters, but there was always a certain amount of bleed over from the animal side into the human characteristics. Hawks mated for life. Their loyalty was unswerving.

Had that blonde woman earned his loyalty?

Rachel flopped onto her back on the mattress, hating the image of the two of them together that rose up in her mind, but incapable of banishing it. They would make an attractive couple, his darkness and her fairness. She was beautiful in a strong, striking way. Not unlike Adrian.

"Stop."

She said the word aloud, hoping it would work to stop the highlight-reel playing in her head.

It didn't matter if he'd gone off to his lover. It made no difference to her if they were soul mates. It wasn't like Rachel had ever had a shot of reclaiming his affection. He would never let himself care for her again—she'd seen that truth in the way he watched her, angry and unforgiving. But it still hurt to think of him with that blonde Amazon.

No sense getting caught up in girlish fantasies of the big, heroic Hawk now. He was her jailer. Nothing more. She needed to focus on that truth, on the present, and forget the might-have-beens of the past. Forget the way he could set her on fire with just a look. The way she'd been clenching her thighs together just sitting across from him at that fucking table.

She had a meeting with the Alpha in the morning. That was what she needed to be worrying about. Would he value all she'd done for them or fixate, as Adrian did, on her sins?

She was exhausted—who knew being in a drugged stupor all day was so tiring—and she knew she should sleep. She needed to be at her best in the morning. But her thoughts wouldn't settle.

She compromised by closing her eyes as she mentally rehearsed what she was going to say to the Alpha, one ear always open for the sound of Adrian returning. But he never did.

Rachel fell into a fitful sleep and must have eventually settled into something deeper, because when she opened her eyes, sunlight was poking through the holes in the curtains and a pile of fresh clothes rested against her ankle.

Her *unbound* ankle.

Somehow Adrian had come in here, unchained her and left the clothes—complete with shoes and socks—without ever waking her. Rachel lunged for the clothes, racing to the bathroom to change before her jailer returned and changed his mind.

The bathroom was a revelation in itself. Lined up in a neat little row behind the faucet were a toothbrush, toothpaste, floss, a brush, face wash and *deodorant*. She could kiss that man—if it weren't for the fact that her privation was due to him in the first place.

She quickly made use of the toiletries and the toilet, then began tugging on the clothes. He'd thought of everything—bra, panties, a soft, long-sleeved undershirt and heavier sweater, and a pair of snug, black slacks. The quality was high— certainly higher than the clothing the Organization had provided for her use—and each item fit as if it were made for her, with the exception of the pants which stretched just a little tight across her hips and butt. Even the shoes fit.

She only hoped he hadn't gotten these things from the blonde. She didn't want to be dressed in his lover's clothing. Though Rachel probably wouldn't have fit in her clothes anyway. The blonde had looked taller, broader across the shoulders and hips, with more exaggerated curves along with all her muscle. Which still didn't explain where the clothes had come from.

Banishing the thought, Rachel smoothed her hair into a snug ponytail and stepped out into the main room of the cabin. No chain rattled at her steps and she was tempted to smile, though the urge faded quickly.

Why had she been released? If Adrian had released her this was probably some kind of test to see if she would try to escape.

She wasn't about to run, but neither did she have any intention of wasting this freedom if this was going to be her only chance to breathe fresh air and get a look at where he was holding her.

There was no lock on the door, just a latch that lifted easily. She stepped out onto the narrow seen-better-days porch and took in her surroundings as quickly as possible.

The dense evergreen forest that shrouded the clearing on every side looked and smelled so different from the Georgia woods she'd played in as a child. The air was crisp and cooler than she was used to, the slight breeze cold enough to sting her cheeks, though there was no snow on the ground. It would be November now, she realized. Well into winter in the northern part of the country—provided they were close to the Wyoming facility where she'd broken Adrian out.

He melted out of the trees as if conjured by the thought—something he was making a habit of. Though as often as she thought of him, it would be more surprising if she *weren't* thinking of him when he appeared.

He'd changed as well—the jeans newer than his usual ragged pair and his preferred Henley covered by a rich green sweater that made his eyes look even more electric than usual. They'd both dressed up for the Alpha, it seemed.

It was surprisingly tempting to sass him about the fact that she hadn't attempted to run away as soon as the chains were off, but her mama's raising asserted itself and she said instead, "Thank you for the clothes and the sundries."

He shrugged, the muscles shifting beneath the green cloth and she shivered—half-cold and half-keen awareness.

"They fit perfectly. Where did you get them?" she asked as he reached past her, grabbing the coat she hadn't noticed hanging on the hook beside the door.

He dropped the coat around her shoulders. "It's a full-service pride."

Whatever that meant. "Well, thank you," she repeated, slipping her arms into the winter coat, instantly grateful for the warmth. Though she wasn't sure whether the sudden heat was from the coat or her body's reaction to his proximity.

He moved away from her to push the door closed and fasten a padlock over the latch. It was a strange dance they seemed to have with one another—frustration and care, anger and gratitude. Nothing could be straightforward with her hawk. A fact that was proven again as he pulled a black scarf from his back pocket and reached for her—at first she thought it was another nod to the cold of the day, but then the black cloth covered her eyes and she grimaced.

Of course she wasn't to be trusted. She, who had rescued over a hundred shifters. She couldn't be allowed to see where they were. God forbid.

"Is this Wyoming?" she asked, smelling the crisp freshness of his aftershave and the pine as her other senses tried to compensate for the loss of vision.

"Montana," he grunted, tugging the scarf tight.

"Would you tell me the truth?" she mused aloud. "What if I led my evil overlords back here?"

"I thought I explained," he said, his warm breath brushing against her neck. "You're never leaving my sight, so we don't have to worry about what you know about us."

She fought down a little shiver of awareness. "Then why the blindfold?"

"If you can't find your way to main pride compound, you can't go there begging for sympathy from shifters who don't know your treachery as well as I do." He took her arm, guiding her down the steps and onto the uneven ground of the forest with a touch that was just firm enough to be comforting.

As he led her through the forest, she was instantly hopelessly lost—a fact which likely would have been just as true if she'd been able to see. Her sense of direction had never been particularly good. She estimated they'd been walking for about five minutes when he stopped her and spun her in a circle until her already confused directional sense was completely obliterated. He caught her hand then, linking their fingers together and pulling her onward. They walked on for another ten minutes down a gradual slope before she began to discern sounds of life beyond Adrian's breathing and her own heartbeat.

She'd never had occasion to wonder what a shifter pride sounded like before, but she strained her ears now, picking out the familiar hum of voices in the distance, the high-pitched shrieks of children on a playground, the occasional crunch of footsteps passing them, though no one spoke to her or Adrian as they passed. Were they staring? Maybe it wasn't strange to see a woman being led blindfolded through their midst. Just another day at the pride.

"How big is the pride?" she asked.

For a moment Adrian didn't answer, waiting until another set of footsteps crunched past them before he spoke. "Almost two hundred strong at last count and growing every day— thanks to the Organization driving us into groups for safety."

Two hundred. "Heavens, it's a town."

"Full-service pride," he repeated. "Steps now."

They fell silent as he guided her up a set of stairs, shifting his grip so one hand held hers and the other braced her hip. She was excruciatingly aware of him, tempted to lean against him, but as soon as they reached the top, he stopped her and his warmth slipped away. She heard the rap of knuckles against wood, the sound of a door opening and a feminine voice. "Adrian. Good. Everyone else is upstairs." A pause, and the female's voice grew dry. "Is that really necessary?"

"Not here," Adrian acknowledged, and she felt a tug and the loosening of the blindfold before the black scarf fell away. "Patch, meet Dr. Rachel Russell. Rachel, the Alpha's mate, Patch Fontaine."

"Jaeger, now," the petite woman corrected absently, avidly studying Rachel. "So you're the Organization doc who changed the game for us, huh?"

"That's me."

Patch didn't look like any alpha lioness Rachel had ever seen. Slim, dark and tomboyish, she had a direct gaze and a sloppy ponytail. And none of the regal hauteur Rachel had expected. "Come on in." The alpha female waved them through the door and Rachel's awareness expanded to take in their surroundings.

They were on the doorstep of a grand house. It was massive, set high on a hill overlooking what did, indeed, appear at a glance to be a small town, filled to brimming with people she assumed were shifters. Did the Organization know about this place? If they did, it was only a matter of time before they attacked. This many shifters in one place was too juicy a target for the Board to resist forever.

Adrian nudged the small of her back and Rachel stepped obediently into the house. The foyer was massive and spacious, with a curving staircase that could have come straight out of *Gone with the Wind*. Patch was already leading the way toward it as Adrian took her coat and stowed it on an overflowing rack. This kind of place, this much infrastructure, indicated a permanence to the pride that she had never suspected.

"I thought shifters were migratory," she whispered to Adrian as they followed Patch up the stairs.

"Not all of us," he replied, one hand resting on her back as they ascended. She wondered if he was even aware of the touch. "The prides and packs are all about territory. But the migratory ones are easier for the Organization to snatch, so those are the ones you see more."

That would explain why there were so few lions and wolves in the Organization cells, even though they were rumored to be the most plentiful breeds. The ones they did manage to catch tended to be nomads and lone wolves. She doubted the Organization was ignorant of the prides and packs. Far more likely they were avoiding the larger threat of the larger groups. For now.

That concern would have to wait for another day. They reached the second floor and Patch opened a pair of large double doors, releasing a buzz of conversation on the other side that quickly fell silent as they entered.

Showtime.

Chapter Thirteen

The room reminded her sharply of the Organization board room where Mr. Washington had first threatened the Hawk. High windows flanked by long drapes and a massive conference table dominated the room. Around the table, nearly a dozen large men and a handful of Amazonian women eyed Rachel as she followed the Alpha's mate into the room.

Patch made a beeline for an empty chair next to the largest man in the room—a big blond behemoth with muscles on top of his muscles and a carefully blank expression. He reached out to brush a hand along Patch's arm as she took the seat at his side—the gesture automatic and quietly possessive.

Two chairs remained empty, at the end of the table farthest from the door. Adrian nudged the small of her back gently, prodding her into the room, and Rachel began the long walk in front of all those curious stares.

"Dr. Russell," the big man said as she crossed the room. "Welcome to Lone Pine Pride."

Apparently they were pretending she was a guest now. Rachel smiled graciously, manners rising to the fore, and slid into the chair Adrian held for her. "Thank you. It's good to be here."

"I'm Roman Jaeger, Alpha here. This is my mate, Patch. And these are our lieutenants—Xander, Grace, Kye, Hugo..."

The names continued, a barrage she couldn't hope to remember as he named the fifteen men and women around the table in rapid succession—though she recognized the golden Grace, who watched her with a small half-smile, her gaze occasionally flicking to Adrian. Because she was sleeping with him?

"Has Adrian explained what we are asking of you?"

Rachel pulled herself out of her jealousy, focusing on the moment at hand. "Somewhat. You'd like me to tell you everything I know about the Organization."

"We would."

"I'm afraid I don't have as much intel as we both might wish. I was never in the inner circle, and these last few months they kept all but the most necessary information well out of my reach."

"I expect you know more than you think you do," Roman remarked. "And all of it is more than we have right now. Why don't we start with what you did for them?"

There was a click to her left. The young boy-band one, Mateo—still pretty even looking ragged with dark circles under his eyes—had just activated a voice recorder.

Rachel squirmed, remembering Adrian's reaction when she'd first told him that the Organization was attempting a breeding program. But if anyone had a right to know, it was these shifters.

"I'm a reproductive specialist," she said, pressing on quickly and keeping her eyes on the Alpha to avoid seeing as many of the unpleasant reactions as she could. "I was initially brought in because of my record with couples struggling with fertility. When I was recruited, they explained about shifters and told me they faced unique fertility issues. I was told that because of the necessary secrecy such special patients required, that I would not have much if any direct contact with them. It was unusual for me to be working strictly in the lab, fertilizing embryos for in vitro without patient interaction, but the science was fascinating and I thought I was helping people."

She'd been seduced by her fascination. The conversations she'd had with the other scientists about the seeming magic of shifter science had stimulated her brain in ways she'd never experienced. How did a human form transform into something with more or less mass? What was the catalyst? Where did the energy for the transformation come from? Where did the excess matter *go*? So many questions—and they didn't even brush the surface. Her own work had consumed her. She'd practically lived at the lab.

"It was months before I met my first patient and realized things weren't entirely on the level. When I threatened to expose them, they threatened my mother. My father had just passed away and she was in such a delicate state. She passed away a few months later and I considered leaving again, but they're very good at disappearing people and they don't hesitate to remind their employees of that if we think about stepping out of line. When they told me no one would miss me, I realized they were right. With my family gone, I was in a vulnerable position, but if I stayed I thought I could do some good. So I pretended to be a team player. I did everything they asked and earned more contact with more shifters. I ingratiated myself to other employees, making contacts who would later be able to help me when I started smuggling shifters out."

"You learned how their Organization was structured."

"As much as I was able to. They're obsessed with secrecy. Most employees only know what is going on with their little piece of the Organization, but their records are meticulous. I knew I couldn't get anyone out unless I had access to the records and could change their status. I was based out of a rural Nevada A Block facility, but when I gave the appearance of being a team player, they started having me travel between the sites. I had access to more shifters, but it would look too suspicious if all the disappearances could all be traced back to me, so we stole codes to falsify the records. Deleting the files raised too many red flags, but changing a shifter's status to deceased? Anyone with a medical passcode could do that."

Several shifters leaned forward suddenly, but it was the Alpha's mate who spoke. "So when you helped a shifter escape, they were listed in that roster you got us as deceased? Not all of those shifters are dead?"

"Not all of them. All told we got one hundred and fifty-two out."

Murmurs rippled around the table. "And you remember which ones," Patch pressed, all but crawling on the table now. "You know their names."

"All of them."

"Dorian Fontaine. Was one of them Dorian Fontaine?"

Rachel's heart plummeted as she matched the name to the one Adrian had given as Patch's surname downstairs. Brother, father—whoever Dorian Fontaine was, he meant a great deal to the Alpha's mate. "I'm sorry. He wasn't one of mine."

Patch lurched back as if struck, blinking furiously. "No. Of course not." Roman reached over and laced their fingers together, his mate gripping his hand with both of hers as if he was a lifeline. Rachel envied them that. She'd never had a lifeline.

"What about Cari, Caridad Amador?"

Rachel gasped, her head whipping toward the softly spoken words. *That* name she recognized. That name, thank God, she could report on with less heartbreaking news. "Yes! Yes, we got her out."

Mateo, the tech-savvy young man with the boy-band pretty face, broke down, bowing his head and covering his face with one hand, shoulders shaking.

Suddenly Adrian was in her space, his lips right against her ear. "You wouldn't lie to Mateo, would you? To try to gain favor? I don't remember any Caridad."

"She was after you were...incapacitated," she whispered back. "There was a coyote from New Mexico, one of the first shifters we got out, he met us and took her south."

"Can you give us the names of all the shifters your group freed?" Roman spoke, forcing Adrian to lean back. Even when he was stiff with suspicion, she missed his warmth along her arm.

"I think so. It may take me a while to compile a complete list."

"Understandable." Roman's thumb continued to rub circles on his mate's. "Some of those one hundred and fifty-two are here, Dr. Russell. We're very grateful for all you managed to do. A one-woman task force against the Organization."

Tell that to the Hawk. "It wasn't one woman. I had help. And anyone in my position would have done the same."

"No. Few would have even attempted half of what you did, let alone accomplished as much. We're in your debt." Roman caught Adrian's eye and gave a slight nod. "But we're also responsible for too many lives to ignore the fact that you were with the Organization for a long time. I'm afraid for the time being, our gratitude must be tempered by caution."

One of the lieutenants spoke, a heavy-set bearded man with thick brown hair just going to silver who couldn't have looked more bear-like if he tried. "What more can you tell us about the Organization's operations?"

"They target isolated shifters. Those who won't be missed. I was only involved in an acquisition one time—" She studiously avoided looking at Adrian, "—so I can't provide much insight into that side of things. I do know that once they are acquired they are assigned to one of four blocks. The A Blocks, where I worked, were for biological research. B Blocks were for psychological or social experiments. The C Blocks..." She cleared her throat, forcing herself to meet the Alpha's eyes. "They were for information gathering. Torture, mostly. And the D Blocks are for detainment and disposal—typically where shifters are sent to die after they are of no use to the other three blocks anymore."

"Those blocks," another lieutenant asked, lifting a hand to catch her attention. "Do they relate to the location codes in the rosters?"

She nodded. "The first four digits of the code are the building, and the rest of the code is the location within the building."

"But none of the buildings on the schematics you gave us have codes," Mateo argued, his eyes now dry.

"They're hidden in the addresses. A Blocks are Avenues, Bs Places, Cs Circles, and Ds are Ways. The first letter of the street name and the last number of the address are the rest of the code. So 785 Monroe Way would be D Blocks and M is the thirteenth letter, so it's D135. The Organization makes sure they're private roads so if they want to repurpose a building, they simply change the name of the access road."

Mateo groaned, closing his eyes. "I'm an idiot. We didn't analyze the street addresses."

Grace bumped his elbow with hers. "Don't beat yourself up. You're one person. And that's convoluted shit."

Mateo didn't respond, he was already bent over his tablet, scrolling through a list of some kind. "What are Lanes?" he asked.

Rachel blinked. "There are Lanes?" The Organization had an entire class of buildings she didn't know about.

Roman leaned forward. "Mateo, can you use the roster to determine where the highest concentration of shifters are being held? That could help us decide where to strike next."

"The ones in the D Blocks are at the highest risk," Rachel said. "Some of the guards would joke that D was for deceased."

Roman gave a sharp nod, turning back to Mateo. "Start with the D Blocks."

Mateo rose with a crisp nod and slipped out of the room. As soon as he was gone, the other lieutenants piped up with questions, grilling her about everything she knew and a dozen things she didn't know about how the Organization worked.

She told them how the Board of Directors used fake names—Mr. Lincoln, Mr. Washington, Mr. Wilson—and how they were constantly on the move. How even the tech guru who had helped Rachel compile the hard drives hadn't been able to locate a central headquarters and each cell operated independent of the others, orders funneling down through the supervisors and managers who traveled from site to site. She described a handful of those managers—including Madison Clarke—but she didn't have much hope that they would be able to capture any of them. Organization members at that level were all true believers. They wouldn't let themselves be taken alive.

The interrogation lasted for hours, some of the shifters excusing themselves and others coming in to take the empty chairs. Food was brought in, but Rachel barely picked at it, her appetite nonexistent. She felt like her brain had been run through a meat grinder by the time Adrian—who had been silent all day—finally spoke up.

"Enough."

Roman started to protest, but Adrian held his eyes, a tacit challenge that made several of the shifters around the table stir uncomfortably.

"She'll still be here tomorrow. That's enough for today," Adrian insisted.

As grateful—and confused—as Rachel was for the intervention, there was one question she had yet to be asked. "Wait, you have Organization prisoners, right? From the lab where you found me?"

Suddenly everyone at the table was very, very quiet. "Why do you ask?" Roman inquired, the words stretching.

"Some of the people who work for the Organization are monsters, I don't deny that, but some are good people. I can help you separate one from the other. I know many of them—"

"Which is why you won't be allowed anywhere near them," Roman said, with a sympathetic grimace. "Sorry, Dr. Russell. Caution before gratitude."

"Come on." Adrian rose, holding out his hand for her when she would have argued.

She was exhausted. And just like the questions they still had for her, it was an argument that would wait for another day. Taking the hand he'd offered, she let him tug her to her feet and guide her out of the room as the pride's lieutenants fell to arguing about what she had been able to tell them.

"They aren't all bad," she said quietly to Adrian as they descended the *Gone with the Wind* staircase.

"Maybe not," he acknowledged. "But you don't get to sort them out."

He helped her into her coat and opened the door, holding it for her as she stepped out onto the front steps. The sun had set while she was inside being interrogated and the pride spread out below her in the cozy glow of yellow light bleeding out of windows and lining the pathways. It was lovely. Peaceful and domestic in a way she'd never associated with the animalistic shifters.

Adrian withdrew a length of black scarf from his pocket. She groaned.

"I'm exhausted, it's dark, and I have the world's worst sense of direction. Is that really necessary?"

"Caution before gratitude."

"That's going to be your excuse whenever you want to get your way, isn't it?"

"Pretty much. Turn around."

She gave him her back and he looped the scarf over her eyes, securing it with quick, deft tugs. Within seconds he was leading her down the steps and through the pride again, and back into the forest. It was strangely relaxing, relying on his eyes. His night vision was far better than hers anyway and she had more faith in his ability to keep her from falling than she did in her own, as tired as she was. She still trusted him completely—even if he couldn't return the sentiment.

She gave herself up into his care, blanking her mind of the concerns of the day and focusing instead on the cool night air filling her lungs one breath at a time and the warmth of the hawk at her side. Even without her sight, she always knew where he was. Her Adrian-sense was well-honed.

She was enjoying the walk, wishing it could stretch on longer—so of course it felt like it passed in half the time of their previous trip. Before she knew it he was tugging at the scarf and her eyes—well-adjusted to the dark now—opened to the shadowy shape of the cabin rising out of the clearing.

"I'm sorry I've run you out of your home."

"You haven't." His hand was back on the small of her back, nudging her up the steps. She went obediently, wondering if he had any idea how often he touched her—little brushes, subconscious gestures, but always in contact, always keeping her near.

"But where do you sleep?" she asked as he pulled a key ring from his pocket and set to releasing the padlock. "While I'm here, I mean." Where had he been last night?

Please don't say with Grace. Please don't say with Grace, she chanted internally, remembering the blonde's knowing smile as she met Rachel's eyes.

"Here," he grunted. The padlock came loose and he opened the door, stopping her with a hand on her hip when she would have preceded him into the shack. He crouched forward as if expecting an attack, slipping into the room and searching it with the efficiency of deadly experience. He acted like they might come under attack here. From the Organization? Other shifters?

A chill danced down her spine and she glanced over her shoulder, scanning the dense shadows of the forest. A dozen shifters could be lurking out there, two dozen Organization operatives, and she would never know.

"Hawk?" she called, her voice quavering.

"Come on in. It's clear."

She stepped into the dubious fortress of the cabin, feeling disproportionately relieved when the door was shut behind her.

The damn thing only locked from the outside, but she was still grateful to have it closed at her back.

Then what he'd said earlier registered.

"What do you mean you sleep here? What about last night?"

He gave her a look that questioned her intelligence. "Did you really think I would leave you unguarded?"

"Do you mean to say you slept outside? In this cold?"

"I don't require much sleep and shifters aren't as affected by cold as humans."

"You can still get hypothermia." She'd seen the studies. Temperature tolerance was a favorite experiment at the Organization because it served the dual purposes of torture and scientific research.

"Relax, Dr. Russell. I still have all my fingers and toes. The specimen is intact."

Rachel had always been able to control her temper before— she'd had to—but tonight, exhausted, cranky and unjustly accused for the millionth time, her hold on her anger snapped. Perhaps this was another of those defining moments—a small one, this time. The moment when she'd finally found her breaking point.

She stormed across the small room, getting right in Adrian's face—or his chest, since he towered over her. She poked him with one stiff finger. "I have *never* treated you, or any other shifter, like a lab rat. I know you're mad at me and yes, I did a terrible thing to you, but you can't cram me into the Evil Organization Doctor box just because you don't want to deal with your feelings for me."

He caught her wrist, stopping her poking. "What feelings are those? Loathing? Disgust?"

"Lust."

Chapter Fourteen

Adrian blinked, rocking back on his heels like she'd swung at him, discomfort written all over his face. "I don't know what you're talking about."

He dropped her wrist like it was on fire and started to push past her, but she sidestepped to block him, her body bumping into his, chest to chest, hip to hip. "Don't you?" she challenged, grabbing his hips by the belt-loops. "Tell me, Hawk, which pisses you off more? That the Organization fucked you or that I did?"

She'd never said that word like that before, actually referring to the act. Her face flamed, but she forced herself to meet his glowing yellow gaze without flinching.

"Do you still want me?" She'd never been bold with him before, but she rubbed against him now, provocative and slow. "Is that why you're so angry?"

His eyes blazed and suddenly he wasn't trying to get past her. One hand gripped her hip as the other closed over her throat, gently but firmly. Her heart rate tripled as he rushed her backward with his body until the rough-hewn wall pressed against her back. The hard heat of him pressed against her abdomen as he loomed over her, a savage light in his eyes.

"Tell me, Doc," he mimicked darkly, "were you just following orders? Did the Organization tell you to fuck me into submission?"

Her heart pounded, need driving the beat. He'd always been tender with her, treating her like she was precious, breakable, but this was different. There was an electric wildness in him now. An edge that she knew should not turn her on, but she was practically squirming with desire.

Her protest was breathless. "I meant it when I told you everything between us was real." *And still is.*

"Everything," he echoed, acid in the word. "Are you proud of yourself?" His long fingertips moved over her neck, softly stroking the delicate skin as his other hand curved around her waist. "Proud of how I fell for you? Proud of how easy it was to trick me? Were you laughing with your Organization friends while you were taunting me in that fucking cell?"

His voice was hypnotic, seductive and low. Rachel felt herself melting under the spell of it and almost missed the significance of the words. *Taunting me in that fucking cell.* "I didn't—"

"Don't lie." His fingers tightened fractionally, not enough to hurt, but just enough to remind her that he held her life in his hands.

Pinned against the wall, she trembled, but not from fear. He would never hurt her. "I never saw you. They wouldn't let—"

"Don't *lie,*" he snarled. "You were there. I know what I remember."

"I swear I'm not lying. I wouldn't lie to you. Not about this."

"And I should just believe you. When everything between us was a lie from day one."

"It wasn't a lie. You were..." Words failed. He'd been *everything.* The only thing in her life that had felt real.

"What was I?" That yellow gaze bored into hers, partial shifting until everything human left his eyes. "Your express pass to the higher echelons of Organization operations?"

"I explained about that. What it let me do. It was necessary."

"If that's what you need to tell yourself."

"Adrian—"

"You should have told me *before,*" he growled. "But God forbid I question Saint Rachel. Does it make you feel good? The

Vivi Andrews

way the shifters here fucking worship you? The *savior*. Did you like the way all the lieutenants looked at you today? Everyone *loves* you. Does it make you feel powerful?" His other hand moved to grip the hair at the nape of her neck, drawing her head back as his gaze roamed down her body. "I bet you get off on knowing I still want you. That you fucking *own* me."

"I never wanted to own you," she whispered. "I wanted..."

"What? You want to be my consolation prize for all I went through?" His hold on her waist lowered to her hip and squeezed before jerking her tight against him so she could feel how hard he was.

"Stop it," she whispered, pressing her thighs together against the heat pooling there.

"Tell me what you want." The words were a dark growl, his face was harsh, but all she saw in him was pain that made her throat ache, and all she wanted was...

"You," she said on a sigh. "I always want you."

"*Fuck.*"

Whatever battle he'd been fighting with himself ended as his mouth crashed down over hers.

The kiss started off fast and fierce, a surge of wild heat and possession. She held on tight, tugging his body closer to hers, but seconds after his tongue plunged into her mouth, he released a low moan and everything changed. His rough grip eased, his lips softened and that erotic darkness in him retreated, transforming into something so sweet and heartbreakingly tender that it was even more impossible to defend against than the initial overwhelming rush.

What began as reckless, undeniable lust became something else entirely.

A tease. A taste. A lazy exploration.

Their bodies were plastered together in a thousand points of heat but he drew back until their lips flirted and brushed tentatively, like a middle-schooler's first kiss.

And perhaps this was theirs.

There had always been layers of lies between them before—Noah and Dr. Russell—but now they were Adrian and Rachel, with all the complications that entailed, and this first soft exploration was so impossibly sweet her heart rose up in her throat and tears pricked the backs of her eyes as her lids fell helplessly closed. Her hawk kissed her like the act had been invented just for them. A flick of a tongue across her lower lip, a nip at the corner of her mouth, the soft press and draw that was so much more than lust and heat and need—it was seduction. Impossible to resist.

His name escaped her mouth on a sigh.

He went still. Shifter still. The motionlessness of an apex predator.

Adrian lurched away from her so sharply she swayed, catching herself against the wall. He was already halfway across the room, the door slamming shut behind him before she could do more than say the first syllable of his name. The sound of the padlock clicking shut was ominously loud—even managing to be heard over the thundering of her heart.

Merciful heavens. Her fingertips lifted to her lips, almost scared to touch them lest she brush away the imprint of him. What had just happened?

They'd been fighting and then... Lord, chill bumps raised up on her flesh just thinking about it. If that was how the man ended an argument, she was going to have to rile him more often.

His anger gave her pause. But if he hated her so much, he couldn't kiss her so sweetly. Could he? All those little solicitous touches. The way he was so hell-bent on protecting her. She kept looking for signs that he still cared for her beneath all his anger, when it might just be the predator being possessive of his kill.

There was emotion there, that was for sure, but it was different, so different than before. He'd always been careful with her before. Controlled. She'd rushed into his arms, afraid each moment with him would be her last and in a hurry to wring each drop of pleasure from their time together as possible, but Noah—*Adrian*—had been patient. Deliberate. Holding her like he would keep her in his arms for an eternity or two.

That was gone now. There was anger where his adoration had been, but when he kissed her...the tenderness was still there underneath it all, confusing things.

He was so certain he'd seen her while in captivity. She'd seen herself how out of it he'd been. The drugs must have done a number on his memory. It wouldn't be the first time a prisoner thought their hallucinations were real. But she didn't know how to earn forgiveness for the crimes his fevered, drugged-out mind had convicted her of.

She wasn't fool enough to think they could go back to where they had been before, but where did they go from here?

Adrian called for his feathers, needing wind currents pressing against the undersides of his wings, but the hawk remained out of reach, dormant, and it was that absence that finally slowed his headlong flight from the cabin. He couldn't go far, couldn't leave her undefended, but neither could he go back. Not when he could still feel the warmth of her imprinted on his body.

He didn't know how he'd ended up kissing her. Or how it had turned so fucking tender. Or why she had melted in his arms like warm chocolate and sighed his name against his lips like he was the patron saint of imminent orgasms.

He just knew he couldn't let any of it happen again.

He could almost forgive her betrayal, almost forgive the syringe piercing his skin and the creeping numbness that felled him, if not for the way she'd tormented him when he was in the Organization cells. And now to lie about it when he had heard her voice, that distinctive southern lilt, a thousand times.

She was still lying to him, proving he was right not to trust her, proving he still didn't know who she really was. Loyal to the Organization? Loyal to the shifter cause? Loyal only to herself?

He'd believed down to his soul that she was *his*, and there had been a purity in that belief, justifying every risk—which made her violation of it that much more unthinkable.

Whatever she was, she had never been loyal to him.

He was close enough to hear when she began moving around inside the cabin, struggling to light a fire. The cabin would be cold, the fire in the pot-bellied stove long since burned out. The urge was strong to go back to her. Light the fire. Care for her. But that way lay weakness. He wasn't sure he could look after her without succumbing to her. His instincts demanded he do the former and his brain insisted on the latter.

No matter how strong his reservations, no matter how completely he *knew* she couldn't be trusted, his need for her was still an animal thing, pressing out against the inside of his skin. Just like it had been from the beginning.

He knelt with pine needles and twigs digging into his knees, staring at the cabin but seeing another night. Another forest.

It had been snowing the first time he saw her.

He wasn't supposed to see her. It was safer if they never met. Safer if he couldn't even identify her on sight. As long as he didn't know who his accomplice was, she couldn't be compromised if he was captured. And vice versa.

For the first two years they'd worked together he'd resisted all curiosity about his counterpart on the inside. But then he'd arrived early at the clearing for a pick-up and there she was. Kneeling in the snow. Tucking a scarf around the neck of an eleven-year-old wolf-shifter, one of two sisters being relocated. It was unusual for the Organization to have wolf cubs—the packs were famous for protecting their young, but somehow these two had ended up in Organization hands. In Rachel's.

As a hawk, his vision was far keener than a human's, sharper even than most other shifters. Even in the low light and through the snow, he'd been able to see her like a diamond shining in the night.

His father had told him the story of how he met his mother a thousand times. Love at first sight. The first look hitting him like a runaway train. Adrian had known that hawks mated for life, but he'd always thought his father's story was romanticized beyond belief. Until the sight of Rachel bowled him over and laid him flat.

The rich mahogany of her hair was thick and swept to one side, falling over her shoulder with a hint of a curl. What he could see of her figure beneath her bulky winter coat was curved, feminine perfection, but it was her face that stole his breath. She wasn't just beautiful. She was exquisite.

Her features were delicate and refined. High, sculpted brows arched over eyes the exact shade of dark chocolate, framed by lashes so thick snowflakes tangled in them. Her nose was a perfect upturned slope, above a mouth so kissably soft he ached for a taste just looking at it. And beyond the individual perfection of each aspect of her face, her personality seemed to glow from every pore. A purity that was somehow unspeakably seductive.

On a scale of one to ten, she was a fourteen. He'd never seen anything like her. Not in real life.

Rachel.

He shouldn't have known her name. It was dangerous to know it. But he'd heard some of the more careless shifters he'd transported say it and now he understood the almost reverent tones used by some of the men when they spoke of her.

That night in the snow, he'd listened to the sweet seduction of her voice, as she'd stayed too long, trying to comfort the cubs. By that age they had teeth and claws sharp enough to defend themselves, but Adrian understood the reluctance to leave them alone in the woods, waiting for the next leg of their journey. Even if it was a necessary measure.

He'd watched her until she faded into the forest that night. And all the nights after.

He'd gotten in the habit of going early to their meets, watching for her, hungry for the sight—until one night a few months later when she hadn't shown up for a scheduled drop.

The shifter smuggling operation was a well-oiled machine— and no one person was more important than the operation as a whole. They all knew that. If she failed to show, he wasn't supposed to wait. He would abandon the op and flee. Those were the rules. They kept everyone safe. But when she'd been five minutes late, he hadn't been able to walk away. Not from her. When her tardiness had stretched to fifteen minutes, then twenty, panic had dug its talons into his heart and he hadn't been able to wash his hands of the op the way he knew he should.

He'd crept closer instead, moving in the direction of the Organization facility, searching for some trace of her, staying in human form so he could keep his gun at hand. His imagination had conjured up a thousand nightmare scenarios before he finally heard the crunch of boots on the brittle frozen leaves and saw her, struggling through the forest with a singularly human lack of finesse, branches tangled in her hair with a small shifter child wrapped around her torso like a baby monkey.

There should have been two—mother and child—but Adrian knew better than to ask after Mama Bear. When he'd spoken her name—*Rachel*, not even supposed to know it—she'd whirled toward the sound of his voice, stumbling and nearly falling to the ground, awkward with the weight of her cargo. Her human eyes had frantically scanned the night until he realized she couldn't pick him out of the darkness and moved forward until her pupils contracted minutely, focusing on him as the moonlight touched him.

She'd been wary, cautious, and there was something fiercely protective in her eyes. He'd known instinctively that she would fight to the death for the little cub in her arms—and that knowledge had reached through the distance he always kept around himself and made his chest ache strangely.

Instead of trying to pry the cub from her arms, he'd broken protocol yet again and led Rachel with her cargo through the forest to his waiting Jeep. They hadn't spoken on the trek. Nor when he'd opened the door and tucked Rachel and her ungainly burden into the passenger seat. They were miles down the road, the cub snoring softly in Rachel's lap as more miles whipped beneath the wheels, before she spoke, thanking him for waiting.

He'd frowned, his gaze never veering from the road ahead. *I shouldn't have.*

Then I'm even more grateful you did.

Then he had looked at her. Rachel. The most beautiful woman he'd ever seen in real life—but this time every hair hadn't been in place. There was dirt on her jaw and a stick snarled in her hair. Dark circles were heavy under eyes haunted by whatever she'd seen tonight. Lines of tension slashed between her eyebrows and at the corners of her mouth. And she was still the most beautiful thing he'd ever seen.

They reached a truck stop where he called in a favor to get her a ride back to within a decent hike of where she'd left her car. The night was cold, so after they settled the sleeping cub in the back seat, they waited in the warmth of the cab for her ride, the heater quickly fogging the windows and giving them a false sense of isolation, of safety. They who knew better than anyone that no one was ever safe.

He didn't remember everything they talked about that night—she'd teased him about filling an ark and blushed when he'd carefully extracted the twig from her hair. Talking nonsense mostly. He'd just wanted to hear her voice, the soft lilt of her accent—but he did remember asking her if it was safe for her to go back. Her soft promise that they didn't suspect. That she would be fine. He'd been surprised by the protectiveness she called up in him. Surprised when he heard himself say, *You don't have to go back.*

The desire to keep her with him, to keep her safe, was a bright burning thing, but she'd just smiled and murmured, *Yes. I do.*

That should have been the end of it. He should never have seen her again, but Rachel tempted him to break every rule he'd ever had. Soft, sweet, innocent temptation.

He'd known from the beginning that every meeting with her could be a trap, but he had wanted to trust her. She had tempted him to go against his instincts, tempted him as nothing else ever had, and here he was, weakening toward her again, if only in his own mind.

She was different now. Fiery. Less restrained. And that fire was a temptation in itself, but he would resist it. He would keep his distance. He was stronger than this.

Or he thought he was. Until he heard the shower turn on and heated memories made him painfully hard. Adrian closed his eyes, but the visions were no less vivid that way. Unsnapping his jeans and taking himself in hand was pure self-defense. He recalled her slick heat, the way her eyes would flare with surprise every time she came—as if each frisson of pleasure startled her anew. His grip tightened and he groaned, jerking hard into his hand until the muscles in his neck knotted and his spine tingled.

Fantasies of her were still more satisfying than sex with anyone else. But the fantasies were all he would let himself have.

Adrian slumped back against a tree. He would get over this. He had to.

The hot water wasn't very hot to begin with, but Rachel stood under the spray until it was downright icy, waiting for some epiphany about how to crack Adrian's anger toward her. Jailer or protector, lover or punisher. Something had to give.

The toiletry buffet he'd left for her that morning had yielded her preferred brand of shampoo, conditioner and body wash. She was clean and floral-scented again when she emerged from

Vivi Andrews

the bathroom to find even more mixed-messages from her hawk.

He was gone again, but signs of his presence were everywhere. The fire blazed in the stove. Cozy flannel pajamas were stacked neatly on the bed, next to another set of clean clothes for the morning. A tray of food was perched on top of the flat top of the pot-bellied stove, staying warm and smelling good enough to have her stomach growling and reminding her how little she'd eaten today.

Rachel put on the pajamas and devoured every last morsel of the meal. The fire had warmed the small room nicely. Warm, clean and fed, the exhaustion of the day rose to the fore and she curled onto the futon, facing the door. She tugged the single blanket over her and wriggled around to find a comfortable position on the lumpy mattress, all the while watching for Adrian's return.

She wasn't chained. He wouldn't go far. He wouldn't trust the padlock to hold her forever. He could be lurking on the porch. Or shifted into hawk form and watching her from a perch in a tree.

The thought stuck. She'd often wondered what his bird form looked like. Would those yellow eyes still hold the force of his personality when he had wings? Would he be larger than the average hawk? Would his wings beat at the air with graceful sweeps? Would he ever trust her enough to show her?

Her dreams were filled with raptors in flight and feather-light brushes against her lips that deepened into long, erotic tanglings of tongues, but Adrian never returned.

Chapter Fifteen

"Looking for something?"

Adrian jerked guiltily, automatically trying to hide the bottles in his hands behind his back, but Grace just lifted one tawny brow and snorted at the attempt. "Relax, Hawkeye." She plucked one of the flowery bottles from the shelf in front of him and rolled it between her hands. "I've seen men trying to figure out how to buy lotion for their girlfriends before."

"She isn't my—"

"I know, I know. You don't care for her even a little bit and you're certainly not in love with her. Which is why lavender versus peach has become like Sophie's freaking choice for you."

Adrian looked down at the bottles in his hands and shoved the peach one back onto the shelf. The general store at the pride was pretty bare bones—if you wanted something, you took whichever brand they had and said thank you—but when it came to feminine toiletries there were an abundance of options. He'd remembered what kind of shampoo Rachel used—the one time they'd showered together was engraved in his memory—but he'd never seen her put on lotion. Didn't know what she'd prefer.

Not that her preference mattered. She was a prisoner.

He shoved the lavender back onto the shelf, plucking up the peach. Or what the fuck was Midnight Mist? Was that better? He started to switch the bottles—

"Jesus," Grace grunted. She shoved the bottle she'd been playing with into his hands. "Go with orchid. Orchid is hot."

"It's not about hot," he snapped. Rachel's face was getting chapped by the harsh winter wind on their walks to and from the compound for her interrogations each day. It was his job to look after her. This had nothing to do with fucking hot, damn it.

"I get it. It puts the lotion in the basket or it gets the hose again." At Adrian's horrified stare, Grace grinned wickedly. "What? I'm funny."

"Says who?"

"My mom. Of course, she also thinks I'd be happier if I was married with a pack of rug rats nipping at my heels, so clearly the woman has been smoking something." Grace grabbed a bottle of her own and started down the aisle. "So how's the good doctor?"

The good doctor was temptation and torment. But he couldn't very well say that.

He'd been avoiding speaking to her as much as possible ever since that...aberration the other night. She was too tempting. Too familiar. His memories too sharp.

She wasn't his lover. She was his prisoner. And he wouldn't blur that line. He'd gotten in trouble before when he'd let his feelings for her rule his actions. He wouldn't be so foolish again. Not when she was still lying to him, playing games.

Their days had fallen into a certain routine. He would collect her each morning after she'd dressed and eaten the food he left for her in the night. He'd guide her, blindfolded, down to the compound and deliver her to the Alpha, his mate or his lieutenants, depending who had new questions for her that day. The sessions were always recorded, but as the days wore on and she was able to provide less and less new information, they grew shorter.

He hovered nearby until the questioning was complete, then blindfolded her again and led her back into the woods to his cabin. She often tried to engage him in conversation, but he'd grunt monosyllabic replies and ignore her as much as possible. After checking the cabin for threats, he would lock her inside, returning only when he brought her dinner tray.

He hadn't chained her again—she'd made no attempt to escape and he didn't want her to be completely vulnerable if someone like Dominec should find where he'd stashed her. Though Adrian was rarely far from her.

He'd constructed a little lean-to in the forest with sight lines on all the approaches to the cabin. It was too cold to be sleeping outside, so when his bones started to ache with the chill in the middle of the night, he'd slip inside the cabin and stretch out in front of the door for a few hours. Rachel slept like a rock. She never even stirred with his comings and goings, but he snapped awake every time she shifted and sighed. His gaze would take in every detail of her sleep-softened face, his vision sharp even in the night-darkened cabin. He'd watch her sleep, sometimes for hours, and then sneak back out into the forest beyond to keep watch—no more settled on how he felt about her than he ever was.

She still tugged at something inside him. Something that refused to give up on her even after the way she'd betrayed him. That part of him argued that he should forgive her, that she'd done what she needed to for the greater good. But another, unforgiving part of him screamed that you didn't betray your mate. Not ever. If she had been his, she never would have been able to hurt him. Not for any reason.

How was she? Intoxicating. Infuriating.

"She's fine."

Grace snorted. "Yeah, if I'd been a slave to the Organization for years, fearing for my life and hating every second of it and I finally escaped, I'm sure I'd just be, you know, *fine* too."

Adrian glared at Grace while she paid for her own items, waving to the lion at the counter to add Adrian's things to her tab as well. He waited until they were outside the store to admit, "Now that Roman has most of what he needs from her, I think she's bored."

"Not surprising. Few people are as good at being inactive as cats."

"I don't think she's used to doing nothing. She's always been an overachiever. I think she was one of those graduated-med-school-at-twenty-three types."

"What, didn't Mommy and Daddy love her enough?"

Grace was joking, but Adrian didn't think she was far off the mark. When Rachel had told him about being the valedictorian, always-the-best-at-everything perfect daughter, he hadn't been surprised to learn she was adopted. She'd protested that her parents had never treated her like she had to be perfect to earn their love, that she'd always known they adored her just as much as if she'd been their biological child, but all that perfection had screamed overcompensation to him.

But it felt wrong to share any of that with Grace, so he shrugged, changing the subject. "How are the other prisoners?"

"Pains in my cute furry ass," Grace grumbled. "We've never needed a jail-type facility before, so we had to improvise, put them in an unused barn at the edge of the main compound—but the thing is hardly Fort Knox and some asshole leaked the fact that we were hiding them there to the pride at large. Three guesses which psycho ass tiger probably spilled that little tidbit. So now every shifter in the pride with a beef against the Organization is camped outside the fucking barn calling for their heads. Loudly. Twenty-four hours a fucking day. I could use you, if you're up for watch duty. Someone with your eyesight would be invaluable on the perimeter and free up some of my guys to babysit the barn. It's getting harder and harder to find guards who'll keep the good guys from going all Tarantino on the helpless bad guys' asses." She grimaced. "Good times."

"Is Rachel in danger?"

"The patron saint of captured shifters? You should hear the way the shifters she's rescued talk about her in the dining hall. Gandhi had a worse reputation."

"But there could be some who don't see her that way. Dominec—"

"Is his own brand of crazy. Don't judge the pride by him."

"I'm not judging anything." But neither was he willing to risk Rachel's safety on Grace's opinion of how the pride saw the Organization doc. Things were volatile now.

Yes, they were striking back against the Organization and even rescuing some of their own, but seeing the condition of those rescued wasn't making the shifters feel any more kindly toward the Organization prisoners. Too many of their lives had been touched or even ruined by the Organization. Too many scars of the both physical and emotional variety could be laid at their door.

The last thing he needed was Rachel getting in the middle things.

And she would get in the middle. She couldn't seem to stop herself from pointing out that not everyone who worked for the Organization was evil. All she had to do was say that to the wrong person and she'd be gutted in seconds flat.

No. Better that she stayed tucked away in his cabin. Bored and safe.

And beyond temptation.

He shivered, tugging his leather jacket closed to keep out the winter wind.

"Do you think the fact that the Organization didn't immediately retaliate or try to get the prisoners back means they don't know where we are?" he asked.

Grace grimaced. "I wish I believed that. Wouldn't it be great to be that naïve? But no. It feels like we're being set up."

"Like they're just biding their time," he agreed.

She nodded. "Wearing us out." They reached a fork in the path and Grace paused, shoving her hands in her pockets. "Everyone who is remotely trained is working flat out, but how can we hit over a hundred facilities before they move everyone? It's like fucking Sisyphus. We just keep shoving that boulder up the hill and it rolls back down to crush us again. And then I think about what Dominec did on the last raid and part of me is tempted to just sic him on them. See how much damage he can do." She had been staring out over the pride as she spoke, but now she turned to him. "What would you do, Hawkeye? We can use someone with your experience. How do you kill an organism that doesn't have a heart or a single brain? Our battles are successful, but we're losing the war because we can only attack one facility at a time."

"At least we're doing that much. Rachel's group freed over a hundred and fifty shifters by smuggling them out one at a time. So we'll fight this war one battle at a time. And we won't give up."

"Even if some among us still think we're doing the wrong thing by attacking at all?"

"What's the alternative?"

"Running and hiding. Avoiding poking the monster." She shook her head. "Never mind. Go bring your doctor her lotion. But be careful, Hawkeye," Grace tossed off as she moved down the left path. "You can keep her in a box, but boredom can make us stupid. If I were you I'd find something to distract her. Or someone."

He was trying to kill her with boredom. That was the only explanation.

Rachel had never been idle in her life. She didn't know how to be. And now here she was. Useless.

After six days of interviews, her time at the pride compound had diminished to under an hour and her hours at the cabin were making her stir-crazy. She cleaned. She wrestled the damn furniture around in an attempt to feng-shui the tiny cabin. She scoured every cupboard and closet for reading material, without success.

She'd taken to spending an inordinate amount of time on her appearance, showering and primping with the ever-growing supply of beauty products Adrian provided for her—always when she wasn't looking, as if it would be too intimate for him to hand her a canister of tangerine-scented shaving cream. A Southern woman knew the power of being well put together. There was persuasion in a pretty face and Rachel wasn't above using every weapon in her arsenal to get back in Adrian's good graces.

Maybe she would be waiting for him naked when he came with her dinner tray.

He'd have to kiss her then, wouldn't he?

Not that she wanted that. Her feelings for him were too tangled and sideways to invite affection right now. But that didn't mean she was above seduction to get her way.

"Oh, who do you think you're fooling?" she asked her compact mirror. "You want him like there's no tomorrow." Seducing him to get her way was just a handy excuse.

He'd been taciturn since the latest kiss, no longer accusing or antagonizing her, but neither did he speak to her. He cared for her in as close to absolute silence as she would let him, never eating with her, just leaving the food and clean clothes— sometimes taking her dirty things away and returning with them freshly laundered the next day.

She'd tried bringing up the kiss once when he brought her dinner and he'd turned and walked out of the room without a backward glance. When she'd dared to bring up the so called taunting the drugs had convinced him she'd done while he was in Organization captivity, rage had pulsed off him in a near tangible wave and he'd stormed out, not returning for hours.

At this point she would talk about whatever he wanted as long as he stayed.

When he shouldered open the door and walked in with her dinner tray and a bottle of lotion that evening, she was ready for him, greeting him with her best company smile. *Catching flies with honey.*

"Adrian. I'm so glad you're back." Latching on to the sight of the lotion tucked under his arm, she folded her hands over her heart like it was a diamond tiara. "Is that for me? That's so considerate of you. And the shampoo was my favorite—"

"Don't," he cut off her ode to shampoo. "They aren't gifts. You're my responsibility."

"Yes, but I still appreciate—"

"Grace picked it out." He set the tray on the table and moved to drop the lotion in the bathroom.

He was going to leave. Even though she was starving, she ignored the food—and the twinge of jealousy at the mention of perfect *Grace*—putting herself between the Hawk and the door so he wouldn't be able to vanish on her. "Won't you eat with me? I miss your company."

He frowned, but didn't immediately charge for the door. Progress. "What game are you playing?"

"I'll settle for anything but solitaire at this point."

Only when his eyes fired with heat did she realize how suggestive the words had come out. Well, she'd wanted to seduce him.

She twirled a lock of hair around one finger and drew it forward so the tips fell into the plunging V of the button-down top she hadn't buttoned up all the way.

"Please stay. You used to enjoy my company."

His expression darkened. "You'd do best to never mention the past to me again."

"It wasn't all bad—"

"*Never.*"

Oookay. She wasn't in a position to push him. Time to change tactics. "There has to be something I can do," she said. "I'll shovel latrines, if you want. Think of it as community service. Please, Adrian. What possible use am I to anyone out here?" Her plea was only somewhat ruined by the growling of her stomach.

"Eat your dinner." He brushed past her.

"Adrian—" She tried to catch his arm, but he just evaded her grip, leaving behind only boredom and the click of a lock. "Shit."

Chapter Sixteen

Adrian didn't come for her the following morning. No blindfold. No escort down to the main compound. Just hours of empty time ticking by second by second. This was her life now. Relegated to the cabin for the indefinite future.

She was debating the wisdom of crawling out one of the windows and trying to make her way down to the main compound when she heard the steps on the path. Rachel stiffened, her heartbeat accelerating, instincts raising an alarm even before her brain caught up enough to remind her that she never heard her hawk approach. He was always so perfectly silent, but these steps tromped noisily up the path, accompanied by a low murmur of voices.

Acutely aware of her vulnerability out here, too far out to call for help, Rachel scrambled for something that could be used as a weapon, landing—ironically—on the length of chain coiled neatly beside the bed. She lifted it, testing the weight, swinging it experimentally. She'd never learned to fight— perhaps she should have invested in karate lessons when she started working against her lethal employers, but she hadn't wanted to do anything to raise suspicion. Now she felt her helplessness keenly as the voices grew closer, the footsteps clomping up the steps.

"Dr. Russell?"

The chain slid from her fingers. She knew that voice.

"Kathy?" She rushed to the door, as if she would open it for the woman, remembering too late that it was padlocked from the outside.

The lock clinked, rattled, and the door swung outward, revealing three women in their twenties and thirties and a slim, dark-haired boy of fifteen.

Kathy, Calliope, May and Hunter—four of her one hundred and fifty-two. Here. Safe. Healthy. *Free.*

An inarticulate sound of joy burst from her mouth and then they were hugging, laughing, everyone talking at once.

She didn't build personal relationships with all of the shifters she smuggled out—she couldn't afford to be seen favoring them before their "deaths", but these four had been different. Special.

Twenty minutes later, when Rachel had sufficiently marveled at how tall Hunter had grown, how lovely Kathy looked, how happy Calliope and May were, they sat crowded around her table—May and Calliope squished together onto one chair while Hunter sprawled on the floor and Kathy perched on the futon. They each frowned when they saw the length of chain she'd dropped on the floor, but no one commented on it.

"We aren't the only ones," Kathy, the unofficial spokeswoman of the group, said as soon as they were settled. The lynx shifter was the oldest of the four—she'd be thirty-eight now if Rachel remembered correctly. Kathy had been one of her first patients and among her first escapees.

Calliope and May were younger—mid-twenties—but the two had spent more than half their lives in Organization custody before Rachel had managed to smuggle them out. As non-predatory shifter breeds, they'd been particularly defenseless. There wasn't much the big-eyed doe or sleek, graceful otter had been able to do to protect themselves. If not for their friendship and the fact that the Organization seemed to see the wisdom in keeping them together, their spirits doubtless would have been broken years ago. Still, by the time Rachel had smuggled them out, they'd both been in such poor shape that it had required little explanation to convince her superiors that one had succumbed and the other had simply faded away after her.

Now they looked like new women, healthy and bright-eyed. Still clinging to one another like the contact was as essential as breathing, but no longer cowering, flinching at every sound. For the first time, Rachel had heard them laugh, even their amusement harmonious and synchronized.

Hunter didn't laugh. He was still the same intense, silent boy he'd been when she met him two years ago. Like the girls, he'd spent more than half his life in Organization facilities, he and his mother taken when he was six years old. He'd later been separated from his mother, who, Rachel knew, had been killed after a riot in one of the D Blocks. Too dangerous to be allowed to live. He may not look it, all elbows and knees, but Hunter shifted into a black bear and even as an adolescent he'd be lethal enough to kill a full-grown man. A prize for the Organization, and one they'd attempted to train like a circus animal.

"There must be two dozen of the shifters you helped escape who've made their way to Lone Pine," Kathy went on. "Not counting the ones who were rescued in the Organization raids. I hear you're responsible for those as well."

Rachel squirmed, uncomfortable with the way they were looking at her. "It wasn't just me. A lot of people put themselves at risk to get you out. And I had very little to do with those raids."

Kathy waved away her protests as May and Calliope just smiled. "Several of the others would like to see you too, but we had first dibs."

"How did you ever talk Adrian into giving you the key?"

"It was his idea!" May piped up brightly. She yipped, flinching and shooting Calliope a glare. "What? Was I not supposed to say that?"

"His idea? Why would he—never mind." There was no point in trying to figure out how the mighty Hawk's mind worked.

"We all wanted to come," Calliope was quick to assert. "We just didn't know we were allowed until he came to us last night."

Rachel reached across the table, squeezing Calliope's hand to reassure the nervous deer. "I'm so glad you're here. And looking so well. You must tell me everything about your lives here at the pride. Don't leave a single thing out."

"It is strange sometimes," Calliope admitted, "being surrounded by animals my doe is convinced want to eat me, but the lions are really quite kind, much better to us than we ever suspected they might be."

"Calliope and I make a point to jaunt off for a beach vacation whenever the lions have one of their silly ceremonial hunts scheduled. Even knowing the elk and moose they hunt aren't shifters, it still feels wrong to be here for the deaths."

"And you, Hunter?" Rachel prodded. "You like it here?"

He shrugged one shoulder in a quintessentially teenage gesture. "There are other bears here," he said, as if that said it all. And perhaps it did. Breed groups often became a sort of family out of necessity. "Kathy's got a mate." Hunter jerked his chin toward the lynx, deflecting the conversation away from himself.

Rachel turned to arch a brow at the blushing lynx. "*Do* you?"

The conversation flowed easily into the afternoon, pleasant and light in a way that had never been possible at the Organization. Kathy had brought a picnic hamper and they feasted on sandwiches and fruit when Hunter's stomach began to growl ominously.

This was why she'd risked everything, Rachel realized, as Kathy told her stories about the romantic love-match between the former Alpha's only daughter and a jaguar who stole her away from Roman, the current Alpha. Rachel had done it so they could have afternoons like these, laughing and trading gossip and just *living*, beyond surviving the next minute, the next day.

Perhaps not everyone she'd gotten out would heal. Perhaps they wouldn't all be happy and healthy, but they had a chance. Tears pricked the backs of her eyes and she swallowed them back. Perhaps she had done more good than harm. Perhaps her father wouldn't be so disappointed in the way she'd spent the last few years after all.

The pale winter light was fading into shadows by the time the four gathered up their things and clambered to their feet, saying their farewells. Rachel hugged May and Calliope, watching the pair dart off hand-in-hand into the forest before catching Hunter and forcing a hug on the not-as-unwilling-as-he-might-want-her-to-believe teen. He grunted, face flushing, and gave her shoulder a single reluctant pat before tugging away. He sniffed the air and muttered, "Going to snow tonight," before following the two young women down the path.

Kathy hung back, fidgeting with her picnic hamper. The cold was sharp, so Rachel shut the door and leaned against the frame as she waited for Kathy to rearrange the hamper to her liking—or spit out whatever she'd hung back to say.

"Kathy?" she prompted gently.

The lynx looked up and grimaced ruefully. "I don't pretend to understand everything that's going on in this pride. I don't know why all those Organization people they captured are being held in that old barn any more than I understand why you're out here with a padlock on your door. Adrian made us promise we wouldn't show you the way down to the main compound before he would give me the key and he wouldn't let us come unless we brought Hunter as a bodyguard—figuring no one would tangle with a bear, even an immature one." Kathy pulled a face. "I don't know about any of that."

Rachel shook her head, unclear what Kathy was driving at. "Neither do I."

"What I do know is you're a good person and a great doctor. You helped me when you didn't have to. Back in that...*place*, you held my hand when I lost that baby and even though that pregnancy hadn't been my choice, you understood that it was still a loss and you grieved with me. I'll never forget that. No more than I'll forget how you got me out of there."

"Kathy, it was—"

"Don't say it was nothing. It wasn't nothing."

"I wasn't going to." She'd been going to say it was her honor to help the shifters, but Kathy didn't give her time to explain.

"I know what you did for the Organization," she said. "Better than anyone, I know. You were their miracle doc. They couldn't get any of us to catch with their in vitro crap until you came along."

"I'm sorr—"

"No, I'm not blaming you. Crud, I'm saying this all wrong." Kathy stood, gripping her hands at her waist. "I want to get pregnant."

Rachel blinked. "What?"

"My mate, he's a good man and he loves me, and we know it's a crazy time to bring a shifter child into the world, but I'm not getting any younger and we both want kids so badly, but no matter how we try—and believe me, we've tried—I just can't seem to get pregnant."

"Kathy, I—"

As if fearing Rachel was about to refuse, Kathy plowed on. "The pride doc has tried to help us, but he doesn't know much about lynx shifters or cross-species matings. My mate, he's a bobcat, you see. And I know the old wives' tales, that our kids won't be able to shift at all, even if I can get pregnant, but we don't care. We want this, Dr. Russell. And when I heard you were here I thought, it's gotta be a sign. You were the one who helped me get pregnant the first time and, yes, I miscarried that baby, but with all the experiments they were running on me and the fetus I figure it was a miracle I made it to my second trimester."

"Kathy—"

"Please, Dr. Russell. We want this so badly."

Rachel didn't know if she could help. Cross-species matings were complicated—some breeds were completely genetically incompatible. But if anyone could help Kathy conceive and carry to term, it was probably her. And after everything she'd done for the Organization, this seemed like a fitting way to even the karmic scales. She wasn't sure she'd even be allowed to help, but she couldn't say no.

"I'll do whatever I can."

Chapter Seventeen

The promise of snow hung in the air, blanketing the pride compound in an expectant hush. Or what would have been a hush without the constant roaring surrounding the building where the Organization prisoners were being held. The most recent evacuees had taken to taunting the prisoners in shifts, so the building walls echoed with roars and angry growls twenty-four-seven.

Even from halfway across the pride compound, it was enough to give a man a headache. Adrian could only imagine what kind of fresh hell it felt like inside those prison walls.

He silently cursed his sharp hearing, trying to focus on what Kye was saying at his side as they walked toward Mateo's office.

"We'll leave at dawn, day after tomorrow. Are you sure you won't come? We're down two without you since we can't trust Dominec to keep his shit together, not after last time."

Adrian vividly remembered the blood-splattered walls. The gun aimed at Rachel's head. It was about time they benched the psycho. But if Dominec was staying at the pride, that was all the more reason for Adrian to stay behind as well. "Sorry. I need to stay here for now."

Kye pinned him with a steady look, but said nothing. It wasn't his style.

In the distance, the timbre of the roars shifted—the angry, threatening snarls turning fiercely triumphant. Adrian froze, lifting his ear toward the sound. "Did you hear that?"

"No. What—" Kye broke off as another, louder roar—unmistakable in its victory—echoed through the compound, followed by shrill human shrieks of terror. "Fuck. The prisoners."

Adrian bolted toward the prisoner building, but the snow leopard quickly outpaced him. He silently cursed his inability to shift and fly to the site. He'd lose the tranq gun on his hip, but a hawk swooping on rogue shifters from above could do substantial damage even without the human weapon.

He pressed on another burst of speed, but by the time he rounded a building and the old barn that had been retrofitted into a prison came into view, all-out chaos had broken loose. The doors were wide open and the shifters were inside the building—foxes in the fucking hen house.

Kye was nowhere in sight, doubtless already inside. Adrian palmed his tranq gun and waded in. The melee inside was more of a free-for-all than any sort of coordinated strike. A knot of prisoners—the smart ones—had barricaded themselves in a stall in the back and were fighting to keep the shifters out. Those who had tried to make a run for it littered the ground—as did a few of the rioting shifters. Kye was putting them down with a fluidity and ease that was impressive, but nothing compared to the half-shifted lethality of Grace.

She tore through the rioters on two legs, but with fangs and claws flashing and a light dusting of golden fur covering her partially feline face. Her dominance was a force that seemed to hum in the air around her, causing some of the smarter shifters to tuck tail and cower rather than engaging her.

Adrian didn't waste time admiring her skill—the rioters may not be trained fighters, but there were too many of them and they were too angry to give up easily. He pushed into the fray, tranqing everyone who wasn't actively trying to stop the battle. When he ran out of darts, he holstered the gun and continued with his fists. As an avian, he didn't have the strength of many of the larger predatory breeds, but what he lacked in brute force, he made up for in training. There was

148

never any doubt in his mind that they would put down the uprising—the only question was how long it would take and how many prisoner casualties there would be before they did.

A heavyset man with more bulk than brains charged Adrian and he snapped out his fist in a jab meant to catch him in the nose and put his lights out, but the bastard turned his head with shifter speed and Adrian's knuckles plowed into the hard bone of his skull rather than the nicely crunchable cartilage of his nose. Adrian hissed, feeling something crack in his hand, but didn't slow, spinning away from the massive man's haymaker and striking his throat with the knife-edge of his hand, sending the big man crashing to his knees as he gasped for breath.

He sensed another smaller shifter at his back and spun, sweeping the legs. He slapped a hand on the woman's shoulder, pinning her to the floor. He fucking hated fighting women. "Stay down," he snapped.

Claws swiped at him, lightning fast, and he barely avoided slicing open his face. A quick thwack of her head against the concrete floor knocked her out—and left him feeling sick to his stomach. Why did they never listen?

Another figure rushed him and Adrian leapt to his feet, engaging again.

When the dust finally settled—quite literally since Grace had thrown a partially shifted jaguar into a wall hard enough to pulverize the drywall—Adrian stood with Grace, Kye and a handful of pride security personnel over the prostrate forms of a couple dozen shifters as the surviving prisoners whimpered pitifully in their barricaded cell.

One jaguar—possibly the same idiot who'd made friends with the wall—feinted at rising and Grace snarled, forcing him back down so his belly scraped the floor in submission.

"Fucking mess," she growled, the words slightly distorted by the fangs still filling her mouth. "Kye," she called, command in her voice—the snow leopard might call the shots on their excursions into Organization territory, but here at the pride

Grace outranked him by a mile. "Get Brandt and Roman down here. Gather up the uninjured idiots and put them somewhere—I don't care where as long as it's far away from here." She raised her voice so the power in it echoed off the walls. "If you don't require immediate medical assistance, go with Kye and be good little shifters. Don't try to sneak off. We have surveillance, you dumbasses, and I have personally memorized each and every one of your stupid faces. Anyone tries to sneak off gets punished twice. Once by the Alpha—because you all fucking deserve it—and once by me, because I'm pissed. And anyone who even *looks* at the prisoners on their way out gets an express pass to the infirmary, courtesy of yours truly. Got it?"

There were rumblings that sounded vaguely agreeable and Grace nodded as if there had been a chorus of "Yes, ma'ams". She waved one clawed hand at Adrian. "Come here. Help me triage this shit. You have any medical training?"

He picked his way through the unconscious and wounded shifters—and handful of desiccated prisoner corpses—to her side. "Battlefield minimum."

She nodded, seemingly satisfied with that. "Look for anyone who's bleeding to death. Try to stop the bleeding. Brandt'll be here soon. Then just do whatever the hell he tells you."

She began moving through the bodies—just as terrifyingly efficient as a medic treating the injuries as she had been causing them. There weren't many in desperate need of medical attention—the prisoners who hadn't barricaded themselves in the back were shredded to the point of raw meat. There was no helping them. Most of the shifters were merely unconscious—tranquilized or knocked that way without life-threatening injuries, in a testament to the skill of Grace and her security forces. It seemed the few direly injured were rioters who had gotten in the way of one another in their frenzy to tear apart the Organization prisoners. A gash from claws here, a snapped bone there. Adrian did what he could until the real medics arrived and then he became a litter bearer, relocating the unconscious shifters out of the building.

Adrian crouched next to one shifter who had managed to fight his way all the way to the stall where the prisoners had barricaded themselves before being knocked out. One of the shifter's arms reached through a hole punched in the wood. Adrian withdrew the arm, taking shallow breaths through his mouth. The stench was worse back here. Not just the smell of carnage, he realized, but the scents of accumulated filth. Inside the stall were buckets filled with days old urine and feces. The surviving prisoners had barricaded themselves in their fucking *toilet.*

"Please."

Adrian focused on his task, ignoring the word whispered through the wood. It came again, and a third time, but he kept to his work, lifting the senseless shifter body and carrying it away. When he returned to move another body—this one the bloody remains of a prisoner—the voice was closer to the other side of the wall.

"Please." Quavering. Feminine.

It could be Rachel. If anyone but him had found her at that raid, it would have been.

Adrian turned his head, meeting a pair of pale blue eyes through the hole in the wood. Stringy brown hair framed a quietly desperate face. The woman from the van. "Please," she whispered again. "I don't know why I'm here. I'm just an administrative assistant. I do *data entry.*" Tears welled in her eyes. She lifted a hand to shove a hank of mangy hair away from her eyes, a tattoo on her wrist catching his eye.

No one was caring for this lot. No one was bringing them lotion and shampoo and three square meals a day. They might all deserve it. But then again, they might not.

Grace called his name and he returned to his task, turning away from the brunette who could have been Rachel.

The first snowflakes were beginning to fall a half hour later, when Grace—now fully human again—grabbed the other end of the stretcher he was lifting and helped him carry the last tranq-victim out into the night.

"Dumbasses, all of them," she muttered darkly.

"What happened?" he asked. "How did they get inside?"

Grace rolled her eyes, disgust coming off her in waves. "Some idiot woman inside snapped from all the roaring and started screaming through the walls at the shifters outside, goading them, challenging them. Some of the guards hadn't exactly been happy with this detail and apparently the two on the front door decided to take a smoke break around that time."

Adrian's eyebrows arched skeptically. Shifters never smoked. It fucked with their sense of smell and tasted positively vile to them. "Are you going to have a word with them?"

"They're being dealt with," Grace said darkly. They set the stretcher case down with the others in the Pride Hall—the pride didn't have another building big enough to hold all the unconscious rioters that wasn't already being used as a prison. Too many prisoners, in a place not equipped for it.

Adrian and Grace nodded to the guards—hand-picked by Grace herself from the security ranks—and strode out into the gently falling snow. It was idyllic, a lovely snowy evening in the Montana wilderness. And they both had dried blood under their fingernails. Adrian flexed his fingers, his knuckles already beginning to swell beyond usefulness.

"We'll have to screen the guards more carefully. And find someplace else to keep the survivors." Grace grumbled as they walked away from the building, footsteps crunching softly. "The barn was never supposed to be a long-term solution anyway. Just the only place we could think of on short notice that would fit them all that didn't have windows the bastards could crawl out of. What a fucking mess."

"What'll happen to that lot?" Adrian asked, jerking his head back toward the mass of unconscious rioters in the Pride Hall.

"Roman'll come up with a fitting punishment. The hell of it is, I don't even blame them." She shoved her hands into her pockets, long legs eating up the ground. "I wish I could, but most of the rioters are from the most recent batch of shifters released in our Organization raids. They're the ones who still wake up screaming every night. Who are we to tell them they can't kill their persecutors? Even if they weren't persecuted by these particular Organization doctors. All the same breed, right?" Grace shot him a sideways look. "Except yours. She's a different kind entirely, isn't she?"

Adrian didn't answer, not sure what she was hinting at and not sure he wanted to know.

Grace stopped abruptly. She turned her head sharply, watching the shadows, her nostrils flaring. Adrian held himself still, waiting for a command, but a moment later her ready stance eased. "Fucking Dominec."

Adrian frowned, searching the shadows, but whatever Grace had sensed, he didn't see or hear it. "I'm surprised he wasn't right in the thick of it, goading the shifters on."

"If he had been, I would have taken great pleasure in kicking his ass into next week. That's a lesson long overdue."

Adrian would have paid good money to see that fight—if he hadn't been a little unsure which of the two would come out on top when push came to shove. Grace was fierce, but Dominec was insane. In those cases, sometimes insanity won.

"I expect the Alpha will bring your doc in to sort the goodies from the baddies now," Grace commented, continuing down the path.

"Is that wise?" He may recognize the need, but Adrian didn't want Rachel anywhere near that charnel house.

"What? You trust her to knock up our kitty-cats, but not to tell us which of the Organization prisoners we need to be most wary of?"

Adrian scowled. "What are you talking about?"

"Don't you know? Kathy-cat came running to the infirmary earlier, bragging about her big news, right before I got the call that the shit was hitting all sorts of fans over here."

"What news?"

"Your doc is gonna help her have kittens. Little lynxy babies. Or bobcat babies. I don't know how that stuff works when you're mixing."

He stiffened. "She wouldn't."

"If you say so. Kathy seemed pretty sure."

He gritted his back teeth. Wouldn't that be just like Rachel, to volunteer to help without a single thought to her own safety. There were shifters in the pride—even those who hadn't been involved in today's riot, who wouldn't take kindly to an Organization doc tinkering around in the infirmary, no matter what she'd done for them in the past.

Images from the bloody fight in the barn rose vividly in his mind—only this time instead of faceless Organization prisoners lying on the floor with their bowels ripped open, it was Rachel's wide brown eyes staring lifelessly up at him.

Adrian shuddered. "She wouldn't," he repeated, as if repetition could make the words true.

"What did you expect? That you'd keep her tucked away in your little hideaway forever? Good plan, champ."

"Am I dismissed?" he snapped.

"Are you reporting to me now? I thought you were all *I'm not part of this pride.*" At his glower, she shrugged. "Sure, you're done. Go pee a circle around your doc."

Adrian didn't dignify the parting jab with a reply. He turned and began jogging toward his cabin. It had been hours, far longer than he normally went without checking on her. Sure, she'd had a bear guarding her most of the day, but he was young, and if Kathy was back at the main compound telling everyone Rachel was helping her, then the others had probably left as well. Rachel was alone. Locked in the cabin. Defenseless.

And Dominec hadn't been at the riot.

Dominec, who could easily track her back there along one of the scent-trails she'd left when Adrian had guided her blindfolded through the woods.

Dominec, who had already made one attempt on her life.

Tired though he was, Adrian poured on a burst of speed, sprinting dead-out toward the cabin.

"Rachel!" He bellowed her name—as if that would help if she was being dismembered—and took the cabin steps in a single leap. The lock wasn't on the door and his panic escalated to critical levels as he yanked the door open and charged inside.

And there she was. Sitting at the table. Calm and cool and collected.

The fear that had driven him instantly morphed into a blinding rage, latching on to the nearest excuse. He slammed his hands down flat on the table, bending down so his head was on her level.

"What the *fuck* were you thinking?"

Chapter Eighteen

Rachel had barely had time to process the panicked shout outside before Adrian was bursting through the door, surging into the room like the devil himself was at his back. It was late, far later than he normally arrived with her dinner, and he looked like hell—exhausted and covered with flecks of rust-brown dried blood. He'd staggered to a stop, his eyes glowing more hawk-like than ever as his gaze raked her from head to toe and back again. A thousand expressions flickered across his face before they were all swallowed in a dark scowl.

She'd been sitting at the table, wondering if she could use toilet paper and eyeliner to make a list of procedures for Kathy to give the pride doctors as a starting point, mentally composing her thanks to Adrian for allowing her the visit. Before she could ask him what had happened to leave him looking like he'd been in a bar brawl he was in her face, snarling accusations.

"I don't know what you—"

"You think an Organization doctor can just start running fertility experiments on shifters here and no one will mind?"

"*Former* Organization doctor," she snapped, rising to her feet, her spine straightening as she realized what had twisted his feathers. Lord, why was it always like this with him? Just when she thought they were making progress, he had to take seven steps back from trusting her again. "And I'm not experimenting on her. I'm helping her. Like she asked me to."

"You think everyone here is going to care about that distinction? Do you know how many shifters only see an Organization doctor when they look at you?" He prowled around the table and she retreated instinctively, forcing herself to stop as soon as she realized what she was doing, her calves pressed against the low futon mattress.

"Isn't that what you see, Adrian? Isn't that why I'm your personal prisoner up here? Because I'm the Evil Organization Doctor Who Can't Be Trusted? When are you going to stop painting me with that brush? Yeah, I betrayed you when we were a team, but you left me behind too. I thought I was going to die and I never blamed you."

He stopped, close enough to box her in but not touching. "Is that why you're bringing it up now? Because there's no blame?"

"I'm only saying neither of us is perfect."

"I never claimed to be."

"No. You just wanted *me* to be. Because if I was a saint and I loved you, then it absolved you of all your sins and you must be a good guy after all, right? All those people you were ordered to kill as a sniper, you were forgiven if Rachel the Madonna loved you."

He backed away from the futon and her, raking both hands through his short hair. "Don't talk about love with me."

"Why not? Because you hate yourself for still being in love with me?"

"Stop." He growled. "No fertility treatments. End of discussion." He turned away, as if they were done and she grabbed the object nearest to hand—which unfortunately was just a pillow—and chucked it at the back of his head.

"This isn't your call!" she shouted as he spun around hissing in anger after her pillow-assault. "It's Kathy's body. Kathy's baby. *Kathy* who trusts me to help her. It doesn't matter what you want."

"I can keep you here where Kathy can't reach you."

"Why? So I can be useless and bored? This is what I'm good at. It's what I was hired for and here I can actually do some good with it. *Let me.*"

"It isn't safe. Do you want to get yourself killed?"

Rachel froze, realization pulling the stopper on her anger and letting it leak out of her like water down a drain. He wasn't trying to punish her. He was trying to protect her. She'd thrown the words about love at him on impulse, but there must be some truth there. He was determined to hate her, but couldn't help worrying over her. Lord, what a mess they had made of things.

If only he would let himself see what he still felt for her.

"Why did you send Kathy and the others to see me today?" she asked softly.

He turned away, moving to the sink and running his hands beneath water that must have been icy, scrubbing at the rust-brown flecks caked on his skin.

"Adrian?"

"To distract you," he answered without looking at her. "Keep you busy so you didn't try to break free and get down to the main compound."

"What's going on at the main compound? What happened today?"

"There was a riot," he said, still without looking up from scrubbing his hands. "Some of the recently released shifters managed to get into the building where the Organization prisoners were being held."

Rachel hissed in a breath. "How many were killed?"

"Not quite half. Nine of twenty-two. Leaving a lucky thirteen."

"Including me?"

He looked up then, frowning at her as if she'd said something disgusting.

"Aren't I one of them? Isn't that what you're worried about? That no one will see a difference?"

"Some won't."

"So show them I'm different. Don't treat me like a prisoner. Let me help Kathy."

He shook his head, turning back to his hands—which were now as thoroughly cleaned as Lady MacBeth's. "I can't protect you down there."

"Adrian, for the last three years I lived with the knowledge that every day when I got to work my employers might decide that today was a good day to kill me. A little danger is nothing novel."

He didn't react. Washing, always washing.

Rachel played her last card. "Am I really any safer here? Locked in a box? Easy pickings?"

His hands went still. A moment later he shut off the water and grabbed the ragged kitchen towel. He winced and Rachel zeroed in on his knuckles. "Are you hurt?"

He neatly folded the towel and tucked it over the edge of one cupboard. "It's nothing." He tried to dismiss her concern, but she caught his hand, cradling it between both of hers as she examined the swollen area.

"You should have this X-rayed. It could be broken."

"Shifters heal quickly." He began to pull his hand away, but she gripped his wrist firmly.

"At least let me wrap it. You won't do anyone any good if you keep reinjuring it because you're too stubborn to get it looked at."

He grunted, but reached into his pocket with his uninjured hand and pulled out a key ring, extending it to her. "There are bandages in the trunk."

She moved cautiously—no sudden moves, as if he was indeed a bird of prey who would be startled into flight. He sat on the futon and she withdrew the supplies from the trunk which seemed to hold a bizarre mishmash of possessions—an extra pair of boots, a well-worn spy novel, a lumpy black duffel bag and a white box with a familiar red cross on the front—all lined up with military precision. Adrian's things. Was this all he had in the world?

She retrieved the first aid box and popped it open. Laying the bandages on the bed, she sat tailor fashion in front of him and drew his hand into her lap, gently probing the injury. It was almost definitely broken, and she wanted to push him to get it seen to properly, but shifters did heal rapidly. It was possible if she bound it today, it would be as good as new in a day or two.

Without pain killers, it had to hurt, but Adrian didn't make a sound as she wound the bandage snuggly over his knuckles, bracing the broken bones in place. How often had he been injured with no one to tend to his wounds?

He didn't look at her, watching her hands moving over his, but for once his gaze didn't feel cold. A strange sort of truce existed between them as she worked. She found herself working slowly, wanting this moment to last longer. She secured the end of the bandage, letting her fingers linger, a light caress over his wrist, the back of his hand. When she heard his breath catch, she dared to lift her gaze to his face, he was close, his eyes all hawk as they fixed on her lips. She let her own gaze fall to the firm line of his mouth, leaning toward him. "Adrian…"

It was just a kiss. But nothing with Adrian was ever *just* anything. Their lips brushed gently, hesitantly, both of them hyperaware that the slightest misstep would shatter their fragile truce. And she didn't want anything to break this moment. She lifted a hand and traced the hard plane of his jaw, his stubble rough against her fingertips. She deepened the kiss, sliding her tongue along the smooth inside of his lip. He groaned. The entire world seemed to shiver and hold its breath.

And then he lifted his head.

"I'll take you down to the infirmary in the morning."

Frustration spiked. "Adrian. That wasn't why I kissed you."

He pulled away as if he hadn't heard her, standing and striding to the door.

"Adrian!" The padlock clicked shut after him.

Part of her wanted to celebrate. This was progress. But another, larger part of her ached. Would he ever stop walking away from her?

A low, distressed sound reached through the night and Rachel cracked her eyelids, blinking sleep away as her half-awake mind struggled to identify the noise. It came again, raw and edged with fear. She rolled to the edge of the futon, searching out the source, and came fully awake as she identified the lumpy mass sprawled blocking the door as Adrian's sleeping form. He twisted restlessly, caught in some nightmare as another low, ragged sound ripped from his unwilling throat.

For a moment she was too shocked to move. He'd been guarding her sleep like this without her knowledge. Perhaps all week. She would never understand this strange man who would look at her like a murderer by day and watch over her each night. Who brought her presents—which he refused to admit were presents—and then turned around and snarled at her when she so much as brushed his hand.

He groaned again and she sat up in bed, wondering if she should wake him. Was he dreaming of the Organization? He may lash out at her if she woke him, but she couldn't leave him in that dream world where he was obviously in pain when she might be able to help him.

Rachel slipped out of bed and crept across the icy floor on bare feet, half-expecting him to come surging awake at every creak of the floorboards, but he was too deep inside whatever nightmare held him. She knelt at his side, careful not to loom over him, and touched his arm—gently at first and then more firmly when he didn't respond. His skin was warm beneath her palm, warmer than human, and harder, like the muscle was closer to the surface, barely contained inside his skin.

"Adrian."

His eyes moved rapidly behind his closed lids, but they didn't open.

"Adrian, you're dreaming. *Hawk.*"

He jerked, flailing wildly, striking her across the cheek and throwing her away from him, eyes still squeezed shut.

Chapter Nineteen

"Adrian. Hawk."

She was calling for him. He heard her, would know her voice anywhere, but he couldn't reach her. He was back in the prisoner barn, but it looked wrong. Stretched. Rachel was vulnerable—outside the cell where the other prisoners had barricaded themselves—but with every step he ran, the distance between them seemed to grow longer. The footing was treacherous and he slipped, going down in a mess of blood and gore, something slick tangling around his ankles. Intestine, he realized, kicking at it, bile rising in his throat as she called again, closer this time. He looked up and could almost reach her, almost touch her, but then Grace was there, smacking his hand down with a swipe of her claws. *We aren't doing enough*, she said. Kye's face swam in front of him, fangs bared. Xander. Brandt. Roman. All those he'd thought were friends barring his way, forcing him away from her, his hands scrabbling for purchase on the blood-slick floor.

Then Dominec was there, his scarred face half-feline as he loomed over Rachel. The tiger dug his claws into her abdomen and twisted. She screamed and Adrian threw off the friends who would hold him back, fighting away their clawing hands. He reached for talons and wings. His hands instantly elongated, the tips sharpening to razor points. A familiar pain split his shoulder blades, wings bursting forth, but they felt wrong, diseased. He tried to flap them, tried to lift his partially shifted body above the fight to get to Rachel, a pool of blood rapidly expanding around her, her mahogany eyes dimming, but with the first downward thrust the bones of his wings snapped, the agony piercing as the brittle bones shattered and his feathers fell to stick in the gore at his feet. He called again to his hawk, but his wings dissolved, crumbling, the pain crippling. He screamed in a thousand points of pain as she said his name again, this time through lips white with blood loss, her eyes already dead as Dominec licked the glistening red of her blood from his claws. He'd failed her. Again.

"Adrian. You're having a nightmare. Please, wake up."

He felt hands on him then, shaking. Heard the sound of another heartbeat racing alongside his own. *Rachel.*

He jerked awake—one moment wrapped in the bloody remains of the dream, in the next splayed on the floor of the cabin, Rachel crouched over him, gripping his shoulders, her face a mask of worry. *Alive.*

He lunged for her, needing the feel of his arms around her more than he needed his next breath. She flinched at the sudden movement, but didn't try to pull away when he buried his face in her hair, breathing her in, holding her close. He could feel her surprise in the slight stiffness of her shoulders, the careful way her arms closed around him in return. He whispered her name, his lips stirring the hair beneath her ear, and that wary stiffness melted away. She sank deeper into his arms, all warm, soft femininity—and so heartbreakingly alive.

It wasn't a matter of conscious thought to lift his head and seek out her lips. It was the completion of a compulsion so irresistible the lack of it would have been unthinkable. She was smooth and sweetly yielding against his mouth, accepting all the desperation and tenderness that surged through him. He held her ever closer. There could be no distance in a kiss like this, no barriers between them, even air. She squirmed against him as if she could climb inside his skin and Adrian coaxed her mouth open, thrusting inside to claim all that she was with a sweep of his tongue. She tasted like heaven—strawberries, the lingering mint of toothpaste and something else. Something that was singularly *hers*. For the first time, he wished he were a different kind of shifter, so he could bathe in her scent, roll himself in the taste of her.

He slipped his hands beneath her flannel pajama top—hating himself for giving her something that covered her lush body so completely. Her skin was silk as he stroked up her back and she gasped, arching her body against his.

He claimed her mouth again, diving deep. He tried to reach her gorgeous breasts, but the damn flannel got in the way. Adrian gripped the shirt in both fists and yanked, sending buttons flying until her lush, delectable curves were his to feast on.

"God, I missed you," she breathed as he bent, palming and massaging her breast, his tongue teasing the nipple with delicate flicks before sucking it fast and hard into his mouth just how she liked it.

She was a finely tuned instrument, and one he remembered exactly how to play. His free hand slipped down the front of her pajama bottoms and found her, wet and willing. Still laving her breast, he gently flicked her clit, making her cry out and twist in his arms, then soothed her with long, sweet strokes, delving his fingers into her sweet, tight channel, and she keened, shoving her pajamas down her hips and kicking them off.

Her fingers yanked at the drawstring of the slacks he'd been sleeping in, shoving down his pants until she found her prize, her fist wrapping around him with the perfect pressure. *"Fuck."*

"Condom?" she asked breathlessly and he swore again. They'd always been careful before. For all he knew he and Rachel weren't even genetically compatible and shifters weren't susceptible to human STDs, but they could be carriers for them and as a non-human Adrian couldn't exactly get a blood test at a local clinic. He'd always protected her.

Please God, let there be a condom.

He dove for the footlocker containing his possessions, wrestling with the lock as Rachel followed, holding her flannel top closed in a strangely modest gesture.

Adrian threw open the trunk, rummaging through it without regard for his usual, orderly packing system. The toiletry bag was buried at the bottom. When he pulled it out of the trunk, his blood-deprived brain almost thought it heard a symphony. He yanked open the bag and there it was. Salvation.

What the fuck was he doing?

That single, rational thought somehow found its way through the lust fogging his brain.

Then she reached around him, plucking the condom from his fingers with one hand while the other wrapped around his cock and all his higher brain functions gave up the fight.

Rachel stroked her hand up Adrian's cock, her face pressed to his shoulder to inhale the scent of him. Her Adrian, back in her arms. *Yes.* She used her teeth to rip open the foil packet and rolled the condom up his length, giving him an extra stroke for good measure.

He turned, hands sliding beneath the loosely flapping fabric of her pajama top, lifting her, placing her against the wall and pinning her there with his body, every point of contact a searing, erotic heat. He nipped her lower lip, her throat. Guiding her legs around his waist, he fitted himself against her core and pushed inside. She stretched around him, every sensation amplified by the fact that it was him. Her hawk.

His yellow eyes gleamed, nothing human left in them as they shone into hers. Deeper, harder, until she was sobbing his name, clutching his shoulders, and that first violent tear of pleasure ripped through her.

He bared his teeth and pounded into her, hard and unrestrained until she felt the prick of his talons delicately pinching her hips as he found his own release inside her with the intense, burning silence that she remembered so well. She whispered his name, holding him to her with arms and legs, as if she could hold on to that fleeting feeling.

Spent, he collapsed onto the futon, holding her against him. She wanted to wallow in the moment, to stretch it out for an eternity, but the jab of his talons was a little too sharp now that her afterglow was fading. Rachel had never been into pain.

"Careful," she whispered. "Your talons are sharp."

Talons. Adrian froze. Moving carefully, slowly, he withdrew his hands. Now that she pointed them out, he could feel them, the sharp points where his fingertips should be, but he needed to see them as well. He hadn't been able to partial-shift any part of his body other than his eyes since he'd escaped from the Organization. Part of him hated the loss of her warmth as Rachel leaned slightly away from him, her eyes questioning, but his thoughts were tangled up in talons and wings.

He lifted his right hand and both of them stared at it—the knobby, bony knuckles tapering to fierce, razor-sharp talons. They may have come when he called them in the dream or after, with her, with his release. He hated to lose them, even for a second, but he called to his human hands, watching as his fingers reshaped themselves into something wholly human.

Was he healed? He probed for the hawk, the other half of his soul, in the dark of his mind, but it was still lost. His talons. His eyes. It came to him in pieces, but withheld the most important part. His eyes burned, shoulders aching for the loss of his wings.

"Adrian?"

He jolted. Rachel lay against him, the length of her aligned to the length of him, but he'd momentarily forgotten her presence—not that he'd forgotten she was there, but more that the presence of her was so natural, such an extension of him that it was simply accepted. Her voice startled him—but it was the rightness of her in his arms that sent a jolt through him, not the disruption.

Shit.

What had he done?

Adrian set her away from him sharply, rolling to his feet and clenching his fists to fight the instinctive urge to help her to hers. He peeled off the condom, dropping it in the trash, and yanked up his pants, securing them clumsily. What the fuck had just happened? He'd reached for her like his long-lost mate and she'd come into his arms as if she belonged there. *Wrong. So wrong.*

She scrambled to her feet, the sounds impossibly loud and clumsy. He should have heard her approach him and woken. She shouldn't have been able to sneak up on him, even in the middle of a nightmare. His instincts should have raised the alarm before she got so close—but it felt so fucking right to have her close.

Wrong.

"Are you all right?" she asked, her voice a little rough. From sleep or arousal. Her heart still beat too quickly, her rapid breath raising her full breasts beneath the god-awful flannel top that she held closed with one hand. The beginnings of a bruise marred the perfection of her left cheekbone and he reached out to brush his fingers delicately beside the spot before he could stop himself.

"Did I...?"

Her slight grimace was answer enough before she said, "I got in the way when you were in the dream."

Regret pierced him. That he could have harmed her felt more wrong than everything else in this chaotic interlude. "I'm sorry." *For everything.*

She waved away his apology. "It doesn't hurt."

He couldn't tell if she was lying.

And that was always the problem with Rachel. He'd never been able to tell when she was lying.

He didn't trust easily, but she had been the exception. It had been too easy to trust her and it would be too easy to do it again. He'd listened to instincts that swore she was *his* in an inescapable way, and he'd been wrong.

And now here he was again, falling too easily into her arms. He could be with her—he couldn't seem to stop himself—but he couldn't let himself be swayed by what she made him feel.

She'd delighted in his pain while he was in captivity. He remembered the malicious cheer in her voice. He couldn't trust himself to trust her now. Not when she could be Mother Theresa or Machiavelli and he couldn't tell the difference because he wanted her—and desire was the great blinder.

She hovered in front of him, on the balls of her feet as if she would rush forward into his arms at the slightest indication that he would welcome it. But no matter how he wanted her, how he ached for her in a way he'd almost forgotten how to feel, he couldn't take that last step. Not with the cruel edge of her voice ringing in his memory.

If she would just admit it...

"How could you do it? Even if you had to, how could you?" She was supposed to be the exception.

Her eyes flared with shock and hurt. "Adrian... I explained. They knew about us—"

"Not that. The experiments. Why did you have to make them think you enjoyed hurting me?" Why had she had to make *him* believe it?

He needed to know, but he saw the denial closing down her face before she said a word. "I never—"

He couldn't listen to her lies. Not tonight when everything was raw.

"Go back to sleep, Rachel." He turned away without waiting to see if she would obey. He didn't want to see the hurt on her face, didn't want the guilt. He snatched his holster from the floor near the door where he'd been using it as a pillow before everything went sideways. He finished fastening his pants on the porch, hooking the holster to his waistband.

The icy night air felt right on his skin, the veil of falling snow just the mask he needed so he didn't have to look at himself—or his desire—too closely. Wrong. She was wrong. It was an illusion that made her feel so right. Mistakes and lies.

He just needed to remember that.

"Damn it, Adrian!"

He leaned against the exterior wall, listening to Rachel cursing inside. She had an impressive repertoire. Surprisingly varied.

He'd never heard her lose her temper before Lone Pine. Not when they were sneaking around, always united, and he'd mooned over her like a freaking puppy. And not later, when he was her prisoner. She'd always been calm then. Chillingly so.

His memories of his time as a guest of the Organization were a foggy jumble at best, but he remembered with absolute clarity the first time he'd heard her voice inside those cells. It hadn't been immediately after his capture. He'd had weeks to build up elaborate rationalizations for why she'd sedated him and handed him over to her bosses.

And all it had taken was the sound of her voice to shatter them all.

He'd been blind—thanks to one of the many operations to investigate the unique properties of his corneas—but he knew her voice, even with all the compassion stripped from it.

She'd been giving orders. The others bowing and scraping to her. He'd said her name, but she hadn't responded—except to tell his jailers to determine the exact amount of pressure required to break an avian shifter's bones. For science.

And he'd fucked her tonight. And it had been fucking amazing. *Fuck.*

Something rustled in the woods, snapping Adrian out of the memory. Rachel was still muttering curses inside, but he focused his eyes and ears on the trees to his left.

If he hadn't been a raptor, he wouldn't have caught the movement. Dominec was that good.

The tiger blended with the shadows, the pale rusty yellow and white of his fur making him all but invisible in the snow. A hundred yards out. Watching the cabin with lazy feline focus.

Adrian had begun to wonder if he was just being paranoid about Rachel's safety, but he didn't feel paranoid now. He pulled the tranq gun from its holster at his hip, holding it loose at his side with his uninjured hand. Grace had handed him a freshly filled tranq gun following the riot. After the day he'd had—the riot, the nightmare, taking Rachel like a fucking animal because his defenses were down and no force on earth could have stopped him—he was primed and ready for a fight.

Just try to get past me, big guy.

For a long, interminable moment, the tiger didn't move. Adrenaline sharpened Adrian's focus, honing his edge. He was in a staring contest with a psycho with six-inch claws and he wasn't going to blink first.

After what felt like an eternity, but was probably only a handful of seconds, the Siberian lifted from his crouch, turning with a flick of his tale and loping back toward the pride.

Adrian leaned back against the exterior wall of the shack, but couldn't make himself relax. The memories of what had been done to those nine unlucky prisoners today were too fresh in his mind.

He wouldn't let that be Rachel. He didn't love her. He couldn't let himself. But she was his to protect. So he settled in to guard, rolling shoulders tense with strain. This was supposed to be a safe haven, but they would never be truly safe.

Chapter Twenty

Rachel stumbled through the snowdrifts hiding roots and rocks, struggling to keep up with Adrian's quick, sure-footed pace far more than she had when she'd been making the same trip blindfolded. She glared at his back as she fought to keep her feet, certain she was on her own if she started to go down—Adrian hadn't come within five feet of her since he'd arrived this morning to escort her down to the main compound. She couldn't even catch his eye.

She certainly wasn't the first woman who had ever been slept with and then ignored, but she would never understand what prompted a man to devour a woman like she was oxygen, make her feel like she would die on the spot if he couldn't keep touching her, and then turn around and pretend she didn't exist. He'd been ravenous for her—and in Rachel's book, that meant something, no matter how distant and taciturn the icy Hawk wanted to play it in the morning light.

Her left foot caught on a tree root and she pitched sideways, catching herself against a tree, both palms lightly scraped by the rough bark. She'd been right before—there was no way she'd be able to find her way back to the cabin without an escort. She was a city girl. The path may be clear to a shifter like Adrian, but to her it was just woods, woods, and more woods.

It was with distinct relief that she stepped out of the forest and onto the wider, more cultivated—and thank goodness, cleared of snow—paths close to the heart of the pride.

She'd seen bits and pieces of the main pride compound—a building here, a bungalow there—as she was taken to various locations during her debriefing, but it was a different matter entirely seeing the scope of it. Not just a glimpse before Adrian blindfolded her, but the breadth of it laid out before her. She understood now what he'd meant in saying it was a full-service pride. Lone Pine was a village unto itself.

They passed a school, two dining halls, several apartment complexes and a general store—which answered the question of where Adrian had gotten all the clothing and other supplies that magically appeared in the cabin, anticipating her every need. The pride bustled with activity in spite of the snow—nothing shut down in Montana because of a little of the white stuff. Not like her Georgia home.

At various points along the path there were laminated maps pinned to posts that looked like they'd just been driven into the ground. Directories, doubtless to cope with the influx of new shifters. And above it all, the Alpha's mansion reigned from the top of the hill, the physical and emotional heart of the pride.

Adrian led her, always without looking directly at her or speaking, through the maze of pathways to a sprawling low-slung building with a giant red cross painted on the stucco face. He held the door for her and she stepped inside, looking around her with interest. They called it the infirmary, but it was larger and better outfitted than the name implied, reminding her of a well-funded private clinic or small country hospital.

A tall man with close-cropped dark hair mixed with gray came forward, his hand stretched out to greet her. "You must be the infamous Dr. Russell," he said, with a ready smile.

Adrian scowled, but performed the introductions. "Rachel, this is Dr. Brandt. The infirmary is his domain."

"I am indeed the master of all you see." Dr. Brandt waved to encompass the waiting cots and sleeping machines. "At least Moira lets me believe myself to be."

"Moira?" Rachel inquired.

"My right hand. She's a registered nurse, but her role here is more as healer and midwife—honoring the old ways. She's eager to talk to you, actually. To pick your brain about shifter

173

babies. It's rare she meets someone whose expertise on the matter outstrips her own."

"I thought you'd be busier today," Adrian commented. He stood apart from them, focused on the empty beds and silent machines so he didn't have to look at her. "After last night."

"Processed and discharged." The words preceded Grace into the room as she strode out of a back hallway. "Shifters make shitty patients. Always checking themselves out against medical advice, right, Adrian?"

"Grace." The hawk's shoulders visibly relaxed as soon as the blonde Amazon walked into the room.

Rachel felt her own shoulders tensing in direct proportion to how much Adrian's relaxed. Did he have to be so relieved to see Grace? She still knew nothing about their relationship. For all she knew, Grace was the one he went running to every time he left her.

Jealousy burned like acid in her stomach, but she did her best to ignore it. She turned to Dr. Brandt, intent on asking for a tour of his domain, but Adrian stepped between them and caught her hand. The fact that he was actually touching her was so startling that she missed the first few words of whatever he was saying to her.

"—so stay here until I come to fetch you and don't leave Grace's sight for a second. Understand?"

He was leaving. A flood of conflicting emotions joined the acidic wash of jealousy in her stomach—relief that she wouldn't have his distracting presence looming over her shoulder all day, pride that she'd earned enough of his trust—finally—to be allowed on pride land without him watching over her like a hawk—ha—and fear that she would be defenseless without him. Not that she didn't trust Grace to protect her, but she felt on some irrational, purely instinctual level, that she was safer with him.

"Rachel," he said sharply when she didn't immediately respond, giving the hand he held a light shake.

"I understand."

"Good."

Adrian dropped her hand, nodded to Brandt and Grace, and turned to march out the door without another word. He did love his dramatic exits. Rachel glared after him for a moment before Dr. Brandt caught her attention, a slight smile touching his mouth.

"Kathy and her mate will be in later," the pride doctor said. "This morning we thought you could start bringing us up to speed on what you've learned and what techniques have proven effective in your treatment of shifters."

Her treatment of shifters. She noticed the doctor very carefully didn't mention the Organization or the word "experiments", but Rachel couldn't help a flush of shame at *how* she'd acquired some of the knowledge she had to share with them. Few of her patients had been willing and she had rarely been able to protect them from the experiments of the other doctors.

Seeming to sense her discomfort beneath his gaze, Brandt turned his head back toward the hallway from which Grace had emerged. "I wonder what's holding up Moira. Why don't I go fetch her so we can get started?"

He didn't wait for an answer, disappearing into the back of the building, leaving her alone with the warrior princess.

Rachel eyed the leggy blonde. "Don't you have something better to do than babysit me all day? Lieutenant duties?"

"Actually, you're part of my lieutenant duties. I volunteered for babysitting duty so I could corner you later and have you look at some photos of the Organization prisoners and see what you know about them." Grace grinned, flashing bright white teeth. "I'm also our field medic. EMT. Whatever. Figure it doesn't hurt to know more about the risks of cross-breed baby-making, because I might be the first one on the scene if we have an emergency." Her smile grew wider. "I also assigned Adrian perimeter duty to keep him busy so he won't hover over you all day like a mother hen. You're welcome."

Rachel said nothing, not sure she was grateful.

"Brandt doesn't blame you, you know. For the experiments," Grace said conversationally, hitching herself up onto one of the empty beds and swinging her booted feet. "None of us do. We're the first point of contact for most of the refugee shifters, treating them for everything from dehydration to...well, you know. Don't you?" She tilted her head studying Rachel with disturbingly direct blue eyes. "They don't all talk about what happened to them, but those that do, speak about you like you're the patron saint of everything good and holy in the world. You had to do some shit you aren't proud of—we've all been there. Nobody's judging you. At least no one in this building. Got it?"

Rachel nodded. She was reluctant to like Grace, but the lioness didn't seem bothered at all by her coolness.

"Nice shiner," she said when Rachel still didn't speak.

Rachel lifted a hand to her cheek, her fingers hovering over the mark. She hadn't had any makeup to cover it up—Adrian hadn't gone that far in his provisions. It didn't hurt unless she touched it and the swelling and discoloration were minor, barely noticeable. She'd forgotten it was there, but she should have known the shifters would notice it.

"It was an accident."

Grace snorted. "That's almost as good as *I fell.*"

Rachel stiffened, irritated by Grace's insinuation. "It wasn't anything like that. Adrian would never," she defended, though the hawk shifter hardly deserved her loyalty after his hot-and-cold routine. But through all their tempestuous history, he'd never laid a hand on her and she knew he never would. It would violate his honor in the most intrinsic way. "He was having a nightmare and I got in the way."

"So you are sleeping together. Damn, I just lost twenty bucks. You positively reek of his scent, but I figured that could always be from staying at his place."

Rachel's face grew hot with the knowledge that her sex life had been the object of speculation and betting. She shouldn't be surprised. The shifters didn't seem to have much in the way of boundaries. It was a wonder her blush wasn't permanent.

Last night was too personal to be public knowledge. She protested, "We aren't—I mean, it isn't like that. We don't—"

Grace's arched brow screamed that she wasn't helping herself with her stammering.

She was a better liar than that. Rachel cleared her throat and tried again. "He guards me. From the floor. He won't get near me."

Except when he did. And the world caught on fire for a few minutes before they both remembered he hated her.

Grace nodded, unsurprised. "Either way, I'm glad he didn't hit you. He seems like a good guy. I'd hate to have to kick his ass into next week."

Rachel frowned. She didn't know what to make of the woman. She and Adrian seemed so close, and then she went and implied that she would take Rachel's side. It could be a ploy to get Rachel to trust her. But even if it was a trick, Rachel was inclined to let it work. She was so tired of being guarded all the time. If only the woman trying to befriend her wasn't also the one she suspected of sleeping with Adrian. Though if Grace knew he was sleeping with Rachel... Grace didn't seem the type to share.

She could make herself crazy speculating or she could ask. She'd been raised that it was rude to ask, but the last few weeks had worn away her need to be polite. "So you and he aren't *together?*"

Grace snorted out a laugh, rocking back and forth on the bed with the force of it. "Oh honey. Me and Hawkeye? No, thank you. Not my type."

Rachel was tempted to ask her what her type was. It seemed incomprehensible to her that Adrian's brand of fierce, intense passion wouldn't be every woman's type, but before she could get the words out, voices reached them from the back hallway and Dr. Brandt emerged with a petite, curvy woman. Moira.

"You must be Rachel!" she exclaimed with undisguised enthusiasm lighting her pale brown eyes. "Adrian spoke of you so often I feel like I know you already. I'm Moira."

Rachel took the hand Moira offered, unsure how to respond to the idea that Adrian's version of her could have generated such a positive welcome. Luckily, Moira didn't seem to require a reply. She pulled Rachel into a tour of the facility, gently but inexorably taking control and putting proof to Dr. Brandt's comment that Moira only let him believe he was in charge. She was clearly the heart of the operation—though she ruled so subtly Rachel doubted most people even noticed she was there.

Her coloring was unusual, a few shades darker than most of the lions Rachel had met—shades of brown tinting her skin, eyes and hair so she looked for all the world like she'd been dipped in caramel. Moira was also much smaller than Dr. Brandt and Grace—who Rachel suspected were both lions. But what was Moira?

"What do you say, Dr. Russell?" Dr. Brandt asked as they completed the tour in the cluttered office he shared with Moira. He tossed himself into one rolling chair, waving Rachel to another as Grace perched on the desk and Moira took the other chair. "Will we do?"

"I'm very impressed with what you've done here," she said sincerely. The infirmary was no back-country sawbones. They had much of the most up-to-date technology, though nowhere near the level of the Organization facilities. "I should be able to do almost everything I need to with what you already have, and if we do need more specialized equipment, we can cross that bridge when we come to it."

"We try to do everything on site," Dr. Brandt explained. "Too much risk in sending blood work to external clinics to be analyzed, but that does limit us. There's only so much we can do with the resources we have—but it's better medical care than most shifters get."

"It's just the three of you?"

"Up until recently there were less than a hundred shifters living here," Grace said, swinging one leg at the knee. "There's a lynx who comes by to run blood work for us as needed and some of our pride mates have basic first aid training to help in a pinch, but for the most part three was plenty. Especially since, as a group, we are notoriously pig-headed about seeking medical help." Grace tipped her head in Moira's direction. "Bears are the worst. You'd think doctors were going to declaw them all with the way they grouse about even getting a check-up."

"Lions are no picnic," Moira put in dryly.

Rachel's eyes flicked to the petite woman. She seemed much too small to be a bear, but there was something very warm and maternal about her and bears were good parents. She wasn't used to meeting shifters without seeing their files first, with their animal designation and medical history laid out before her.

"Is it rude to ask what kind of shifter a person is?"

Grace laughed and Brandt did as well, but Moira took pity on her. "It's not rude, no. It's just that few shifters would have to ask so they forget that not everyone can smell the differences on them. Grace and Brandt are both lions. I'm a Kodiak bear." Rachel's jaw dropped and Moira laughed, a soft, gentle sound completely at odds with Rachel's image of bears. "Yes, I know, it surprises most people who can't smell it on me. But someone has to remind the lions they aren't the top of the food chain. And my strength comes in handy if we have a shifter mama with a difficult delivery."

"That it does," Brandt agreed. "But first we have to get to full-term. Which, with cross-breed pairings, has been quite the challenge. With pairings of the same breed, our shifters seem to be so fertile we've had to develop birth-control shots to keep our population from rising too rapidly, but cross-breeds are a different story."

Moira nodded. "We have so many old wives tales about what happens with the offspring of cross-breed pairings, but we have no real data. And here at Lone Pine, with so many different breeds mixing, more and more cross-breed pairings seem to be popping up."

"Which is where you come in." Brandt turned to her. "So what can you tell us about your work, Dr. Russell?"

"Call me Rachel."

Chapter Twenty-One

"Dude. Are you really the Hawk? Like, *the* Hawk?"

Adrian eyed the young soldier looking up at him with what could only be described as glazed hero-worship. "Just call me Adrian." He hadn't been *the* Hawk in a while.

The kid's jaw dropped. "Holy crap, you are. I thought you were a myth! One of the guys was telling a story the other night about you being like...what's his name? The Greek dude who ferried souls? Only you did it for shifters. Ferrying them from hell back to the real world with new names and shit."

"Charon."

"Right! Only you're, like, ex-Special Forces, right? Green Beret or something?"

"Army Ranger."

"Dude. I can't believe you're real. I thought you were just something shifters had invented to make themselves feel better when everyone was disappearing without explanation."

Adrian kept his gaze trained on the tree line from the crow's nest guarding the perimeter wall, wondering if he just ignored Soldier Junior if he would take the hint and go away.

"Dude, if you're the Hawk, what are you doing here?"

No such luck. "Perimeter watch."

"Well, *yeah.* But why aren't you out freeing more of us?"

"I'm not a superhero, kid. I can't do anything without someone on the inside sneaking the shifters out to me." If he had been the ferryman, Rachel had been Persephone, trapped in the Underworld.

"So you just stopped?"

"We didn't just stop," he snapped, wondering if he had ever been that young and obnoxious. "They caught us. First me. Then her."

"But you got out."

"Yeah."

"And now what? They win?"

Adrian wondered if punching the kid was frowned on. "They don't win," he snarled. "We're still fighting them."

"But you're here."

He didn't have anything to say to that. The fucking kid was right about that much. He could say he was still recovering, but that felt like a cop out. He could say he was looking after Rachel, but what was he really doing? Hiding out.

He'd lost more than his wings during his time at the Organization. He'd misplaced that piece of himself that made him the Hawk. The one this kid gawked at like he was some kind of miracle worker.

He *wasn't* doing everything he could to bring down the Organization. He was doing everything he could to protect himself and protect Rachel.

The next Organization raid was scheduled to leave tomorrow morning. He should be on it. But would Rachel be safe without him? He couldn't help remembering the tiger stalking through the woods. Or the feel of her hot and eager in his arms. And he didn't know which one was more dangerous.

He didn't know if he could be the Hawk, reclaim that part of himself, and still keep her safe.

He could speak to Grace. As soon as he had a shift break, he would go back to the infirmary. The Hawk had been dormant too long.

"When they first brought me in," Rachel avoided saying the name of her former employers, even though it was just Brandt, Grace and Moira with her in the office, "none of the captured female shifters were catching and the human females they impregnated with shifter sperm kept miscarrying. For the human women, fertilization wasn't the problem—there was something about their body chemistry that seemed to be incompatible with the fetus. By studying some of the other data on hand, it became apparent to me that the physical presence of other shifters could cause both humans and shifters to produce a unique hormone. I became convinced that the isolation of our subjects was limiting this hormone which made it impossible for the women to carry to term.

"It made sense to me that the hormone would be required for reproduction—a sort of biological failsafe to prevent shifter children from being born in an environment where there were no other shifters to care for them. The presence of a shifter father—or other shifter support system—would cause the mother to produce the hormone and enable her to carry the child to term.

"I was unable to convince my employers to lessen the isolation of my subjects, but I was able to isolate and reproduce the hormone, which I injected into our subjects as a supplement. The human women continued to miscarry—though much later in their pregnancies—but the real breakthrough was when I applied the hormone to shifter females. Their fertility instantly skyrocketed."

"But we're surrounded by shifters," Grace interrupted. "That shouldn't be a problem with us."

"With cross-breeds it might be," Rachel explained. "The hormone is very breed-specific. If you are, let's say, a lynx mated to a bobcat, your body might not produce the hormone at all without another lynx in the vicinity. Though they're both felid species, the hormone appears to be extremely picky."

Moira nodded. "Lion shifters living in prides would be more fertile, flooded with that hormone. As would wolves in packs.

183

That would also help explain why even our more independent shifters tend to feel the need to bond into family units far more frequently than their animal counterparts."

"We called it the community hormone. Several of our shifter subjects associated the injections with a feeling of comfort or home—some even reporting hallucinating familiar scents as a side effect. The humans were less affected, but the feelings generated seemed to be positive there as well, just to a lesser degree—it would be logical for shifters to seek out that sensation in the wild. The comfort of the community."

"I understand this shifter community hormone makes the mother's body a fertile environment for the fetus, but what about the babies themselves?" Moira asked. "What would they shift into?"

"Even after I began having some success, I was never allowed to see the mothers through to the end of their pregnancies, so while I believe there were a handful of successful births, I never actually saw the children or learned if they could shift. In the wild, certain animal species can create hybrids—lions and tigers can have offspring together—but based on genetic testing of the fertilized ova, it appeared the breed of a shifter child was determined almost entirely by the breed of the mother—the only exception to this being the very rare cases of humans carrying latent shifter DNA being impregnated by shifter males."

All three of her listeners straightened sharply. "Humans with latent shifter DNA?" Brandt pressed. "We've never heard of such a thing."

"It's rare."

"Do you have it?" Grace asked, which shouldn't have surprised Rachel.

Of course they would think she would be more sympathetic to them if they shared some genetic marker, no matter how buried. Rachel had wondered herself, when she first saw that certain humans carried the shifter gene. She was an orphan, after all. Her parents could have been anyone or anything. But then she'd performed the test on herself.

"I'm just human."

She imagined she saw disappointment on their faces—she wasn't one of them after all—or perhaps that was just her projecting.

"So this hormone, that's the magic bullet?" Brandt asked.

"It does a lot, but some pairings are simply incompatible. The fetuses aren't viable in any environment. Ursine-feline, for example."

Or avian-human, like her and Adrian. Not that she should be thinking along those lines. Lately, he didn't even seem to like her, even five minutes after loving her senseless.

"And you have data on which breeds can successfully cross?"

"At the fertilization level, yes. I had reams of it which should be in the computers taken from the raid of the lab where I was found. We had hundreds and hundreds of samples—every mature shifter brought through Organization labs was harvested for reproductive material."

"*Jesus.*"

Rachel whipped around at the raw curse from the doorway behind her.

Adrian stood in the hall just outside the office's open door, horror and disgust warring for dominance on his face as he stared at her. He turned on his heel, stalking away without a word.

"Adrian!" Rachel scrambled out of her seat and after him, replaying what he must have heard in her head.

She'd been talking to colleagues, people who were as fascinated by the science as she was, but to a shifter who had been experimented on, she didn't know how it would have sounded. How much had he heard?

The way he'd looked at her...

She caught him near one of the patient rooms, catching his arm between both of her hands in an attempt to slow his rapid stride. He spun, startling her with the quick about-face and caught her by her arm, half-dragging her into the patient room and kicking the door shut behind them before dropping her arm like the touch of her skin burned him.

"*Harvesting for reproductive material?*" he snarled, stalking to the far window before spinning to face her with the breadth of the room between them. "Did you do the job yourself or did you have assistants for the hands-on portions? Did you get bonuses if you got us off quickly or were you paid by the hour?"

"Don't be insulting." She tucked her arms against her chest, defensive.

"What am I supposed to be, Doc? How many little hawks were you trying to breed from me?"

"None. They never drew sperm from you. I rescheduled the procedures whenever they tried to do those things to you. I couldn't do much, but I swear I tried to protect you from whatever I could."

"So of all the tests you were perfectly happy to watch them perform, you drew the line at that one. Lovely. Is that supposed to make me feel better?"

"Can anything make you feel better?" she challenged, her own anger rising. "We both know you're never going to forgive me, so what are you doing with me? What do you want? Every day it's hot and cold. You want me, you hate me, I get it, but I am sick of being the villain in this pairing. What more do you want me to do?"

"I want you to be who I thought you were!" he shouted.

She froze, startled as much by the raw honesty of his words as the volume.

"I want you to be the woman who would never betray me for any reason," he went on, quieter now, though there was no lessening in the fierce intensity of his glowing yellow gaze.

She met his eyes, though it was a struggle to do so. She felt like she was shaking apart from the inside out. He would never forgive her. "I'm sorry I was too human to live up to your lofty ideals."

"So am I."

Chapter Twenty-Two

I want you to be who I thought you were.

He hadn't meant to say that. He hadn't even known he was thinking it until the words were out of his mouth and then the profound rightness of them had sent shockwaves through his soul. He couldn't seem to forgive her for not being the woman he'd wanted her to be. He *hated* all the reminders of who she was, what she'd done, because she was supposed to be his. His mate. His everything. The one who would never, *ever* betray him for any reason. Not even to save the lives of a hundred others.

Because he wasn't sure he would have made the same call. He might have let all those shifters she saved fry if it was a question between her and them. And he wasn't sure if that made him a better man or far, far worse.

Rachel was still stunned and he took advantage of her shock to stride past her and out of the building. Grace was there. Grace would watch over her. Right now, he couldn't be around her. He couldn't be around anyone.

He'd rushed back to the infirmary after his stretch on the perimeter. He'd been on edge all day on the wall, worrying that someone would make an attempt on Rachel the first second he wasn't watching over her. But when he'd hurried through the infirmary, chasing the sound of her voice, her words had begun to penetrate and his blood had chilled.

He'd known she was an Organization doctor. Obviously, he'd known. He remembered. But hearing her talk about her subjects like they were nothing more than genetic material to be acquired and manipulated...it had shifted something dark inside him, reminding him once again of those awful months.

He'd been fighting his memories of last night all day and this was the perfect example of why. He couldn't let himself want her. Couldn't allow himself to believe she was who he'd once thought she could be to him. Wanting her was a weakness that had destroyed him before.

It wasn't just that he wanted her to be the ideal that he'd envisioned before they met. He needed to be able to trust her and he didn't know how he was ever going to be able to let himself do that. He didn't even know what he was doing with her anymore, what kind of role he was playing.

He jogged away from the busy pathways of the main compound, reaching instinctively for his wings and hissing with frustration when his hawk remained stubbornly dormant.

He needed to fly. He wasn't whole without his wings. That piece of himself, his hawk soul, was missing, perhaps forever, and it felt like an amputated limb he was left struggling to balance without.

There weren't many avian shifters left—he knew his parents had feared that he was the last of his kind—and now even he had lost his wings. Surrounded as he was by other shifters, he was still as alone as ever. Separated from those so like him, but so crucially different. Separated from his hawk. Separated from Rachel.

He'd been alone much of his life—isolated even in the band of brothers that was the military. Ever since his parents died, he'd kept his own counsel and he'd never minded the solitude. He was a solitary creature. It suited him. But now he ached. Ached for the mate who was not to be. Ached for the hawk that had abandoned him.

Adrian ran, pushing himself through the snow that had fallen the night before, and his soul ached.

"I take it our little birdie left."

Rachel's head snapped up at the dry voice from the doorway. When Adrian had run out, she'd dropped onto one of the beds, momentarily defeated. She didn't know how long she'd been sitting there before Grace found her.

The lioness eyed her, reading something on Rachel's face that made her step into the room and flick the door softly closed. "You okay, Doc?"

Rachel released a soft, exasperated breath. "I don't know what I am anymore."

Grace plopped onto the other bed, facing her. "That sounds like a good start. Like that whole *the wise man knows first that he knows nothing* bullshit."

Rachel snorted. "Something like that."

Grace waited, surprisingly patient, until Rachel found herself spilling everything she'd been holding on to for the last week—hell, for her entire life.

"It isn't fair," she said. "I lived my life by the rules, always trying so hard to be perfect so my parents would never regret for a second the choice they made to love me. My mother worried that I pushed myself too hard. My parents were wonderful. Love was never conditional for them—they were so good to me. I never understood why God decided to bless me with them. Why me, right? So I tried to be perfect enough to earn it. Always doing everything exactly right."

"How'd that work out for you?" Grace said dryly—clearly not a woman hindered by playing by the rules.

"It worked great until I fell in with the Organization and my parents passed away and all of a sudden I was in a new cage. Lies and danger and trying so hard to do the right thing. Always wondering if I was doing more harm than good, never free to be myself. Always playing three different games, trying to stay ahead of suspicion."

Rachel pinched the bridge of her nose, a headache starting just thinking about those years. "It was so isolating, so lonely, and then Adrian came along and I felt like I could relax with him—even though I knew it was stupid. I knew I shouldn't let down my guard, because the Organization was watching. Always watching. And then they wanted him." She swallowed thickly. "I didn't know what to do. I didn't know how to get out of the cage I was in—so I made the shitty call. I told myself the Organization would have captured him anyway and that I should use the opportunity to gain trust so I could save more shifters. I told myself it was the greater good, but I hated who it made me. So I pushed back. I freed more shifters, I freed *him*, and the Organization put me in an even smaller cage. Their pet M.D. Until y'all found me."

She closed her eyes, remembering the moments of adrenaline and hope. "Waking up in that cabin with a chain around my ankle was the first time in my entire life I can ever remember being truly free to be whoever and whatever I am. No pretense, no expectations. Here I may be a prisoner of sorts, but I'm more free than I've ever been. I could love it here, if Adrian would just let me. But he's too busy hating me. Everything is just *wrong*."

Especially the way she felt for him. "I can't figure him out," she heard herself confessing to Grace. "One second he's angry, the next he's protective. He touches me so tenderly I just fall apart, then pushes me away and won't even look at me."

"He's a man. He doesn't know what to do with all the feels," Grace said in what Rachel was coming to recognize as her usual dry way. "If it's any help, he refused to leave you if I wasn't personally guarding your cute little ass. So he's clearly got a hard-on for keeping you safe." She shrugged. "That's something."

"Am I really in danger?"

"From most of the pride? No. But there are one or two who might still want a piece of you."

"Like Dominec." Rachel shivered, remembering the man with the heavily ridged scars twisting his face.

"Maybe," Grace admitted, though she didn't sound certain. "None of us really know him."

"But he's part of your pride. Your...family."

"Sort of. Keeping Dominec around is kind of like having a pet dragon. Some days it makes you powerful and some days it makes you barbeque. Can't always tell which kind of day it's gonna be."

"So I should listen to Adrian."

"In terms of your protection? Not a bad idea. He knows his shit. As far as the rest of it? Hell, what do I know about damaged shifter men with more instinct than brains? All I can do is wish you luck, girl, because if you decide you want him, you're going to need it. Now, you ready to look at some prisoner mug shots?"

If you decide you want him...

Those words haunted her for the rest of the afternoon as she looked at the photos and identified nine of the remaining thirteen prisoners. Most were harmless—the most aggressive having been killed in the riot—but Rachel flagged two of the guards as assholes to keep an eye on. For a moment she thought one of the women, a cowering brunette with her hair covering most of her face, might be Madison Clarke, but when Grace told her the name on the woman's badge was Marta Torres, she vaguely remembered a receptionist by that name and kicked herself for seeing bogeymen everywhere. Madison would never let herself get taken alive. Adrian's paranoia must be rubbing off one her.

If you decide you want him...

The words still echoed in her brain into the evening as she explained the hormone therapy to Kathy and her mate and worked alongside Dr. Brandt to create a balanced hormone cocktail for the pair, listening with half an ear for Adrian's return.

If you decide you want him...

Funny how she'd never before thought of it as a choice. Ever since that snowy night when he'd first swept into her life, he'd occupied a central point in her world in a way no other man had, filling up her thoughts and taking up space in her hopes. But was he really what she wanted?

He was strong and loyal and stubborn and moody and so intense she felt as if every second she spent in his presence saturated her soul and fired her senses. There was more feeling packed into a minute with him than in a month without and she wanted more of that intensity. More of the way he touched her when he didn't seem to realize he was doing it. Gentle, solicitous, taking such care with her in a way that was automatic.

If only he didn't stop himself from that automatic affection whenever he noticed he was doing it.

Was he what she wanted? She felt stronger when she was with him, like the most fierce and authentic version of herself. She wanted to be that woman. The one he inspired her to be. Not a perfect angel, but something much more real.

And not the woman he seemed determined to think she was.

So yes. She wanted him. But only on her terms. Only if they could start fresh and move forward, without the past hanging over them like a guillotine blade always waiting to fall. If they couldn't have a fresh slate, then there was no point punishing herself wanting him. She'd taken everything he'd thrown at her, scarcely defending herself because on some level she'd felt like she deserved it, but that was over now.

No matter how many defining moments she had, no matter how much she told herself she'd changed, she was still that little girl trying to earn love. She'd spent half a lifetime trying to earn it from her parents and now here she was, ready to spend the other half trying to be worthy of Adrian's affection. Something had to give.

She was done being sorry, done apologizing. He would either accept her thousand attempts to make amends and forgive her, or she would find a way to separate herself from him. She didn't want to leave the pride—she liked it here—but she would, if they would let her. If that's what it took to get away from Adrian.

It was time they both decided if they wanted this. If he wanted her, he needed to get past her past. If she wanted him, she had to show him how. Starting now.

Chapter Twenty-Three

Rachel was sprawled on her back on one of the beds in the emergency room of the infirmary when Adrian returned to take her home. She propped herself up on one elbow as the door slammed, blinking sleepily at him. It wasn't that late, but she looked utterly drained, with dark circles smudged under her eyes.

He eyed her, unsure what reception he would get after the way they'd left things, but she just smiled wearily and swung her legs over the edge of the bed. "Hey, Hawk."

"Did you get dinner?"

"Moira fed us. She's an incredible cook." She came to her feet, stretching her arms high above her head, back arching so her breasts were outlined perfectly against the material of her soft woven shirt.

"Is she?" Adrian mumbled, knowing he sounded dazed, but unable to take his eyes off the feast of her body.

"Mm." Rachel grabbed her coat and tucked her arms into it, zipping up and hiding all those delicious curves from his view— though she was no less erotically enticing to him hidden by all the fluff. "I was thinking," she continued conversationally. "You should teach me to defend myself."

He scowled, pulled out of his pleasant lust haze by her words. "Why?"

"It seems like a waste to have the toughest fighters in the pride babysitting little old me."

He frowned. Grace should be here. Rachel couldn't be left undefended. Admittedly, she was fine, but still.

"If I wasn't so helpless, you wouldn't have to escort me around," she went on, breezing past him into the winter night beyond.

He quickly followed, frowning. There was something different about her tonight. She looked exhausted, but there was a bounce in her step, a challenge in her eyes. More fight to her, though she wasn't combative. Just asserting herself.

She stalked ahead of him, tossing over her shoulder, "Unless you don't trust me not to use any tricks you teach me against you."

He lengthened his stride to keep up with her. "I don't."

She huffed out a sharp, aggravated sigh and glared at him, saying nothing. Definitely something different. Had something more happened today? He felt like he was missing something since their fight.

She charged forward down the path, doubtless fueled by irritation, then stopped so abruptly he nearly tread on her heels. Rachel whirled to face him, hands on hips. "I don't know where we're going."

He pointed to a path on the left and she marched down it until the next fork where she paused again until he took the lead. She didn't try to start another conversation and he wisely kept silent as he guided this new, feistier version of Rachel back to the cabin.

He didn't know what to make of her like this, though he didn't entirely dislike it. The new wildness was oddly compelling—and would probably be downright erotic if it hadn't been sparked by anger that was aimed directly at him.

Adrian didn't delude himself that she would hold in whatever she wanted to yell at him about forever. Five seconds after the door to the cabin closed behind him, she spun, hands back on hips, mahogany eyes shooting sparks.

"What's it going to take?" she demanded.

"I don't know what you—"

"Stop it," she cut him off. "You know exactly what I'm asking. What is it going to take for you to forgive me? For you to even begin to be able to trust me again, because I have done nothing but prove myself ever since that *one mistake,* so what the heck is it going to take, Hawk?"

"It isn't you."

"Bullshit." She blushed as she said the word, as she did every time she cursed, but it was no less forceful for that.

"It isn't. It's me I don't trust where you're concerned."

She muddied everything with lust. He'd been an idiot, led around by his dick, and he refused to be made a fool by his desires again.

He meant to leave it at that, but at the bewildered look on her face, he found himself going on. "I trusted you when I shouldn't have last time. You batted those big brown eyes and tempted me into mistrusting my instincts—and look how that turned out."

"Then it is me," she snapped, stripping off her jacket with quick, angry movements. "I'm the evil temptress who led you astray. It's always the woman's fault when a man wants her, isn't it?"

"Stop. I never said that."

"That's exactly what you said." She flung the jacket at him and he caught it, flicking it aside. "I seduced you with my *big brown eyes.* It couldn't have been your fault. I made you want me against your will."

He drank in her flushed cheeks and the rapid rise of her chest. "It was never against my will."

"No, just against your precious instincts."

"What do you want me to say?" He prowled toward her, crowding against her when she refused to give up ground. "That you don't overwhelm my senses and drown my instincts in need until all I can think of is tasting you?"

"That's a start." She sucked in a breath, her breasts rising to brush against his chest. Her pupils were the size of dinner plates.

Shit. How had he gotten here? So close all he had to do was lean and they would be flush against one another. He'd be breathing in the air she breathed out, looming over her like he could intimidate this woman who would never bend, never break. Her core of internal strength wouldn't allow it.

And he fucking loved that about her. Loved that she would never be defeated, no matter what. She was a queen, a warrior, a thousand times stronger than he'd suspected the first time he saw her, soft-hearted and sweet, in that forest. Tempered steel and southern silk. And he'd never wanted anything in his life the way he wanted to take her, lift her to his mouth and seal them together, never to let her go. He ached with it, this desire for her—not just where his erection was swelling and pressing against his zipper, but in a tight, vulnerable spot just behind his heart.

"Rachel." He couldn't do this. She was his weakness, his Achilles' heel. He lost all perspective where she was concerned. He needed to walk away. Far away. Beyond the boundaries of the pride. Distance was the only cure. When he was with her, she found all the cracks in the walls he'd built to keep her at bay and slipped through them until she was here, inches away, looking up at him with eyes that had gone dewy and yearning.

"Please," she whispered, and the last thread of resistance broke.

He'd thought he would enjoy the sound of Rachel begging him. He'd thought there would be no sweeter sound in the world.

Fool.

That plea grated on his soul.

He caught her to him and she came so readily into his arms it was as if her body was responding to his thoughts. Her arms twined around his neck and he claimed her lips in a caress both urgent and lingering. She pressed against the length of his body, the softness of her curves draining the blood from his brain and channeling it all to his throbbing cock. He slid his hands down to her taut ass, gripping the perfect curves and grinding her lower body against his hardness until she moaned against his lips and tugged on his sweater, trying to yank it off him without allowing even a centimeter between their bodies. Her eagerness fired his hunger to a new level and he lifted her, carrying her two steps to the futon which groaned beneath their combined weight as he knelt on it and lowered her onto her back. She clung to him, dragging him down with her, still sucking and nibbling at his lips, teasing him with little flicks and languid strokes of her tongue. When his weight pressed her down into the mattress, she moaned again into his mouth, and executed a slow, sinuous body roll that made his higher brain functions shut down in defeat as she arched against him from hips to shoulders.

He broke the unending kiss long enough to rock back and jerk his sweater and shirt over his head. Rachel squirmed beneath him, still pinned to the bed from the hips down, shoving at her own top. In a fit of chivalry, he helped her with it, dragging the clinging cotton up, reveling in the smooth, silken softness of her skin beneath as he did. He tugged the shirt over her head and flicked it aside. Her hair lifted with static electricity and he took a moment to smooth it down with both hands. Gazing down at her, it was hard to imagine anything had ever been more beautiful than she was in that moment. The pupils of her wide brown eyes were blown with lust and gleamed with eager anticipation. Her lips were rosy, full and swollen from his kisses, her face flushed, and her perfect, silken curves rose out of the cups of her lacy pink bra. She was heaven and he was sure he'd die if he couldn't get inside her soon, but there was still so much of her body to explore.

He trailed his fingers down the sides of her neck, over her collarbones and around the outer curves of her breasts, caressing them through the material of her bra. She reached for the front-clasp, but he brushed her hands away, shaking his head. Bending his head, he scraped his teeth over the plump upper curve of her breast, tugging at the lace briefly with his teeth before sucking the point of her nipple into his mouth through the fabric. She gasped, her head falling back and her hips twisting against his, pushing to get closer. He hollowed his cheeks, sucking harder, framing and shaping her breasts with his hands, then switched to give the other breast its deserved attention. When he was finally satisfied and she was writhing helplessly, clutching his head to her breast, he flicked open the front clasp and tasted the silken sweetness of her bare skin. He tongued the firm peak of her nipple, rubbing his cheek against the swollen curve of her breast. She'd been made for this, all lush femininity. He wanted to wallow in her curves all night, but his jeans were downright painful and the need to get inside her was pressing every other thought out of his brain.

He rose up to his knees, struggling with the fucking zipper from hell, and Rachel sat up as well, her legs sprawled wide with him kneeling between them in a way that did nothing to help his ability to fit into his jeans. He cursed and closed his eyes, concentrating on his breathing and the fastening of his jeans—and then there was another pair of hands there, helping him in a way that was both insanely erotic and not at all helpful. Adrian swore with feeling and nearly embarrassed himself like a teenager, only stopping himself from coming in his jeans by grabbing her hands and yanking them away, locking their fingers together to buy himself time to remember how to function.

When he opened his eyes, she was looking at him with moist lips and dark, eager eyes and his heart rate went right back into the red zone.

"Take off your clothes," he demanded, releasing her hands and standing up to get rid of his own jeans. He'd call his talons and shred the fucking things if he had to. But thankfully that wasn't necessary. The zipper from hell cooperated and he kicked off his boots and dragged off his jeans, underwear and socks in one move.

Rachel froze in the process of shimmying out of her own jeans, her eyes locking on the length of him, thrust out in front of him. He took a step toward her, another surge of blood rushing to his cock at the way she licked her lower lip, never looking away from him.

"I got some more condoms from the infirmary. Coat pocket."

He practically launched himself at the discarded coat as Rachel finished shucking her shoes, socks and jeans. Rummaging through the pockets, he found three foil-wrapped condoms.

We're going to need more than three.

But that was a worry for later. Adrian grabbed the condoms and somehow stopped himself from sprinting back to the front of the bed and Rachel.

She splayed on her back on his bed in only a pair of lacy pink underwear. Underwear he'd bought for her at the pride store, telling himself the entire time that he wasn't fantasizing about seeing her exactly like this. Lying to himself.

She rolled to her side, propping herself on one elbow and watching him as he ripped open the packet and slipped on the latex. She crooked a finger at him, eyes gleaming wickedly, and he was done for. All he could do was fall on her like a beast, stroking every inch of her silken skin he could get his hands on and pressing the fiery heat of his body against her softness.

She welcomed him into her arms, kissing him back just as fiercely as he kissed her, and tangling her legs with his. His cock bumped up against her pussy, separated by layers of lace and latex, and he groaned, his hips thrusting so the length drove up between them, rubbing against her clit. She gasped and squirmed and he reached between them, his palm flat against the soft curve of her abdomen and then teasing beneath her panties, threading through her curls and brushing against the slick, wet heat of her labia. He found her clit, gently pinching it between two fingers and then stroking through her folds to spear a finger inside her. Rachel moaned, tipping her hips up to take him deeper. He withdrew his finger and thrust back with two, curling them inside her until he found the spot that made her scream, arching beneath him as she grew even wetter against his hand.

He needed to be there.

Adrian withdrew his hand enough to yank her panties down. She helped him, urgently shoving them off and spreading her legs wide. He fitted himself against her, closing his eyes against the drowning depth of sensation. She was tight for the first thrust, allowing him in only an inch, but so wet it took only three strokes to seat him fully. He hilted inside her and she moaned, the muscles of her pussy tightening around him in a way that would have made his brain seize if he'd had any brain left. He picked up a rhythm, all instinct and need, grateful she was with him, gasping and straining for her own peak because he didn't think he could have stopped then for all the armies on earth.

She threw her head back and screamed, quaking beneath him as she found her release and he let slip the last fragmented reins of his control, pounding into her. He heard the pitch of her cries change, going higher as another orgasm built, and he drove into her like a madman, going rigid with his release as sperm shot out of him and he came hard enough to lose a piece of himself in her.

He collapsed onto her, utterly drained but trying not to crush her with his weight. Sweat coated his skin and stuck her hair to her forehead, but she'd never looked more beautiful. Dazed and breathless, but breathtaking too. His Rachel.

Shit. He'd been lying to himself. All those times he'd told himself he didn't love her anymore. Lies.

Chapter Twenty-Four

Adrian slipped out of the clasp of her body and rolled away to dispense of the condom. His good sense tried to return with the flow of blood to his more thoughtful regions, but he ignored it. Rachel still lay on his bed, gloriously naked and turned on her side. He climbed in beside her, ignoring the way the old frame groaned beneath his weight, and rolled her into his arms, tugging the blanket over both of them to keep off the winter chill. He would need to stoke up the fire in the potbelly stove soon. Their activities had distracted him from the icy bite in the air, but his human lover would catch a chill if he didn't warm the room.

But not now. Now he would warm her with his own heat, curling his body around hers and forcibly ignoring the niggling doubts that tried to burrow into the back of his mind.

He wouldn't let himself trust her. Fine. He would keep that last barrier intact, but this—this had been inevitable from the moment he saw her. She was his on a level he couldn't question or hope to understand. She belonged here, curled in his arms, warm and weary from his lovemaking. The rest would wait for morning.

Rachel lay in her lover's arms, sated—and completely confused. She'd been in a state of mindless bliss for about five minutes after he climbed back in bed to cuddle—and then her brain had woken up, loud and dubious. What did this mean? Where did they stand? Had he forgiven her? Had anything changed?

On the plus side, he hadn't run—which seemed to be his usual defense mechanism when he felt threatened by his feelings for her. That had to be a good sign. And in the bed department she was beyond satisfied—he'd aptly demonstrated once again that her memories of his prowess had not been exaggerated. But now they lay twined in each other's arms and Rachel was no closer to understanding what the hell had just happened.

She'd hoped for the best, that he would forgive her and she would fall into his arms—that was why she'd picked up the condoms from the infirmary in the first place—but she had never suspected it might actually work.

She didn't have the first idea if he'd really forgiven her and she was afraid to ask—especially knowing her self-respect wouldn't let her stay if he hadn't—but the question still loomed.

She lay half-beneath him, she on her back, he more or less on his stomach, spread over her like a not-entirely-human blanket. His face was buried against her shoulder, one arm tucked beneath her head like a pillow, the other idly exploring her hip and the dip of her waist. Her arms were looped around his back, stroking across the muscular plane of his shoulders.

He was lean and strong—not heavy like the cat shifters, but then hawks weren't bulky.

She'd never seen him as a hawk, she realized. His eyes would be the same—that keen, yellow intensity. Would his feathers be brown or more gray? Did he fly often? Perhaps that was where he went when he ran from her. How often had he watched her from the sky when she didn't know to look up?

The questions crowded to the front of her mind, safer than asking about forgiveness and begging to be answered. She could tell he wasn't asleep. Just silent.

"Did you go fly today? When you left me?"

Her hawk stiffened. It was so subtle she would not have felt it if she had not been wrapped around him. He didn't answer.

"Adrian?"

He moved then, pulling away from her even as she tried to hold on to him, climbing out of the bed. "Are you cold?" he asked, not looking at her, striding to stoke the fire.

He clearly didn't want to talk about this, but shifting was the most natural thing in the world for shape-shifters. There was nothing taboo about the subject. Unless he still viewed her as an Organization doctor. But this was deeper than that, even chillier than the cold shoulder he gave her work.

"When was the last time you shifted?"

He looked at her then, something dead behind the gleaming yellow of his eyes. "I don't, anymore."

Why? She wanted to ask, but it felt like the wrong question. "For how long?"

"Since your—" He stopped himself. "Since the Organization."

She wished she could take it as a victory that he wasn't calling them *her* people or *her* friends anymore, but all she felt was a horrified loss on his behalf. Months. He'd been unable to shift for months. For a creature that traded shape daily, that must be torture.

She'd read that in his file, she remembered now—that he hadn't shifted in captivity, defying the scientists who wanted to study the process. But she'd thought it was only that—defiance. She hadn't realized that something had happened to him to prevent the change.

"Have you talked to Dr. Brandt about it?" She sat up, tucking the blanket around her. Adrian was naked, crouched by the stove, as unself-conscious about his nudity as any shifter.

"Brandt is a lion doctor," he said, attention on the logs. "It was a chemical cocktail designed to force feline shifters to change that broke my ability to connect with my hawk in the first place. I doubt the kitty-cat doc can help me."

"Have you told anyone?"

"No. Just you."

Rachel had no idea what to make of that. Adrian wasn't the sort to ask for help, but to only tell her...it was a mark of unexpected trust. She was surprised he'd told her at all.

And even more surprised when he went on, volunteering on his own, "Dr. Brandt knew I couldn't shift when I first arrived at the pride. He thought it was all the shit they'd been pumping into me. Figured once it got out of my system I'd be good as new. I just haven't told him I'm not."

Rachel remembered the way his eyes would change, the pupils vanishing into yellow, and the way his talons had nearly cut her after his dream. Physically, it seemed he could still shift, at least partially. So perhaps the block wasn't chemical or physical. Perhaps it was mental or emotional instead. Was Adrian somehow stopping himself from calling his hawk?

His head snapped up, gaze whipping to the front door and then he was moving quickly, striding to collect his jeans. "Someone's coming."

Her heart rate accelerated and she realized she'd seen him like this before. Battle mode. He'd been arming himself as the Organization men crept down the hallway at the hotel. The night she'd jabbed the needle into his back. "Adrian?"

"Get dressed." He was already lacing up his boots, further testament that he couldn't shift. Few shifters worried about clothing going into a fight.

Rachel scrambled out of the bed and pulled on what she could find of her clothing. Her bra was MIA so she went without, pulling on underwear, jeans and just tugging her shirt over her head as a knock sounded at the door.

Adrian was crouched beside the door, gun out and held in an easy grip at his hip.

"Adrian?" a voice called through the door, and the Hawk instantly relaxed his ready stance.

"Kye." Adrian stood, daring a glance out the window, then checking to make sure Rachel was clothed before reaching for the latch on the door.

The man who entered was one Rachel recognized from her various interrogation sessions, but didn't remember well. He hadn't spoken much, just watching her with the same quiet, steady gaze that assessed her now. She felt her face flushing, knowing a feline shifter would instantly be able to scent the sex in the room, though his nostrils didn't so much as twitch in acknowledgement.

"Roman needs Rachel," he said, all business. "They're here."

"They?" Adrian demanded.

Oh Lord. Her heart rate quadrupled. The Organization had come. They were handing her over to them.

Kye shot Adrian a mildly incredulous look. "What rock have you been living under? The ambassadors from Three Rocks. The ones everyone has been expecting for months?"

Adrian frowned. "I don't pay much attention to pride gossip."

Kye looked back toward Rachel. "You can take five minutes. Don't be longer than that." He slipped back out into the night, leaving the door open behind him.

Adrian closed the door and turned to her, a frown crinkling his brow.

"What's Three Rocks?" she asked.

"Another lion pride in Texas. There have been some rumors that they're stirring up trouble, talking about the Organization and threatening to come out to the rest of the humans so the Organization can be exposed for what they're doing to us. That kind of thing. I didn't give much credence to the talk."

"And now they want to talk to me?"

"If they are here—which it looks like they are—they're using the Organization as their bogeyman to scare people into agreeing with them. Roman probably wants you there to vet whatever information they have on your people."

And there it was. They were *her* people again.

And she had five minutes to get ready to face the Alpha.

Rachel grabbed a change of clothes and ducked into the bathroom. Doing the quickest standing-over-the-sink wash-up ever, so she wouldn't reek quite so strongly of Adrian and sex, she emerged from the bathroom with thirty seconds to spare.

"Let's go."

Chapter Twenty-Five

The delegation from the Three Rocks pride was in a way both exactly what Rachel had expected and nothing like she had expected.

They looked like lion-shifters; that was undeniable. The woman was tall, blonde and looked like she could arm-wrestle a Viking without breaking a sweat. Her mate, sprawled in the chair at her side with his arm draped along the back of hers, actually bore a strong resemblance to Roman. Large, muscled and radiating authority with a feline's lazy confidence.

But that was where Rachel's expectations faltered. It was the woman, not the man who gave off the I'm-the-big-bad-Alpha vibes, who was the spokesperson for the pair. She spoke quickly, animatedly, gesturing with her hands, and sounding more like a sitcom character than a diplomat—all slang and quick comebacks.

When Kye guided Rachel and Adrian into the room, directing them to a pair of chairs set up along the wall behind Roman, away from the main conference table where the others were gathered, the ambassadors were already well into their plea. Patch and Roman faced the couple across the table, flanked by Grace and another of the lieutenants, who Rachel mentally placed as Hugo, the bear shifter. Rachel sat, Adrian beside her, one thigh brushing against hers, and Kye propped his shoulders against the wall on her other side.

It was a much smaller group than had been involved in her initial interrogation and Rachel couldn't be sure if that was because these two had dropped by in the middle of the night—though a quick glance at the clock showed it was just past ten—or if this information was somehow more sensitive than what she had carried from the Organization.

Judging from her position along the wall, Rachel took it she was supposed to be seen and not heard, so she focused on listening to the gesticulating lioness.

"I know the tradition demands secrecy," the woman was saying, "but you guys obviously aren't hung up on traditions or you wouldn't have a cougar Alpha's mate and a bear sitting across the table from me. So what's the problem?"

"Zoe," the man said softly, though it did nothing to check her.

"Our best bet is to come out to the humans," the woman—Zoe—insisted.

"And become side-show acts," Hugo rumbled in his big bass voice.

"If we do it together, strategically, we can come forward from a position of strength. If they out us, we won't have that. We'll be the victims of our own story. This way we choose."

"Why now?" Roman asked, calm and unmoved by the woman's theatrics.

It was the man at her side who spoke. "There are more abductions every day. The Organization is getting bolder."

"We were kidnapped right off our own land," Zoe growled.

"That's been happening for twenty years," Patch said, with a decided edge to her voice. "What makes you so special? Other than the fact that your abductors were more incompetent than most Organization operatives."

"They were a splinter cell," Zoe admitted. "But we were able to capture one of them and she gave up everything she knows. We know more now than ever before. We're in a better position to expose them."

Rachel realized with a jolt that these two shifters had no idea that the Lone Pine Pride had Organization captives of their own or that the Lone Pine group had been moving against the

Organization for weeks. She sat up straighter and Kye's hand fell on her shoulder, reminding her to stay quiet.

"If we come out," Roman said with soft authority, "what happens to all the shifters in Organization captivity now?"

Zoe rocked back in her chair, clearly not interested in answering that question.

Roman raised his voice slightly, though he didn't turn. "Rachel?"

Kye lifted his hand. Apparently it was time for her to perform.

"They die."

The lioness across the table speared her with a sharp, unfriendly stare. "All right, who's the human?"

"We have our own sources of Organization intel," Patch said, with distinct satisfaction.

Roman did turn then, waving Rachel forward. "May I present Dr. Rachel Russell, late of the Organization."

She rose and came to stand next to the table, Adrian shadowing the move. Zoe glowered at her, studying her with no small amount of hostility.

"You decided not to take your suicide pill when you were captured?"

"I defected." Or she would have if she hadn't been rescue/captured first. "And to the best of my knowledge only the security personnel and C Block interrogators were issued with suicide pills in a false tooth—the personnel most likely to wish for a quick death if the shifters should get loose. With the rest of us, they found it much more effective to use trackers, explosives and threats."

The lioness frowned, mulling that over.

Rachel went on. "The reason there are more abductions is because the Organization is larger and better funded than they used to be. Money is power and in the last few years they've suddenly had plenty of both. This splinter cell of yours, how long ago did they break off?"

The pair across the table exchanged a look and it was the male who admitted, "We don't know. The one who survived, who is giving us all our information, was never part of the Organization. She joined them after they'd already broken off."

Rachel nodded. "That explains why they haven't been more aggressive about eliminating her. The others must have broken away long enough ago and had relatively insignificant positions within the Organization or they never would have been allowed to survive breaking away."

"You survived," Zoe pointed out.

"They haven't found me yet. Frankly, I'm surprised even minor members would be allowed to leave. Though for all we know there was an Organization hit squad on their way to take care of the problem when you saved them the trouble."

"Would that information be in the files we have?" Roman asked. His tone was casual, but she knew the question was very deliberate. He wanted these two southern lions to know that Lone Pine was not only larger and more influential than their little Texas pride, but that they were better informed too.

"It should be."

Roman nodded to Grace, who whipped out an iPad and pulled up the database Mateo had built from the Organization hard drives. "Names?" she asked, all business.

"You have access to Organization files?" Zoe demanded, but her mate provided the names.

Grace typed in the first one and there was only a second's delay before she announced, "He has a file. Listed as deceased. Security officer who left the Organization after his repeated requests to be considered for positions with more active interaction with shifters were denied. Considered loyal to the cause and not a threat, but marked for continued observation. There's a note at the bottom of the file. *See incidence log Zoe King; Tyler Minor.*"

The couple on the opposite side of the table jerked as if they'd been tased. "They have our names?"

Grace tapped into the database. "Whole files on you by the look of it."

The man—Tyler, apparently—reached over to put his hand over Zoe's fist on the table where her knuckles had gone white. "What about Ava Minor? Or Landon King?"

Grace nodded, typing rapidly. "They have files too. Nothing much. Just *Known Location* and some coordinates."

"Jesus, they know about our whole pride." Zoe lurched up from the table, pulling a cell phone from her pocket and quickly dialing. She stepped away from the table, her voice low and urgent when someone answered. Every shifter in the room would be able to hear what she was saying—and possibly the other end of the conversation as well—but to Rachel's human ears the words were indistinct, though the edge of fear to her tone was readily apparent.

"Her brother is Alpha of our pride," Tyler explained quietly. "We've suspected they knew about us, but he'll want to know about this. How long have you had their files?" There was a slight edge to his voice, as if he felt Roman should have shared this information with the rest of the shifter community, but it was restrained, as everything about him seemed restrained.

"Only a few weeks," Roman admitted. "We're still learning the extent of it ourselves."

The large lion on the opposite side of the table nodded, somewhat mollified.

Rachel wasn't sure if she was only supposed to speak if she was spoken to, but her curiosity was killing her. "How did you escape? When they captured you?"

She'd never heard of shifters breaking free during an acquisition—not that it had never happened before, but if it had the Organization had been quick to cover it up. Bad for morale, no doubt.

"They had us in a box truck. I kept shaking off the drugs they gave me faster than they expected—I could hear Zoe through the wall—"

"They transported you in the same vehicle?" Rachel frowned. That went against all protocols she'd ever read. "I was never in acquisitions and even I know that mated pairs are *always* separated immediately after capture. They're too dangerous in close proximity to one another."

Tyler frowned. "Candice mentioned something like that. Psychic mating bonds or some such ridiculousness. We thought it was just a function of the fact that she read *Twilight* too many times."

"To the best of my knowledge, the Organization never actually proved the existence of a psychic mate bond, but there was something different about the mated pairs."

Zoe returned to the table then, tucking away her cell phone, and Roman resumed control of the meeting.

"What do the other packs and prides think of your proposal?" he asked.

Zoe grimaced, visibly annoyed. "They all want to know what Lone Pine is going to do."

Roman nodded as if he'd expected as much. "Lone Pine hasn't decided yet," he said with quiet authority. "Kye, find a place for our guests to spend the night. We'll discuss this more in the morning."

The leopard stepped forward, but the lions did not immediately rise in the face of their dismissal.

"We can't stay hidden forever," Zoe insisted. "The world is getting smaller, thanks to technology. We can't even be sure that the Organization is the only group that's figured out our secret."

"I'm not suggesting staying hidden forever," Roman said. "But we won't rush into a course of action that will put more shifters at greater risk. We'll discuss this *tomorrow*."

Tyler rose, all but dragging Zoe up with him. "Until then, Alpha."

His mate, obviously less accustomed to bending the knee to another's authority, gritted her teeth and gave a little chin jerk of goodbye before following the ever-silent Kye out of the room.

There was a lingering moment of silence as the door closed behind them and they all waited for the group to get beyond the range of sensitive shifter hearing. Grace was the first one to speak.

"I don't like her."

Patch snorted. "That's because she's *you.*"

Grace gasped in mock horror. "Bite your tongue."

The alpha's mate chuckled. Roman held up a hand to forestall their conversation and turned to Rachel. "What do you think?"

"Their information is outdated, but they aren't wrong. Coming out to the humans would put the Organization in a bad position—but it would also force them to get rid of the evidence of their wrong-doing and that could be very bad for any of the shifters they are holding when you go public."

Roman nodded. He didn't need to say more. They all understood the gravity of the situation. "Thank you, Dr. Russell. I won't keep you from your bed any longer."

There wasn't so much as a hint of innuendo in his voice, but Rachel felt her face heating with a fiery blush as Adrian placed his hand on the small of her back to guide her to the door.

Had they been able to smell the sex on her? She wasn't sure she was embarrassed even if they had. Sex seemed to be treated like a natural part of life here in the pride, not a sin to be ashamed of. She just wasn't sure she was ready for everyone to be thinking of her and Adrian as a matched set, the same way they did of Patch and Roman or this Zoe and her Tyler. Rachel didn't know where she stood with Adrian and it seemed unfair somehow that the shifters could *smell* their connection when even she didn't know how far their affair would extend.

Adrian kept his hand on her back as he guided her home. They passed a few other shifters on the pathways before they reached the forest. It was not yet midnight and there were still several pride members out and about. They nodded greetings to Adrian and Rachel as if there was nothing odd about a bird-shifter and an ex-Organization doctor out for a stroll through the pride lands. They had to know who she was—there weren't that many humans allowed to remain here, wandering about freely—but no one came after her with tar and feathers.

It was possible she could someday be accepted here. As an actual member of this wild and wonderful pride. It startled her how keenly she found she wanted that, to be part of this community. Especially if it meant Adrian at her side.

Her stomach clenched.

She was getting ahead of herself. Just because he'd shagged her silly didn't mean anything would change. For all she knew when they got back to the cabin he would resume the same old routine—locking her in and only coming inside to stretch himself across the door after she was asleep. Perhaps the incendiary passion they'd shared was just an aberration to him. They hadn't spoken about it. She was terrified of starting that conversation.

She fretted the entire walk back to the cabin. By the time they crossed the threshold, she had worked herself into such a state she couldn't even look at the bed where she'd writhed beneath him only hours before. It was the world's most uncomfortable mattress, but for those minutes it had been heaven.

And now the thought of curling up there without him as he stomped off into the night was almost unbearable.

"Thank you."

Her heart suspended its beating for a moment when he spoke so close behind her. What was he thanking her for? Advising Roman? Sex? She didn't turn to face him, still looking anywhere but the bed. "I don't know what you—"

"I know you're on our side," he said, so close now his breath stirred the hair at her nape where she'd swept it up into a knot. "I know I've acted like you might betray us, but I wanted you to know that I can see that you aren't out to hurt shifters."

It was a magnanimous concession—and she wanted to punch him for it.

As if she needed his gratitude. As if she should be thanking him for realizing she wasn't the devil incarnate. Rachel pulled away from the warmth at her back, stalking to the bed without hesitation now. "You're quite welcome," she said with all the sugary sweetness of her southern upbringing.

She caught his expression—sharp, unfiltered confusion— from the corner of her eye as she dug into her small stack of clothing, pulling out the bulkiest, ugliest flannel pajamas he'd brought for her.

"I'm trying to apologize," he said irritably.

"Oh, were you?" she asked sweetly. "I must have missed that part."

"Rachel—"

But she was already safely closed inside the bathroom, pressing her palms against cheeks warmed by anger. The pleaser instinct that had always ruled her life urged her to open the door, accept his apology—even if he hadn't actually *said* he was sorry—and throw herself into his arms. But she didn't want to be that woman anymore.

Another defining moment. Rachel Russell wasn't the doormat anymore. Turns out she wanted amends.

He'd been treating her like a criminal for weeks and she deserved a proper apology, not just thanks-for-not-being-a-slimy-Organization-lowlife-after-all.

She took her time with her shower and her evening toilette, giving him plenty of opportunity to storm off in a huff while she armored herself in layers of flannel. But when she emerged from the bathroom, he was waiting for her, leaning against the table in only a pair of flannel pajama bottoms, arms roped with wiry muscle crossed over his bare chest. Her heart lifted at the sight. He hadn't run.

"I'm sorry," he said as soon as the door opened. "I was wrong. Whatever happened between you and me, you've always helped shifters. I shouldn't have doubted that."

Oh my. Those words might as well have been aphrodisiacs. Her knees turned to mush, her heart thudded eagerly, and her feminine parts clenched and heated in anticipation. "Well, all right then."

His lips didn't so much as twitch, but she saw amusement sparkle in his eyes at her sulky response. "You wanna come over here and let me make it up to you?"

"It might take a while to convince me you're really sorry." She had no idea where that flirty tone came from—a lady was never so forward—but her hawk didn't seem shocked or appalled, if his slow, wicked smile was any indication.

He straightened from the table, unfolding his arms as he crossed the few feet between them. He reached out and hooked a finger between the top two buttons of her top, using it to tug her toward him. He lowered his head until their lips were a whisper apart.

"I think you'll be impressed by how dedicated I am to earning your forgiveness," he murmured.

Then his lips played over hers and for the next two hours Rachel found herself very, *very* impressed.

Chapter Twenty-Six

"Will you teach me kung fu?"

"It's after midnight," Adrian muttered sleepily. He'd done his level best to exhaust her and they'd both dozed for a while after the last bout, but a few minutes ago he'd heard the shift in her breathing and her fingers had begun walking over his chest as she lay curled against his side.

"Are there designated kung fu learning hours?"

He groaned and squeezed her waist without opening his eyes. He'd put on the flannel pajama pants and she wore the matching top to stave off the cold, but they were mostly keeping one another warm, pressed together tightly as they had to be in the small bed. "There are designated sleeping hours, and this is one of them."

She squirmed against him and he knew without looking that she was propping herself up to frown down at him. "What if I'm attacked by a horde of angry ninjas tomorrow?"

"Run. Never try to fight angry ninjas."

"Adrian." She shoved him in the ribs.

He forced himself to wake up enough to consider her request. There was no way he'd be able to train her enough to take on a shifter in one night, but he could at least give her a few pointers that might buy her a little time. He should have already.

She must have sensed his capitulation because she gave a triumphant little squeak and climbed out of the bad, dragging him with her. He reached for the sidearm he'd left beside the bed and caught her hand, tugging her toward him and pressing the grip into her palm.

"Lesson one. You will never be as fast as a shifter. Tranq first, ask questions later."

He pulled her into the lee of his body and showed her how to aim. She cuddled back against him. "This is a very distracting instructional position."

He swatted her behind. "Concentrate."

She gave a breathy little laugh, but obediently sighted down the barrel.

He frowned, taking in her stance. "You've done this before."

"Skeet shooting. My mama had a thing for guns." She smiled sweetly.

"Okay then. Just remember that a dart won't have the range of a bullet."

"Do I get my kung fu now?"

He snorted, taking the tranq gun from her hand and setting it aside. "Lesson two. You will never be as strong as a shifter, so avoid a fight at all costs. Scream as loud as you can and then run like hell."

"I thought that would incite them to chase me."

"In some breeds it might trigger an instinctive reaction to hunt you, but playing dead doesn't work when the wild animal in question has a human brain."

"Lesson one, tranq. Lesson two, run." She ticked them off on her fingers. "I am not very badass."

He brushed a thumb down her cheek. "You're human. And most of these animals have been brawling with one another in one form or another since birth. So make fighting your absolute last resort. But if you do get cornered, there are a few tricks I can teach you."

For the next hour he ran her through the basics, teaching her vulnerable places to strike and how to identify weak points in holds and use surprise and her weight to twist out of them.

She caught on quickly, but it would still be a while before the movements became automatic.

When her attempt to get out of a hold landed them both flat on their backs on the floor, Adrian caught her before she could scramble to her feet for another try. "Enough. It's late. You win."

She sat up, throwing a leg over him to straddle his stomach. She ran her hands slowly over his bare chest. "So I do. What's my prize?"

My heart. He looked up at her, the most beautiful thing he'd ever seen in real life, and felt that tug at the base of his soul.

She bent down, kissing him long and slow and deep, and then lifted her head just enough to murmur, "I'll take you."

He barely stopped himself from saying he was already hers.

The arrival of the Three Rocks lions was like the spark to a fuse Rachel hadn't known was there. Within twenty-four hours, Grace left on some super secret mission to another shifter pack, taking Dominec and the representatives from Three Rocks with her. Kye's team postponed their latest mission and began working with Mateo and the rest of the lieutenants on something big, though Rachel knew better than to ask for details.

Save the absence of Grace, her life at the infirmary was remarkably unaffected.

Kathy was responding well to the hormone treatment and was convinced she was already pregnant, though that was merely optimism, as it was much too soon to tell.

The other Organization prisoners had been moved away from the main compound, though Adrian had mentioned they were still on pride lands. She wondered about them sometimes. How they were faring. What would become of them. But they didn't feel like her people anymore. If they ever had.

She'd asked Mateo about helping her track down the others who had helped her smuggle shifters out, her little rebel team, to make sure they were all safe, but it looked like it might be a while before he had a chance to breathe, let alone help her.

In the mean time, she worked at the infirmary and gave her heart ever more inextricably to Adrian. They'd fallen into a new sort of routine. Another careful truce.

He walked down to the infirmary with her each morning, leaving her to work with Moira or Dr. Brandt. While she helped there, he worked with the security forces during the day—either on the perimeter wall or helping establish contact with the various shifter prides and packs he'd visited over the years as he'd helped shifters escape. He returned for her each evening to walk her back to the cabin where they would eat together whatever food he'd brought from the dining hall and talk in front of the fire before inevitably falling into bed together.

Their strangely normal routine.

They were both well accustomed to being alone, having spent most of their lives that way, but it felt remarkably natural to be together.

But no matter how comfortable she was, there was always some small, subtle reminder that he was keeping distance between them. No matter how they went through the motions of togetherness, he still kept a wall around himself that she could not seem to scale.

Last night as she'd been drifting off to sleep, she'd found herself thinking about improvements to the cabin—a bigger bed, a dresser for their clothes—but when she'd mentioned it, Adrian had climbed out of bed on the excuse of tending to the fire, changing the subject.

Escaping.

She sometimes wondered if he'd always been that way, long before they met and been marked by the Organization. If they'd met under different circumstances, as friends rather than co-conspirators, maybe their path to love would have been smooth and uneventful. But if neither of them had gotten into the shifter extraction business to begin with, maybe she would have looked right past him without even noticing. Maybe her heart wouldn't have stuttered a step the first time she looked into his eerily yellow eyes.

But maybe she wouldn't have to fear the return of that look of disgusted betrayal in them either.

Things in the infirmary were quiet, most days. Grace hadn't been exaggerating about shifters avoiding medical care at all costs.

This afternoon it was a ghost town. Brandt had taken the day off and Moira had slipped out to grab them something from the dining hall for lunch, so Rachel was alone, babysitting the machines that concocted Kathy's treatment when the main door burst open.

A shifter guard came in, supporting one of the prisoners. The guard was extremely young and dark, the prisoner older and pale, with the beginnings of a white beard starting to form on his chin, though his hair was still more gray than white.

"Dale."

She'd seen him in the pictures, she'd known he was here, among the prisoners, but it was different seeing him like this, face to face. They'd only met a handful of times, but he'd seemed a nice guy, much too soft-hearted to thrive in the Organization. He was a neurological researcher with the kind of compassionate spirit that would have tempted her to recruit him for her operations, if not for the fact that he also had an air of weakness—and a daughter in Cleveland the Organization threatened to keep him in line.

And right now he had a bone sticking out of his arm.

"What happened?" She rose quickly, moving to his side, focused on the injury, though she flicked a glance to the young, dark-haired guard, trying to see if the patient—as Dale had become as soon as he walked through the infirmary door—was afraid of him.

Vivi Andrews

"It wasn't me!" the younger man yelped, all but shoving Dale into her arms. "One of the other prisoners did it to him."

Rachel took him by the shoulders, careful of the forearm, and guided him to the nearest cot. "Hi, Dale."

"You know him?" the guard asked.

"I'm sorry," Dale mumbled, letting himself be coaxed onto the cot. It was his left arm and it only took a glance to determine that both of the bones in his forearm had to be broken for one of them to have pierced the skin the way it had. Luckily, from the dearth of blood, none of the bone fragments appeared to have sliced through his major veins or arteries.

"I'll give you something for the pain, Dale, and then we're going to need to X-ray this to see if the bones are broken in more than one place before I set them, okay?" She hadn't set bones since her ER rotation in med school, but hopefully it was like riding a bike. Or perhaps she could just make him comfortable and wait for Moira.

"I'm sorry, Rachel."

"Hush, Dale, you don't need to apologize." By the looks of it, someone had taken a blunt object to his forearm. Like a baseball bat. Rachel would have to have words with the guards about how exactly another of the prisoners could have done this to him.

"It's Leslie," Dale said urgently, blue eyes pleading. "You remember."

"Your daughter. Yes, I remember Leslie. We'll get you back to her. But right now I need you to tell me if anything else hurts." He may have taken a blow to the head or the ribs. Internal bleeding...

"I never had a choice."

"I know, Dale. I understand. Does anything other than your arm hurt? Do you feel dizzy at all? Nauseous?"

"He's not gonna die, is he?" the guard asked, hovering on the other side of the bed. "Xander will kill me if I let one of the prisoners die on my first shift."

224

Dear God, the kid was as green as he was young. Hopefully there was someone more qualified watching the rest of the prisoners while he was here with her. "He's going to be fine."

"I'm sorry, Rachel," Dale said again.

She had his left arm cradled between her hands, focused on the injury, so she didn't notice right away when his right arm moved. Neither she nor the young guard were expecting the old man to move so fast. His hand was around the guard's tranq gun before she'd even registered the motion.

Three darts quickly appeared in the boy's stomach and he went down like a tree, nearly braining himself on the next cot.

"Dale!"

He swung the tranq gun toward her and she reacted, striking his wrist as Adrian had shown her to weaken his grip so she could knock it out of his hands. The gun hit the linoleum and skittered away beneath another cot, but Dale didn't give up so easily. His right fist swung toward her and in the process of dodging it, she stumbled, catching herself on the edge of the bed. While she was righting herself, he was diving for the instrument cart next to the cot. She had only a second to be grateful that the blades were kept locked up before he was lunging at her with a hypodermic.

"Dale! What are you doing?" She scrambled back.

"I have to, Rachel," he grunted, going for her face with the needle. "For Leslie."

Holy God, he really was trying to hurt her. Maybe even to kill her. Part of her mind frantically began to pray, even as another piece tried to remember what Adrian had taught her.

Lesson One: Tranq first.

But Dale was between her and the gun.

Lesson Two: Scream and run.

Check.

Rachel opened her mouth and let loose like a banshee—the sound taking the shape of Adrian's name.

She pivoted and bolted for the door, but Dale leapt after her in a flying tackle, his weight hitting the back of her legs and slamming them both to the ground—a move that must have been excruciating with his arm, but he didn't so much as whimper. *His arm.*

She almost hadn't thought of it. The instinct to *do no harm* made it almost impossible to even consider, but she twisted, grabbed his injured left arm, and squeezed.

He shrieked, but didn't move his weight off her. Didn't he have any self-preservation instincts?

The door burst open. Rachel twisted her head toward the sound, relief already slamming into her. *Adrian.*

But the figure that charged through the door was decidedly feminine.

Petite little Moira hit Dale like a freight train, lifting his weight off her and flinging him halfway across the room. He slumped to the floor in a heap and didn't move.

Moira moved quickly to where he lay, a menacing growl rumbling in her chest. She tested his vitals with much less care than she showed her usual patients, muttering "Unconscious," with what sounded like disappointment. Then she turned back to Rachel, wicked black claws retracting as her hands went fully human again.

"You all right, honey? I heard a ruckus."

Rachel sat up, taking stock of her shaking limbs. "I'm fine, I think." Though from the feel of it, there was a hypodermic needle sticking out of her left shoulder blade. *Dale Schmetterling just tried to kill me.* Her brain couldn't make sense of it. "Check the kid."

Moira moved to see if the young guard was all right as Rachel used a bed to help her stand. She'd found her feet and twisted to yank out the needle when another form flew through the door.

"*Adrian.*" The needle fell from her fingers, clattering to the metal tray.

"Are you all right?" He was breathing hard and made a beeline for her, his hands lifting to gently cup her face.

"I'm fine." She curled her arms around his waist. "You look like you've run a marathon."

"I was at the perimeter when I heard you. I tried to fly, but—" He shook his head. "Thank God you're all right."

"Thank God for Moira."

Adrian's attention swiveled to the bear, who was gaping at him. "Did you say you were at the perimeter and you *heard* her? I didn't hear her until I was twenty feet away."

"Hawk hearing," he said, brushing her awe aside. "Thank you for being here when I couldn't."

Moira didn't look like she bought that explanation for his presence, but she accepted his thanks graciously. "We all look out for one another here." She glowered at the unconscious prisoner. "What do we do with that?"

"I'll ask Xander. He's in charge of the prisoners." He nodded toward the unconscious boy. "He'll probably have something to say about that as well."

"It wasn't his fault," Rachel protested—though, come to think of it, the boy had been standing stupidly close to the prisoner and allowed himself to be tranqed with his own gun. A reprimand might be the least he deserved.

Adrian turned his raptor focus back to her, his yellow eyes searching her face as if he could X-ray her for internal damage. "Are you sure you're all right? I thought my heart would stop when I couldn't get to you fast enough."

The man did say the sweetest things when he wasn't even aware of it. "I did awesome, but I think we probably need to practice self-defense some more. Especially if I get rewarded afterward like I did last time."

His lips quirked, that half-hearted almost smile she loved. "If you're flirting with me, you must be all right."

"I'm not flirting. I'm seducing. Is it working?"

"Every time you look at me."

Vivi Andrews

"Aw," Moira sighed dramatically. "You guys are adorable. Now who wants to help me move the bodies?"

Adrian stalked toward the cabin where the remaining twelve prisoners were being kept with Xander on his heels, the lion lieutenant for once not making smartass remarks along the way.

Dale was handcuffed to a bed back at the infirmary. Adrian would have thrown him back in the cabin, broken arm and cracked—courtesy of Moira—ribs and all, but Rachel had insisted on treating him. He'd come to and refused to give them any information on why he'd done it. Just kept crying that he'd failed Leslie.

Rachel had explained that Leslie was the daughter the Organization used as leverage to force Dale to do things. Which explained *why* the mild-mannered older man had tried his hand at homicide, but that wasn't the whole story. Someone had broken his arm to get him in range of Rachel and given him the order. So one of the prisoners was more than they seemed.

He knew he was barely keeping it together—but he figured in situations like these, barely counted. Someone had attacked Rachel. That was *unacceptable* on such a fundamental level his entire being raged. The idea that he hadn't been there to rip the man's head from his shoulders was similarly unacceptable. But he could do this, now.

Xander waved to the two guards positioned on either side of the cabin. They were young, almost as young as the one who'd nearly gotten Rachel killed, and the sight brought home the reality that while Lone Pine may be filled with predators, they were dangerously understaffed when it came to skilled soldiers. They couldn't fight the Organization with these inexperienced children.

But that was a worry for another day. Today he was focused. Merciless.

Xander unlocked the door and Adrian felt his talons flash out in a partial shift as he walked over the threshold. The cabin was a single decent-sized room, not unlike his own. The prisoners huddled against the walls, most of them cowering, though a couple stared back at him defiantly. Adrian stood in the center of the room, his sharp gaze missing nothing as he flexed talon-tipped fingers.

"Who broke Dale Schmetterling's arm?"

Silence greeted him, but it was a tense silence. The silence of secrets rather than the silence of ignorance.

"Obviously one of you did it. I can review the tapes and see for myself, but then I'll be back and I'll be twice as pissed off as if you just tell me right now. Who. Broke. Dale's. Arm?"

A sound, no louder than a mouse stirring, drew his attention to a lonely corner of the room where the young woman with the brown hair hiding her face cowered. In a move almost too subtle to follow, she straightened a single finger without lifting her hand from where it rested against her leg, pointing unerringly across the room, to where one of the men they'd identified as an Organization guard sat.

Adrian moved so fast one of the women gave a startled scream, swallowing the sound almost immediately. He was on the guard, with his talons gently pressing into the soft skin of the man's throat, before he had time to blink.

"Did you arrange the attack on Dr. Russell?"

The man's eyes flicked over to the corner where the brunette huddled.

"Don't look at her. Look at me. And answer the question."

The guard looked up, struggling to swallow with Adrian's hand on his throat. He nodded jerkily.

"Why?"

The man's eyes flared with panic—as if he'd been asked a test question he didn't know the answer to—then hardened into resolve. "She's a traitor and she deserves what she gets."

Adrian nodded. "Wrong answer."

Two quick moves and the bones in the man's forearm snapped. The man shrieked. Adrian straightened, glowering down at him from his full height. "That's a clean break. As I see it, you have two choices. Find something to splint it yourself and hope it sets properly, or ask the pride for medical care. Your call. Ever had a bone set by an angry lion?"

Adrian didn't wait to hear his answer. He stalked out of the cabin. Xander caught up with him on the path back to the main compound.

"I thought you weren't going to hurt them," Xander asked, zero condemnation in his tone.

"He went after Rachel."

"Fair enough. But give me some warning next time. I'll sell tickets."

Chapter Twenty-Seven

Rachel lay in Adrian's arms that night, holding on to him a little tighter than usual, as he held her just as fiercely. He'd come when she'd called, even though Moira was convinced there was no way even a hawk could have heard her from that distance. He'd known that she needed him. Just like he always seemed to know.

She'd always felt there was something remarkable about their connection, the power of it, but now she had to wonder if it was more than just her emotions running away with her.

"Do you believe in soul mates?" she whispered against his shoulder.

His muscles jumped, going rigid and she instantly regretted the question. Just when things had finally seemed to be good between them too.

"Not that I think we—just, you know—" She started to pull away but his arms didn't loosen in the slightest. The awkwardness was going to swallow her whole.

"Rachel."

She spoke quickly. *Nothing to see here, folks.* "The Organization separates mated pairs because they're harder to control when they're fighting for their loved ones. Isolate them, take away their mates, and most of them become despondent. And there seems to be something to the idea that shifters are specially connected to their significant others. Or are there just as many shifter divorces as any other species and I just haven't had reason to hear about them?"

Divorce seemed like a safer topic than soul mates.

He grunted something affirmative. "Shifter couples split up, but the ones who've gone through the mating ceremony tend to stick together. Just a different attitude toward what that kind of commitment means, I think."

She made herself relax against him. "My parents were like that," she murmured. "It meant something real to them. Not every day was easy, but they made the choice to always put the two of them ahead of everything else, the choice to love one another most." She felt some almost unnoticeable movement in him and clarified, "Not that they didn't love me. They made sure I knew I was loved from the day they got me. But it was like they couldn't have loved me that much if they hadn't loved one another more, you know?"

She'd never loved anyone like that. Until Adrian. But if she told him that, she was afraid it would shatter this moment...and she needed to stay in his arms.

"My mom said my dad would have been so proud of me," she whispered, feeling the guilt of those words anew. "Proud of the work I was doing, helping women who had difficulty conceiving. They'd never been able to have kids, but they showed me what love was." She traced a pattern on his skin. "I think they were soul mates. My mom just sort of faded away without him. She kept up with the church, but she was a shadow of herself and followed him less than a year later."

She lay there, listening to his breathing. Maybe he was asleep. Maybe all of this was just her talking into his dreams. But then he spoke.

"My parents died together." His voice was low, barely audible. "Car accident. But my father used to make my mother promise that she would go on living a fabulous life if anything ever happened to him. *Entertain me in heaven.*"

She smiled against his shoulder, wishing she could have met his parents, seen how he was with them.

"They believed in soul mates," he went on. "Not as some magical, metaphysical bond, but that there was someone out there you were meant to love." He shrugged, the movement shifting the shoulder where she rested her head. "And maybe when you believe that, there is."

She wanted him to believe in soul mates. To believe in her. For a while, he'd seemed to. She just wished she knew how to get back there. Beyond this guarded truce.

"Did you have any aunts or uncles?" she asked, not wanting to miss this rare confessional mood of his. "Cousins or siblings?"

"No, it was just us." He stretched his arm, resettling her against him. "My parents were lucky to find one another. They believed we might be the last of our kind, that bird shifters are headed for extinction." He shrugged, but her chest ached and she knew how raw that thought must make him. "A lot of breeds that don't have the protection of the prides and packs have been dying out. We wouldn't be the first. There've been rumors for years now that bird shifters have stopped breeding true. That even mated pairs have children who can't shift anymore. Or maybe it's all of us," he said dryly. "Some bird shifter disease that explains why I can't shift anymore either."

Rachel stirred restlessly against his side, unsure if this was the right moment to air her theory. "I don't think it's physical."

"What?"

She felt the tension tighten his body and propped herself up to meet his eyes. "Your inability to shift, I don't think it's physical. The involuntary shifting of your hands and eyes would seem to indicate that you *can* shift, but there is a mental or emotional block preventing you."

"So you're a shrink now?" His tone was edged with that angry defensiveness, but at least he didn't push her away.

"No, but in my work, I've dealt with men feeling the pressure to perform, feeling responsible for their wives' lack of conception and—"

"It isn't the same. I'm not impotent. My hawk is gone." He closed his eyes, his expression pained. "Go to sleep, Rachel."

"I just think—"

"Go to sleep."

"You can't just tell me to go to sleep whenever I say something you don't want to hear."

Adrian made a low, frustrated noise and rolled over, pinning her beneath him as he claimed her mouth. She made a muffled sound of protest and shoved at his shoulder, but he kept kissing her until she went soft and malleable beneath him. The kiss stretched on and on, until her blood was molten. He only released her lips as he slipped on a condom and fitted himself to her.

"Don't think you can just kiss me into submission whenever you want," she grumbled petulantly, but she wrapped her arms around him and pulled him down to her with a broken sigh as he slid home.

She clenched tight around him, gasping and rising up to meet each deep, deliberate thrust. And when she came apart in his arms, she didn't worry about holding on to her soul, because she knew he would catch it for her. He always had. Her hawk.

Adrian watched Rachel slip inside the infirmary the next day and had to force himself not to charge in after her. Brandt was there. Moira was there. Rachel had the tranq gun he'd insisted on strapped to her hip. And still he was barely fighting down the panic.

He'd almost lost her.

And a sleepless night obsessing over it hadn't brought him any closer to calm.

When she'd asked him if he believed in soul mates, it was all he could do not to tell her that of course he did, because she was his.

He'd almost lost her.

And if he didn't learn to let go of the lingering anger toward her he was hanging on to, he would lose her. And that was unacceptable. Intrinsically unacceptable. She was *his*.

But he didn't know how to get over it. How did he forget when the nightmares still woke him up some nights? Could he forgive when he couldn't forget?

For Rachel, he had to.

Chapter Twenty-Eight

The boy was bawling when his mother carried him in. There was a lot of blood—a scalp wound, from the look of it, and those could be deceptively bloody. Moira and Rachel both dropped what they were doing and rushed forward to meet the pair. The little guy had an impressive set of lungs, but at first glance the wound looked shallow—a glancing claw swipe during playtime that got a little too rough, most likely.

Moira spoke soothingly to the mother as they led the pair to the nearest cot. Rachel reached to brush the boy's baby-soft hair away from the wound.

The woman's nostrils flared and her eyes rounded with horror. Suddenly her claws flashed out and she lunged over the bed. "Get away from my child."

Rachel stumbled back, barely missing the wicked claws.

Moira frowned and murmured, her voice low and soothing, "This is Dr. Russell—"

"I know who she is. She reeks human," the woman snarled. "Not her. Not an Organization doctor."

The boy's sobbing had cut off and now he watched them all with wide, terrified eyes—startled out of his hurt by his mother's reaction.

"*Susan*," Moira scolded.

"No, it's all right. I understand." Rachel retreated quickly to one of the patient rooms, taking herself out of sight so the frantic mother would stop upsetting her child.

She closed the door and leaned her head back against it, suddenly fighting tears.

She didn't know why she was so rattled. It had been bound to happen eventually. And she *did* understand. But that didn't make the distrust hurt any less.

Any more than understanding why Adrian still held that piece of himself away from her made it hurt any less.

And suddenly she was bawling as badly as that cub out there.

It had been two weeks since Dale's attack. Two weeks of *almost* perfect.

Grace was still off on her secret mission, and Rachel had taken to wearing a tranquilizer gun on her hip when she wasn't at the infirmary or with Adrian. As much as she wanted to be independent, Rachel hadn't been sure it was smart, PR-wise, to arm a former Organization doctor with a tranq gun, but no one had asked her about it yet. It was almost like she was a real member of the pride.

But she wasn't. Today had proved that.

It was a good life, a life she found tempting in the extreme, but it wasn't hers.

Perhaps Adrian had been right to keep a part of himself separate from her. No matter how she might want to, she couldn't stay with him. Her presence here was tolerated and she might even have the illusion of acceptance, but she was still human. Without latent shifter DNA, she would never be able to give him children who could shift and just hearing her hawk talk about being the last of his kind made her desperate to find a female hawk for him—even if it would mean losing him.

Perhaps that was what love meant. Being willing to sacrifice your own happiness so the one you love could be happy.

If only it wouldn't make her miserable in the process.

"Rachel?"

"Just a moment." She sniffled and swiped at her face, before turning and opening the door for Moira. She must have been back here longer than she thought if the boy and his mother had already been taken care of.

She opened the door to find Moira frowning at her with concern.

"Oh honey, tell me you weren't crying," Moira said, though obviously she had been. "Susan is a right bitch. Don't fuss about her."

"No, I—it doesn't—it wouldn't hurt if I didn't understand exactly why she did it."

"She should know better. They should all know you were the one who helped more of us than any of *them* ever have."

"I can't blame her."

"You should. You are not responsible for every human. You aren't the Organization, honey. You are your own actions. And no one else's."

Rachel wanted to believe that. But she couldn't seem to stop paying for where her actions had taken her.

Adrian sensed something different about Rachel the second he arrived at the infirmary to escort her home. There was a distance in her eyes, a reserve in her demeanor that had him instantly on edge. Her monosyllabic replies that she was fine and her day had been good did nothing to ease his mind.

She may have heard about the latest Organization raid. The incursion team had arrived too late, finding only slaughtered remains in the cells of the D Block building. A bloody message that the Organization was cutting its losses. The security team had tried to keep the information quiet—not wanting to incite another riot, but talk around the pride was leaning more and more in favor of outright war against the Organization.

He didn't know how much longer Rachel would be safe here. Neither of them would ever be truly part of the pride, no matter how the lions played at accepting them.

Adrian unlocked the padlock securing the cabin and slipped inside to check for threats. Rachel waited silently until he gave her the all clear, then moved past him to the bathroom without a word. He'd gotten used to their evening routine, he realized. Talking about their days while they set out the food he'd brought. Eating together. Brushing their teeth and him watching her go through her evening ritual of lotions and cleansers before they retired together to the lumpy futon where she would roll into his arms.

He had the food laid out by the time she exited the bathroom in her fuzzy flannel pajamas. She glanced at the food and said, "I ate at the clinic. I'm going to turn in early."

She beelined for the bed and climbed into it, winding herself into a knot of blankets and burrowing in, facing the wall.

Adrian frowned at the lump of her shoulder, hoping for some clue what the hell he'd done. He'd be tempted to blame her behavior on PMS, but she'd had him pick up *those* supplies for her ten days ago and he knew she was no longer binging on Midol and chocolate. But something had changed.

He ate his own dinner, stored the leftovers and went through his own evening routine, preoccupied by the lump of Rachel breathing softly beneath the covers—but not with the even rhythm of sleep. He could hear that she was still awake when he turned off the light and climbed in beside her, but when he brushed her shoulder, she feigned a snuffling sigh and shrugged him off.

"Rachel," he whispered.

No response. What the fuck?

Adrian flopped onto his back, his body awkward and strangely hollow without her tucked against his side, cuddled close.

It was so unlike her to pull away. Rachel, who had always come into his arms eagerly from the very first, as if she was afraid he would be torn from her at any second. It was she who had never let him put any distance between them—except that one night.

The only other time she'd pushed him away.

The hotel room had been fancier than their usual meeting places. He'd tired of meeting her at seedy roadside hotels with shoddy surveillance systems. The glitzy honeymoon suite had a balcony he could fly to, so no one would be able to see him coming or going. He'd had a bag with clothes for him to change into after the shift delivered to the room—along with roses and champagne.

He'd planned to propose in the proper human fashion and convince Rachel to leave the Organization, to come away with him—to Lone Pine of all places—so they could work together to free shifters from the outside, but she would no longer be in daily danger of discovery. They'd only been seeing one another—always in secret—for a few months, but he'd known beyond a shadow of a doubt that she was *his*.

But when she'd arrived that night, she'd been jumpy, nervous. She'd pulled away when he'd tried to kiss her, moving around the room, fidgeting, agitated. He'd asked her if she thought she'd been followed and instead of answering she'd told him he should fly, get away from her—but he hadn't been able to leave her behind. Not even when he'd heard the telltale sounds of a strike team creeping down the hallway.

He'd armed himself from the bag he'd had delivered, prepared to defend Rachel with his life—right up to the moment when he'd felt the needle sink deep into the flesh of his shoulder muscle and heard her softly spoken apology as the door broke open.

He hadn't dreamt of the Organization for almost two weeks, but given the drift of his thoughts it was no surprise when the familiar shape of the dream took form in his mind as it hovered on the edge of sleep.

"Just shift, lover. Just shift for me and all the pain will stop."
Her voice. Her beloved, familiar voice now made bile rise in his

throat—or perhaps that was the pain. They'd blindfolded him again. Other voices faded in and out of the black, "—sure, doctor? Don't want to risk damaging—", "—delicate bone structure—", but hers was always close and clear, "He can take more. Can't you, baby? Hit him again." Pain swamped him, dragging him into the dark. They must have expected him to stay unconscious longer than he had, because when he cracked open his eyelids, the blindfold was gone. Her hands were above him, adjusting the rigging that kept him immobile but suspended midair for their manipulations. Long, graceful fingers. Perfectly manicured nails. The edge of a tattoo peeking out beneath one sleeve. "Awake already, darlin'? My, but you shifters do heal quickly, don't you?" He tried to say her name, tried to plead, but there was nothing but pain again. The endless cycle of pain.

Rachel knew the second Adrian slid into the nightmare. His body went rigid, jerking the bed, and his breathing grew choppy and short.

She shoved at the covers that tangled around her, fighting free of the blankets until she could reach for Adrian, gently gripping his shoulders—and watching carefully for flailing hands and elbows that might give her another black eye. "Adrian."

Cold sweat glistened on his brow, clammy and horrible to see. She hated hearing the nightmares, hated the idea of him reliving those months when he had been helpless, and she had been helpless to save him. "Adrian, wake up."

She was braced for him to lash out, but he woke with sudden stillness, his eyes flying open. "*You.*"

In that instant, she knew the bright, fierce terror that he might actually hurt her. He may not have woken up at all, eyes open but still seeing the nightmare. "Adrian?"

He launched out of the bed, his lean, rangy body halfway across the room before she had any awareness that he'd moved, shifter-fast. He was back—just as fast—and pushing at her sleeves, turning her wrists this way and that, then dropping them, and across the room again, at the window, the door, the stove, moving so fast she could hardly track him—like a bird trapped in a house.

"Adrian? Can I do anything—?"

"You don't have any tattoos."

Rachel frowned, not following, but willing to talk about whatever he needed to. "No. My mother thought they were vulgar. I never really saw the appeal of getting one and it certainly wasn't worth courting her disapproval."

He nodded, more to himself than to her. "They weren't your hands."

"Whoever's hands they were, it was just a dream—"

"No." He pivoted, then spun again, and suddenly he was in front of her, crouched beside the futon. His yellow gaze was fierce, burning with a desperate intensity. "I need you to answer a question and I need the absolute truth."

"Of course."

"Swear it."

"I swear."

"On your father's soul."

"On everything I love," she swore. "Adrian, what's this about?"

"Did you take part in my torture when I was in captivity? Did you direct it?"

Her breath whooshed out. "Of course not. God, no. I would never."

"It was your voice." He straightened, shaking his head as if to shake the puzzle pieces into something that made sense. "I heard your voice. It haunted me. How did they—recordings?"

Realization shuddered through Rachel with painful force. She should have known, should have suspected, but she'd thought Adrian was just confused by the drugs he'd been given, mixing dreams and realities. She hadn't suspected they would use *her* to hurt him. Her voice...

"Madison," she said. "There's a woman who works for the Organization. She believes in their cause whole heartedly and wouldn't flinch at hurting you—and she has an amazing ability to mimic voices. I've heard her do it. But her name was never attached to your file— Oh God. Of course they gave me a dummy file."

Adrian stood stock still in the middle of the room, his hands loose at his sides, eyes wide and breath quick. "It wasn't you they were calling by another name. You weren't there. You really weren't there."

"I tried to protect you," she vowed. "I'm so sorry, Adrian. I know I didn't—"

His lips cut off the rest of what she would have said. His long fingers framed her face, holding her steady as he kissed her, long and sweet and aching with all the pain they'd put one another through.

"You're *mine*," he whispered when he finally lifted his head and let her come up for air.

"*Yes*," she breathed.

Clothing fell away as if it had never existed. There could be no obstacles between them tonight. No more misconceptions, no more apologies. Tonight there was only need, pure and untainted by everything that had come before. He fitted himself to her and she sobbed at the sweet perfection of it, gazing up into eyes that no longer held anything human until pleasure blinded her to everything else. Adrian shouted, for once not silent, talons scraping the futon frame before he collapsed over her, his breath puffing against the sensitive side of her neck and sending delicious aftershocks shuddering down her spine.

"We need a bigger bed," she whispered, and felt him smile against her skin.

"Agreed," he mumbled, and she felt something unlock, something that had been afraid to hope this might mean forever. Furniture was permanent. It meant something. She threaded her fingers through his at her shoulder, careful of his talons. "Your eyes shifted again," she murmured.

He hummed something vaguely affirmative, then his body jerked, going stiff. She tightened her arms around his shoulders, fear spiking at the thought that he was pulling away again, but when he lifted his head, there was awe-struck wonder in his hawk-gold gaze. And tears. *"Rachel,"* he whispered.

With a rush of air—almost silent, like her ears popping— feathers exploded above her, wings erupting from his back in an arch of golds and browns. He was off her like a shot, rushing toward the door, still naked, massive angel-sized wings tucked tight to his back. He threw the door open and flung himself off the porch. Another pop of air and a hawk arrowed through the air where her Adrian had been, wings beating firm and strong, lifting the lithe body into the trees.

Rachel clutched the blankets to her chest and stared after her lover, her heart racing at the sight of him leaping into flight—even as part of her crumpled at the realization that she could never ask him to be with someone who couldn't pass on that gorgeous legacy.

He had forgiven her, she had felt the difference in his arms, but he could still never be hers.

Chapter Twenty-Nine

Adrian reveled in the lightness, the soaring expansive freedom of wind pressing against the inner curves of his wings, lifting him above the trees. He felt the last leaded weights of fear and doubt releasing from his heart—the fear that he would never have this again, never again feel the wild exhilaration of flight.

His hawk was back. Whatever dark recess of his soul where it had been hiding had been flooded with light and he was whole once more. Lighter than he'd ever been as the chill winter air buffeted his feathers. This was who he was. The cool, sharp predator high above the earth, filled with the clarity only flying had ever brought.

He wanted to push himself higher, faster, to stretch his long-neglected wings, but even the hawk half of his soul knew something important waited for him back at the cabin.

Rachel.

He tucked himself into a dive, flying like an arrow loosed from a bow down into the clearing. He called for the shift mid-flight, stumbling only slightly as his bare feet hit the ground with jarring momentum. He was out of practice, but the two halves of his soul still knew one another, still folded seamlessly into one being, each half stronger for the presence of the other.

Just as he was stronger for the presence of Rachel.

He'd always been alone before, had been good at being the solitary hunter, but Rachel had taught him how to trust the first time and taught him again these last weeks when he had fought so hard against forgiving her—when she hadn't needed his forgiveness at all. She *was* his exception. The one who would risk herself to save him—even if it meant stabbing him full of sedatives and handing him over to the Organization. He would have died fighting rather than be captured, but Rachel had made sure he lived—protecting him even from himself. And then she had gotten him out.

And he'd treated her like shit.

The door to the cabin was still open. He wasn't sure how long he'd been gone—the bird's sense of time was so different from his—but Rachel was still awake, curled against the wall on the futon with a half dozen blankets twined around her to combat the chill coming through the open door.

Adrian entered and quickly shut the door, moving directly to the stove to stoke it higher. "I owe you an apology," he said as soon as he felt the warmth of the fire pushing against his skin.

A strange soberness shadowed her chocolate gaze. "No. We're beyond even."

"I should have believed you when you said you weren't involved in my treatment in captivity."

"I was the reason you were there."

"If I hadn't been there, I would have been dead." He crossed to the futon, sitting facing her.

"You could have flown away. They never would have been able to track you."

"And what would they have done to you, if you had warned me?"

"Put an explosive on my ankle and put me in a lab, no doubt."

"But there would have been no hard drives. I never would have been able to find you." He gently cupped her cheek. "We never would have gotten here."

Her somber gaze couldn't hold his, lowering to the mattress between them. "Maybe we weren't supposed to."

"I'm sorry," he said again. "I should have trusted you, but until I remembered that tattoo, I was so sure it was you who had taken pleasure in making my life hell. I didn't know how to look beyond that." He grimaced. "Hell, maybe everything does happen for a reason. If there hadn't been a riot at the barn, I never would have seen that woman with the tattoo on her wrist in the cells, and that memory might never have been triggered."

Rachel's gaze bounced up from the mattress to lock on his, eyes widening. "What woman?"

Adrian shrugged. "Just one of the prisoners. An administrative assistant in the wrong place at the wrong time. She has this tattoo on her wrist—" He pointed to the spot on his own arm, but Rachel had gone unnaturally still.

"Madison Clarke was there the day you rescued me from the lab. I thought she was one of the ones killed. I believed she wouldn't let herself be taken alive because I *wanted* her to be one of the dead—I don't think I've ever wished that of anyone else. She has a tattoo on her wrist. Brown hair. About my height."

"Blue eyes?"

Rachel nodded, gripping his hand. "She's not some secretary. She's dangerous. A human chameleon. She plays parts, manipulates people, and she *believes* in the Organization cause with a devotion that is truly terrifying. She's the Board's personal errand girl—torture, acquisitions, she does whatever they want of her. If she's here, she'll be gathering information, looking for cracks in our security, finding a way to escape—"

Adrian rose, pulling Rachel to her feet. "Get dressed." He moved to grab his own clothes. "You can identify her?"

"Absolutely." She didn't hesitate, her long legs already disappearing inside a pair of jeans. "Oh Lord, the photos. She was always hiding her face."

He finished dressing then helped her on with her jacket, making sure her tranq gun was loaded and strapped to her belt. He handed her a red knit cap and gloves—not the color he would have chosen, too much of a beacon in the forest, but Rachel loved the scarlet—and donned his own jacket and mottled brown hat.

He took her gloved hand and led the way quickly into the night, weaving through the forest, steadying her when she stumbled in the darkness. They skirted the edge of the main compound, moving more quickly along the wide, cultivated paths that abutted the livestock corrals, then slower again as they wound down a narrow, uneven trail into a small gulley on the eastern edge of the pride lands. At the base of the gully was the cabin—and it was teeming with activity.

Adrian's hand tightened on Rachel's. "Something's wrong."

There was too much movement for this hour of the night, too many members of the security team moving with brisk efficiency through the gully. Grace was there. He hadn't even known she was back yet.

Adrian led Rachel toward the cabin, until Grace spotted them and broke away from the conversation she'd been having to intercept them, her face devoid of its characteristic insouciance, filled instead with the same cold, hard deadliness she'd had during the riot.

"She can't be here now." Grace pointed to Rachel, baring their way to the cabin.

"What happened?" Adrian asked.

Rachel simultaneously protested, "I think I have information about one of the prisoners."

"Several of the prisoners escaped," Grace answered him, adjusting her stance so she could keep an eye on the guards back at the cabin, several of whom were frowning at Rachel.

"Madison," she whispered.

"How?" Adrian demanded.

"From what we can tell, one of them got a hold of a dinner knife, stabbed the everloving shit out of one of the other prisoners, painted herself with blood and then claimed to be injured. When the guard opened the door to check on her, she stabbed him in the throat."

"You only had one guard?"

"One at the door, one walking the perimeter. We're short staff," Grace snapped. "The kid at the door called in the problem before he went inside, but by the time his partner got back he was bleeding all the fuck over the place, so this bitch got a head start."

"How long?" Adrian demanded.

"Thirty minutes, give or take. First priority was getting our injured man to the infirmary. At least three of the other prisoners took the chance to run and they all went in different directions. I sent out some trackers already and I'd be after them myself if I didn't worry any guards I leave behind will kill the injured prisoners as soon as I leave."

"I can help with the injuries," Rachel offered.

Grace grimaced. "No offense, Doc, but I don't think it's wise for you to be anywhere near here until—hang on." She brushed past them jogging to greet a pair of soldiers rushing up the path. "Xander, Kelly, thank you for coming. I need you to keep an eye on things out here while we track down our runaways." She led them up to where Adrian and Rachel waited. "Doc, this asshole is Xander and the cowboy here is Kelly. I trust them to keep you safe if you want to patch up the prisoners. I'll take the rest of this lot with me." She jerked her chin toward the knot of guards watching them warily. "Adrian?"

The others were already in motion, getting ready to move out or taking up posts by the cabin door.

"I can cover more ground from the air." He had a vested interest in capturing the bitch who had tortured him in captivity, but his hand was still wrapped around Rachel's and he wasn't sure he wanted to let go. He met Grace's eyes. "Are you sure...?"

"Xander and Kelly are solid."

Adrian nodded and turned to Rachel brushing a thumb over her frost-chilled cheek. "Stay safe."

"Be careful," she whispered back. "She's dangerous."

He smiled, and he knew it wasn't pretty. "Not as dangerous as I am."

Adrian joined the other shifters hurriedly shucking their clothes for the shift. The cats separated, lunging into the forest to chase scent-trails, and Adrian leapt into the air. It was instinct to reach for his hawk—instinct so long denied that he released a sharp half-human caw of triumph as talons burst through his fingernails and feathers rippled over his skin in a lightning wave. Wings exploded out of his shoulders and the sweet pain of the shift compressed his body into a sleekly lethal form. He rocketed into the air, wings beating the wind hard, taking a heartbeat to enjoy the pressure and lift. Free and on the hunt.

Rachel didn't think she would ever tire of the sight of her lover transforming into a raptor. It was a moment powerful and pure in its beauty. But she didn't have time to stand around gawking now.

She didn't have any supplies beyond her own hands, but if she could help, it was her duty to do so. She approached the cabin, unsure what she was going to find inside. She didn't know how the prisoners had been treated. But as she stepped through the door the one called Kelly held open for her, she saw they were in better shape than ninety-nine percent of the shifters they'd helped hold captive. Seven somewhat familiar faces looked back at her, an eighth slack with unconsciousness.

Rachel didn't speak and the seven ragged prisoners watched her silently as she moved first to the unconscious eighth. The massive pool of blood beneath her on the floor was damning, so Rachel wasn't surprised when no pulse met her fingertips. She moved on to another woman—one struggling to apply pressure to a wound in her thigh.

"What happened?" Rachel asked as her scarf became a tourniquet. "Did Madison do this?"

The woman didn't speak, simply staring back with wide eyes as Rachel improvised a bandage, ripping strips from the lining of her coat. She supposed she shouldn't have been surprised by the silence. She wasn't one of them anymore. Never really had been.

Focused on her work, she barely registered the muted thuds outside—until the door creaked open and a shadowy silhouette filled the door.

She finished binding the wound and looked up as Dominec stepped into the light, his scarred face twisting in a smile.

"Hello, Doc. Fancy meeting you here."

Chapter Thirty

"Where are Xander and Kelly?" Rachel asked, fighting to keep her voice calm and steady as she looked into the face of the pride's resident psychopath.

"I didn't *kill* them," Dominec protested, as if offended by the implication. "They're just taking a little nap outside." His lifted his hand away from his side, calling attention to the tranquilizer gun he held, twirling it like a gunslinger before shoving it into the pocket of the black duster he wore.

Rachel sidled away from the wounded prisoner and Dominec's eyes tracked her. He kicked the door shut and strode to where she sat on the floor, brushing back the sides of his duster and crouching down with feline grace so they were just inches apart. She wanted to reach for her own tranq gun, but she was reasonably certain she wouldn't be able to draw it before he mauled her. She'd seen how fast her hawk was with his shifter speed, knew Dominec to be even faster.

He inhaled deeply, his head canting to the side. "You smell like the bird."

Rachel nodded, wetting her lips. "I'm on your side," she whispered, proud when her voice didn't shake. "I helped one hundred and fifty-two shifters escape from the Organization. I got them out."

"You didn't get me out."

Something about the simple way he said it, so frank and calm, made her heart rate quadruple. "No. I didn't."

He nodded and his eyes shifted to feline and back to human, so fast it was dizzying to watch. His teeth were pointed, making him work extra hard to enunciate. "You think I'm crazy?"

Hell yes. "No."

"I am." He smiled again, his head tilting so the light played grotesquely over the mangled scars that dominated one side of his face. "I'm a killer. But I wasn't always. Your Organization did that."

"They aren't mine," Rachel whispered, incapable of more volume. "We're on the same side."

"So you'll let me kill these people?" he asked conversationally, tipping his head toward the silent prisoners who sat motionless and staring. "You won't stand in my way?"

Rachel swallowed, her throat a desert. "I can't do that either."

Dominec cocked his head, studying her. His eyes kept partial shifting, along with his hands, flicking between forms in a way she'd never seen before. "I can smell your fear."

"I know."

"Smells good."

Every cell in her body was quiet and alert, hyperaware of the fact that these could be her last breaths. *I should have told Adrian I loved him.* He must know, but she should have said the words.

He would go after Dominec when he found her body. Would the tiger kill him? They'd had a confrontation over her once before, back at the labs. She remembered thinking at the time that it had been a miracle neither of them had died that day. Somehow Dominec's madness had been leashed.

When Grace arrived.

Rachel swallowed, trying to force moisture down her throat. *Please let this work.* "Grace is my friend. She wouldn't want me hurt."

"Why do I care what Grace wants?" he asked, but a welcome gleam of clarity entered Dominec's eyes. He straightened, shuffling away.

Rachel wasn't sure whether he was angry and viciously clever or genuinely mad, but either way, some of her terror eased its grip as he walked to the far wall, propping himself against it and waving a hand at her. "Go on. Heal them."

It was hard to concentrate on her work with one eye on the madman, but she managed to do a rough approximation of first aid until Dominec straightened suddenly. Rachel flinched, cowering down to make a smaller target—but then she too heard the footsteps and the rasped curse.

Grace burst into the room, taking it all in with a sweeping glance. "Dominec, what the fuck?"

The tiger simply nodded to her, like he was greeting her on a stroll in the park, and walked past her into the night.

Grace swore, and Rachel slumped against the wall, all the rigid tension leaving her body in a rush.

"How did you know?"

Grace slanted her a look, most of her attention still on the door through which the tiger had retreated. "Kelly wasn't responding. He's a pain in the ass on security detail because he can't go for five seconds without flirting over the coms, but he'd been silent for almost ten minutes. Figured he had to be unconscious or dead."

"Dominec tranqed him."

Grace nodded, still glaring after him. "He's going to be a problem."

"Wasn't he always?"

Grace grimaced, finally wrenching her gaze away from the door. "Believe it or not, he was keeping together relatively well before. But ever since the raid where we picked up you, when he went batshit crazy, he's been chugging the extra special psycho Kool-Aid."

"Lucky us," Rachel grumbled.

"Lucky you." Grace studied her, speculation lighting her pale gaze. "How are you still alive, Doc?"

Rachel didn't know how to say she'd used Grace's friendship like a talisman against Dominec. Somehow it didn't seem like the kind of thing the lioness would react well to. "I reminded him I was on his side."

Grace's golden eyebrows flew up. "And that worked?"

"I'm alive, aren't I?" Before Grace could ask more, she asked, "Did you find Madison?"

"Still looking. Bitch knows how to cover her tracks. She found the fucking lake and swam to throw off her scent trail." Grace pulled a face. "Come on. Let's get you and your patients to the infirmary."

The sun was rising and Adrian had just decided to leave the tracking to the lions when movement far below him snagged his attention. He'd located one of the other escapees and returned him to the lions' care earlier, learning at the same time that only Madison Clarke remained at large. So it was with particular eagerness that he fell into the dive, rocketing toward the figure moving furtively along the eastern border fence.

She never looked up.

Adrian shifted ten feet off the ground, letting his full weight fall onto her back and drive her to the ground. Her shriek was cut off by the dirt filling her mouth—but she was far from cowed. She twisted and thrashed, spitting curses. Adrian, without any clothes or anything to restrain her, struggled with the prisoner for a moment before managing to capture her wrists, using his weight to pin her legs. The neck of her shirt stretched in the struggle, revealing part of another tattoo that threatened to trigger a memory, but he pushed it down. He would not think of what she'd done to him. She was a job. Nothing more.

"You're caught, Madison. May as well come quietly."

She went still at the sound of her name. He could almost hear her brain working frantically. When she spoke, it was with the reedy, girlish voice she'd used in the barn. "I don't know who you think I am, but I swear—"

"Madison Clarke. Organization henchman. Give it up."

He ignored her continued protests. A narrow leather belt wound around her waist. He partially shifted his hands and used a talon to slice through the leather—which sent her into screaming fits, bucking and shrieking.

"You will not violate me, you animal! I'd sooner die! You'll have to kill me! I'll not submit!"

He cuffed the side of her head, as much to get her attention as shut her up. "No one is violating you. I'm just short on restraints at the moment."

Getting the belt around her wrists and tight enough to do any good was a battle the entire way, but after several minutes he finally had her contained enough to flip her over. No longer seeming concerned for her virtue, her eyes raked over him as soon as he let her up enough to see him. The look in her eye screamed that she was seeing an object, not a man. She no longer looked young or innocent, just the light in her eyes adding ten years to her age, and he realized what a spectacular actress she was.

"I know you," she smiled. "You're Rachel's toy."

"Nice try." He would not let her get to him. Grabbing her by her bound wrists, he dragged her to her feet and shoved her back in the direction of the main compound. "Walk."

Madison obeyed, but not without editorializing. "She's one of us, you know. She always will be. A human can never be one of you."

"Shut up."

"A war is coming. You know it as well as I do. When the day of reckoning is here, she'll either die for standing with you, or be killed by your own animal brethren."

"You're the animals."

"Are we? So when your righteous shifter army is raining down hell, are they going to care about anything other than the fact that she smells human? I've seen what you creatures do when you're pushed to violence."

"Then don't push me." He cuffed her again on the back of the head. "Walk."

Chapter Thirty-One

Waiting was never one of her favorite pass times, but waiting to hear if the love of her life was all right and the bitch-of-the-universe had been recaptured or would be leading the devil himself to her doorstep at any moment? That had to be a new kind of hell.

Rachel had tended the wounded. Later, Brandt and Moira had insisted that she stay at the infirmary with them rather than going back to Adrian's cabin alone and she had taken absolutely no persuading to accept their offer. She'd tried to sleep on one of the open beds—and failed miserably. No matter how exhausted her body might be, her mind refused to allow even a second's rest until she knew Adrian was all right and Madison was safely imprisoned again. Or dead. It might make her unchristian, but she wouldn't mind dead—especially after hearing of Madison's role in Adrian's torture.

Around four in the morning, Rachel gave up on sleep entirely and began the meticulous task of synthesizing more of the lynx hormone for Kathy. It kept her busy until just past eight, when the door to the lab swung open.

Rachel's head snapped up, but it wasn't her hawk who walked through the door, rather the alpha's mate and a tall, lovely blonde.

"Patch," she said, hoping she didn't sound as disappointed as she felt as she rose to greet the pair.

"Have you met Lila?" Patch asked.

The pretty blonde extended one perfectly manicured hand and Rachel realized this was the former Alpha's daughter. The one pride gossip told her had been originally supposed to marry

Roman before the love stick had hit her upside the head and made her choose a jaguar architect instead. Roman had apparently been relieved to be free to pursue Patch—which Rachel would have expected to make the women rivals, but they were still, by all accounts, the best of friends.

"You're here awfully early." Rachel took the offered hand.

"I didn't want to wait." Lila took a deep breath, visibly nervous. Then wrinkled her nose. "Are you all right? You smell of blood."

"Lots of it," Patch added, her own nose crinkling.

"There was a little problem last night with the prisoners."

"That explains why Roman got up in the middle of the night. *No, baby, stay in bed, everything's fine.*" Patch made a face.

"Another riot?" Lila asked.

"No. More of an internal dispute."

Lila bit her lip. "We should go. This isn't important and you're busy."

"No, I could use the distraction. Right now I'm just waiting for news. What can I do for you?"

Lila glanced at Patch, who gave her a little nod of encouragement. "We hear you can help cross-breed couples conceive. We want to know how it's done. And if you can do it for us."

Patch held up a hand like a stop sign. "Don't include me in that. I'm not even sure I want kids. You're the one who's so desperate to breed."

"Not right *now*," Lila protested. "Santiago and I are still planning our mating ceremony. I just need to know that we can. So Santiago will stop freaking out that I'll stop loving him if we can't have children—which is ridiculous, but he's determined to give me babies."

"Because he's seen the way you go all mushy every time you even see a freaking Pampers commercial," Patch said dryly.

"Regardless of why." Lila shot her friend a quelling glare. "I need to know that we can have kids."

"We aren't positive that you can," Rachel admitted. "Not yet." She had never given her patients false hope and she wasn't going to start now. Especially with such a high-profile patient. Something uneasy worked through her. "Are you sure about this? Did you hear about Susan?"

Patch arched a brow. "Susan?"

"She didn't want me treating her son. And Adrian is nervous about me treating Kathy. I don't know how it would go over in the pride if I were treating you two."

Lila just smiled. "That sounds like a PR problem, and PR happens to be my specialty. You leave your image to me. And I'll leave the medicine to you. Deal?"

Still Rachel hesitated. "I can give you a better shot than you would have on your own—and the fact that you're a lioness, surrounded by lions in this pride should help you, but we're still learning about shifter biology. I can't give you any guarantees."

Lila nodded. "I understand, but can you give me a chance? Will you at least try?"

"That I can do." Adrian was going to kill her. Provided he was all right. He had to be all right.

Marching through a snowy forest naked with a bitching woman who seemed to think it was her duty to periodically make a run for it was officially on Adrian's top ten list of activities never to repeat. By the time he got back to the pride, his feet were half frozen and cut up to hell and back and his temper was worse. He turned Madison over to Hugo, who had temporarily taken over prisoner duty and seemed to enjoy growling at the woman until she nearly wet herself.

Adrian wanted nothing more than to find Rachel and fall into her arms, but he'd had the chance to do a lot of thinking on the walk back, and as much as he hated to admit it, Madison Clarke had a point. Rachel would never be safe here. So no matter how much he had grown to like it here, it was time to leave. His mate's safety came first.

He showered quickly and grabbed a change of clothes in the barracks, then borrowed a computer to type up a quick letter before heading to Grace's office. Anyone else might have been taking the morning off after their busy night, but he knew Grace didn't know how to rest. He knocked on her door and at her call, marched inside and tendered his resignation from the Lone Pine security team.

Grace looked at him, nonplussed, when she was done reading his letter. "You're an idiot."

He wasn't surprised by the declaration, but he raised his eyebrows anyway. "Excuse me?"

She waved the letter. "What is this?"

"My resignation."

"I noticed. It's all nice and official. Why are you resigning?"

He pointed to the letter. "I told you. Rachel and I need to leave the pride. She'll never be safe here."

"Stop being a dickhead, Adrian. Rachel will never be one hundred percent safe anywhere. But she's part of this pride now. If anyone touches her, they answer to the Alpha. Not to mention half a dozen other badass lions most shifters would rather not tangle with. Hell, even Dominec seems to have decided not to kill her." She flapped the letter. "But I don't think that's what this is about. You can drop the self-sacrificing bullshit."

"I don't know what you mean."

"Oh, that's right, I forgot you were brain damaged from testosterone poisoning." She looked him dead in the eye. "*You* are part of this pride too, Adrian Sokolov, hawk-man. It's not going to kill you to let yourself be one of us. So man up and feel the love, dipshit." She ripped the letter neatly in two. "Resignation rejected. Get back to work."

Adrian didn't move. He wasn't sure what to make of this forcible acceptance. Community wasn't a comfortable feeling for him. He was better at being alone. This sense of belonging somewhere, with someone, it was hard to take in.

Grace eyed his poleaxed expression and snorted. "God, the two of you are ridiculous. So much nobility and martyrdom in one couple. It's positively revolting. I think you deserve each other."

"Rachel—"

"Is staying right here. Unless *she* wants to go. You aren't the boss of her. And if you try to take away our fertility specialist, you're gonna have a fight on your hands, boy-o. Lila and Patch have plans to use her for their baby-making, so unless you want to tangle with the Alpha, I'd slow your roll."

He scowled. "What are you talking about?"

"Didn't you know? She promised to help Patch and Lila get knocked up."

Adrian felt all the blood leave his brain in a panicked rush. "She did what?"

Grace rolled her eyes. "Do I really need to say it again?"

"Where is she?" he demanded, barely recognizing his own voice.

Grace's eyebrows arched. "I don't have a tracking device on her, but my best guess is the infirmary."

Adrian didn't say another word. He bolted out of Grace's office, running through the pride compound toward the forest. His feet were too slow. Too fucking slow. He wanted to reach for his hawk, but he didn't want to be naked when they had this argument. And it was going to be an argument.

It was one thing to treat Kathy, but Lila? And the freaking Alpha's mate? When the pride found out, there was no telling what the reaction would be. And if something went wrong, if either of them were hurt in any way, there would be a lynch mob. No one would care whether it was Rachel's fault or not. All they would see were the darlings of the pride hurt by the ex-Organization doctor. He wouldn't be able to protect her then.

Fuck. When had he begun to care more about her safety than anything else in the world? She was more necessary to him than breathing.

He would forbid it. He couldn't let her risk herself. She didn't need to prove herself to the pride. Not like this. They'd just found one another again. He couldn't lose her now. It would destroy him.

She was fidgeting with a machine of some kind when he burst into the room she'd taken over as her lab at the infirmary.

"Adrian," she gasped, and then she was running toward him, flinging herself into his arms with such force that he could either swing her around in the air or let them both crash to the ground. He chose to make her fly.

"Did you get her?" she asked breathlessly, before her feet even touched the ground.

"Madison Clarke is back in shifter hands." He set her on her feet, though she kept her arms around him as she tipped her head back to meet his eyes.

"I thought you might have killed her," she murmured, and he thought he detected a note of hope in her voice.

"Maybe next time." She clung to him—and the feel of her, heaven in his arms, only reinforced his ire. "I hear you were busy while I was gone."

She shrugged. "I was scared, but it was all right. He didn't hurt me."

Confusion broke through his anger, shattering it. "What?"

"Dominec. He didn't touch me. I'm fine."

"What. Happened."

As she explained, he felt his arms tightening around her and had to forcibly restrain himself from crushing her to him. She could have died. Tonight. On the pride lands. And he hadn't been there to protect her.

"We need to leave the pride."

She cocked her head to the side, withdrawing slightly, though still in the circle of his arms. "Adrian, don't be ridiculous."

"Non-negotiable. You'll be safer somewhere else."

"The Organization will kill me somewhere else. This pride is the best and only protection I have."

"I'll protect you."

"Adrian, darlin'. Relax. I like it here. And so do you. I like who I am here. I can help. I can do good. We both can. You won't convince me that doesn't mean anything to you."

"You mean more."

Chapter Thirty-Two

This. This was what the poets meant when they said their hearts melted. Hers felt like chocolate oozing over a s'more. But no matter how her heart melted, she couldn't yield now. Adrian would shatter the world to protect her, but she wanted the life they shared to be one worth living.

"I don't want to run. This is home now."

His gleaming yellow eyes were adamant. "You're my home. You're the only home I need."

"And you're mine, but—"

"I didn't want to let myself love you, but I always did. If you're hurt, I would lose my mind. I tried to keep my distance from you because to love you so much is to risk my very soul, but you are *everything*, Rachel. Do you understand?"

She pushed back in his arms, but he didn't let her go. "Adrian... I can't. I can never give you children. And even if by some miracle I could, they'd never be able to fly. You may truly be the last of your kind."

"You can do anything. I've seen you work miracles. You gave me back my wings."

"I didn't do any—"

"You gave me back my heart. And I have faith in your ability to make science bow to your will. We'll in vitro, or adopt or whatever you want. And whether we ever have children or not, you will always be the one I love the most. You are my soul, Rachel. A hawk mates for life and you are all I will ever want— even if you reject me now because I don't deserve you."

The words made something wonderful unfurl like a flower in her chest. "I think I must mate for life too, because it's always been you. I've loved you from the first second I saw you. Though I've wanted to smack you a time or two since then. But it was only ever you for me." She smiled up at him. "It's about time you came back to me."

Love shone in his eyes as he lowered his lips to hers.

It was, Rachel decided, quite possibly the most perfect kiss ever in the history of kisses. The walls were gone. Everything he was poured through his lips to hers. Her love. Her soul. Her mate. He was finally *hers*.

Every cell of her body felt like it was radiating joy like gleaming rainbow light. No moment could ever be as perfect as this one—except for the next, and the one after that, with the knowledge that there would be a million more moments to come with this man.

She didn't know how long they stayed like that before he lifted his head, his eyes somber as they met hers. "I'm sorry."

"For kissing me?"

"For being a fool for so long. For losing faith in you. For trying to stop myself from loving you. Can you forgive me?"

She smiled. "On two conditions."

"Anything."

"You can't keep making these unilateral decisions for both of us. Leaving the pride? We have to be a team again."

"We are. But I will still be overbearing and obnoxious in my attempts to keep you safe. And you will do the same for me."

"I guess I can accept that. But this time, we stay. We'll be careful. But this is where we belong, Adrian. It's home."

"For now. But we have to discuss this thing about impregnating Patch and Lila. Do you have idea how risky it is to experiment on them? If the pride turns against you—"

"Lila has a plan to deal with my image—whatever that means—and I promise I won't try anything with them until I've had some success with Kathy."

"You'll talk about it with me first?"

"Of course I will. We're a team."

"And the other condition?"

"Never stop loving me."

He smiled, that small, secretive hawk smile. "Never."

The ceremony had been Lila's idea. A special Thanksgiving Thank You. A public statement of trust and gratitude for all Rachel had done for shifters in general and Lone Pine Pride in particular. They'd dedicated the entire feast to her.

Roman, Patch, Grace, Dr. Brandt and Lila had all said a few words. Adrian had watched Rachel blushingly accept their praise, hoping it would be enough, that any shifters who were against her would be swayed by the show.

So far, it seemed to be working.

He wouldn't stop guarding her and never again would he doubt her. It had been unnatural not to forgive her, so unnatural he'd cut out a piece of his own soul. He would never be whole without her and he would never do that to both of them again.

Madison was under lock and key, isolated from the other prisoners and being questioned on a daily basis, though she hadn't revealed anything about the Organization. Yet.

Adrian had taken over the training of the new recruits for the security team, putting them through their paces since it wouldn't be long before they would all be needed in the fight against the Organization. When Rachel wasn't working with Kathy, she'd started giving classes on first aid and battlefield triage to as many of the shifters as were interested. Each class was larger than the next. Everyone sensed that something big was coming.

After the meal, the celebration devolved into a dance party—the cats would take any excuse to play, especially now when there was an air of last chance desperation to the frivolity.

As if this might be their last night on earth. But if it was, Adrian knew there was only one person he wanted to spend it with.

He tucked Rachel against his side and the two of them slipped out into the snowy night. She hugged him against her side and lifted her face to the sky as the flakes drifted down and they crunched away from the Pride Hall.

"They should have celebrated you too," she grumbled softly. "We did it all together."

"Yeah, but I'm a cranky ass with a face like a lawnmower and you're the hot, compassionate doctor. You're easier to love."

She turned to face him, twining both arms around his neck. "I beg to differ."

For a moment, looking down at her, Adrian couldn't speak. His brain had lost all the words he'd ever known. All he could do was cup her face in his hands—still and always the most beautiful face he'd ever seen in real life—and tip her lips up to meet his.

"Fly for me, Hawk?" she whispered when he finally lifted his head.

"Always."

About the Author

An Alaskan born and raised, award-winning paranormal romance author Vivi Andrews still lives in the frozen north when she isn't indulging her travel addiction by bouncing around the globe. Whether at home or on the road, she's always at work on her next happily-ever-after. For more about her books or the exploits of a nomadic author, please visit her website at www.viviandrews.com, or find her on Facebook and Twitter.

When she's in heat, there's no cooling down...

Taming the Lion
© *2014 Vivi Andrews*
Lone Pine Pride, Book 2

Wilderness guide and cougar-shifter Patricia "Patch" Fontaine has known the dangers of lone-shifter life since she was ten, when her parents mysteriously vanished. All grown up now, she thrives on her hard-won independence.

When rumors of a new rash of shifter abductions crop up, she's forced to come home to the Lone Pine Pride for protection—right as the man she's always secretly wanted is about to marry her best friend. And right as she's going into heat.

Roman Jaeger values his role as Alpha heir apparent, but he isn't thrilled about his arranged marriage to the Alpha's daughter—especially when his bride is just as nonplussed as he is—but he'll do his duty for the pride. Seeing Patch again challenges his noblest intentions. The wildness in her sets him on fire, and he can't resist the chance for one last fling.

Both know a future together is impossible. But when chemistry and sowing wild oats grows into a need deeper than lust, their bond could threaten the very heart of the pride they both love.

Warning: This book contains a strong sexy Alpha-to-be, an independent cougar-shifter who knows her way around a lion's heart, secret affairs, arranged marriages, politics, passion, and a pride full of lions and tigers and bears. Oh my.

Available now in ebook and print from Samhain Publishing.

It's all about the story...

Romance

HORROR

www.samhainpublishing.com

CPSIA information can be obtained at www.ICGtesting.com
Printed in the USA
LVOW11s0614240115

424188LV00004B/58/P